CLAIMING HIS DEFIANT MISS

Bronwyn Scott

Published in Great Britain 2017
by Mills & Boon, an imprint of HarperCollins*Publishers*
1 London Bridge Street, London, SE1 9GF

© 2017 Nikki Poppen

ISBN: 978-0-263-92578-4

Bronwyn Scott is a communications instructor at Pierce College in the United States, and the proud mother of three wonderful children—one boy and two girls. When she's not teaching or writing she enjoys playing the piano, travelling—especially to Florence, Italy—and studying history and foreign languages. Readers can stay in touch on Bronwyn's website, bronwynnscott.com, or at her blog, bronwynswriting.blogspot.com. She loves to hear from readers.

Visit the Author Profile page
at millsandboon.co.uk for more titles.

For Catie, Tonia and my Brony,
who came up with the name for this hero.
Thanks for helping me create a memorable hero.

And to all the girls out there. If there's one lesson
I want you to have from this story, it's that
love will find you—sometimes you just have to wait.

Chapter One

Preston Worth might very well die this time. Liam Casek stripped off his shirt and tore away a wide strip with an efficiency born of too much experience—he'd patched up Preston more than once. But tonight might be the last time. He pressed the wad of cloth to the gash in Preston's chest, alarmed by its location so near a lung and alarmed by the size of the crimson spread. It was too much for a mere strip of linen to staunch.

'Case!' Preston groaned with hoarse urgency, frantically grabbing at his arm to make him listen. 'Leave me, they might be back.' 'They' being the ambushers who'd come upon them on the road at dusk. There'd simply been too many to fight off, yet they had succeeded, at the price of Preston's wound. It might have been Preston's wound that saved them. The ambushers had retreated, perhaps convinced the natural course of events would finish off their prey.

'Be still,' Liam growled, all gruffness as he tied another strip around Preston's chest to hold the bandage in place. 'We have to get you stitched up.' But the bleeding had to stop first. He racked his brain for a plan. The nearest town was two miles back. 'Cover the bandage with your hand and press hard.' Liam got his hands under Preston's armpits. 'We're going to get you to the verge.' He hated moving Preston, but the middle of the road was no place for a wounded man in the dark. It made an easy target for careless carriages and returning thugs.

Preston grunted against the pain as Liam hauled him to the side, no easy feat considering Preston was as tall as he was—a few inches over six foot, and nearly a dead weight—hopefully not about to become more dead. Liam propped his friend against a sturdy tree trunk and examined the bandage as best he could in the fading light. It would be entirely dark soon. Damn winter! There was never enough daylight and Liam desperately needed some now. He could feel rather than see the blood soaking the bandage.

'I hurt, Case,' Preston admitted and there was the briefest flicker of fear in his eyes.

'Pain is good,' Liam offered encouragingly. 'You're doing great. You're conscious, you're talking, you're not numb.' Numbness was what Liam feared most, a sure sign of impending death. He'd seen it too often in the wars. He was no doctor, but he was a veteran of battle-fields.

'Those men,' Preston ground out, 'Cabot Roan sent them.'

Liam nodded, too busy with his triage. He was not surprised. The attack tonight confirmed what they'd feared. Cabot Roan was a wealthy businessman suspected by important men in both the Home and Foreign Offices of leading an arms cartel. The cartel was made up of wealthy, private citizens who had manufactured arms for England during the recent wars and were missing their incomes now that the wars were over and there was no need for arms contracts. Now, those businessmen were selling arms to various revolutionary efforts across Europe. It went without saying that many of those efforts did not necessarily align with the British Empire's own foreign-policy aims, which made these men traitors. But proof was needed that Cabot Roan was behind the arms deals. That was Preston's job. If the ringleader was indeed Roan, the man was to be discreetly stopped. *That* was Liam's job.

'The hunches must be right, then. That's good news. Roan wouldn't have sent his thugs if there was nothing to hide.' Liam kept talking, kept smiling. He didn't want Preston to panic. He thought the bleeding might be slowing down at last. There was still too damn much of it, though. He couldn't wait any longer to get help. 'Do you think you can ride? Just a couple of miles?'

Preston nodded. 'Even if I can't, we have to try. We can't stay here and this is serious. You're going to need light to work by, Case.' As opposed to the other times Preston had been shot, knifed or otherwise needed his attentions, Liam thought wryly. If the situation wasn't dire, he would have laughed. As it was, Liam thought he needed a sight more than light to make Preston right again.

Liam moved to help him rise, but Preston stayed him with a hand. 'Wait, before you do that I have to tell you something.' Liam heard the unspoken message. *In case I become unconscious because moving hurts too bloody much.* Which was better than the other unspoken message: *In case I become unconscious and don't wake up. Ever.*

'You can tell me after the doctor has you stitched up and you're resting.' Liam didn't like Preston thinking in those terms. It was always bad when the patient recognised how serious the situation was.

Preston grabbed for his arm. 'No doctor, Case. No inn. Promise me.' He was breathing hard with the force of his words. 'It's too public. Inns are the first places Roan will look for us and doctors will be the first people he'll question.'

Liam nodded in understanding. He had a plan now. He'd remembered something. 'There's a farmhouse not far back. But you have to let me go for a doctor.'

Preston shook his head, adamant. 'You can be my doctor. You've stitched me up enough to know how to do it right.' He tried to laugh and grimaced against the pain.

'None of that now.' Liam held him upright until the spasm passed. 'We'll laugh about this later.' He doubted he'd laugh about this ever. But it was just like Preston to offer reassurance even when he was the one bleeding on the roadside.

The spasm over, Preston drew a shaky breath.

'Now, will you listen to me? I found proof about Cabot Roan and the cartel yesterday, before you joined me.'

This was good news. 'Where is it?' If anyone had thought Preston had the information was on him the thugs would never have left him alive. Liam hoped it wasn't in the saddlebags of the horse that had bolted.

'I mailed two copies of the proof. One, straight to London and another to my sister in case the London mail is intercepted.' Preston continued to grip his arm. 'She's in Scotland, outside Edinburgh in a small village with a friend. You need to go to her and keep her safe until the information can be used to bring Cabot in.'

Liam didn't like the sound of that at all. He didn't like the sound of anything that involved May Worth. 'Why would Roan even think to go after your sister?' After all these years, it was still difficult to speak her name.

'Because…' Preston was growing agitated '…Cabot Roan knows I'm the one who broke into his house. I was sloppy, he saw my face. He'll go after May, Case, and I can't be there to protect her.'

Obviously. Wounded, Preston could do nothing to protect anyone. But even hale, Preston would be a beacon leading Roan straight to May if he tried to reach her. Roan would be watching Preston's every move…if he lived through the night. 'Give me your word, Case. You will protect May.'

'With my life,' Liam promised, because he would have promised Preston Worth anything, even if it was walking into the special hell that was May Worth. 'Now, let's get you up on that horse.' He owed Preston more than he could repay. He just wished he didn't owe Preston *that*.

He had a thousand questions. What was May *really* doing in Scotland? It seemed an unlikely place for the daughter of an influential Englishman like Preston's father. Which village? Preston hadn't given him a name. But questions would have to wait. There was no chance for them now. Preston was unconscious before they'd even gone a quarter-mile, his body sagging against Liam's as they rode, exhausted from the fight, the pain, the loss of blood. It was probably better for him this way, but it sure made it deuced hard to get off the horse with an unconscious man.

'I need help! I have a wounded man!' Liam called out as he nudged his horse cautiously into the farmyard. It was full dark now and strangers at this hour would make an isolated farmer wary. 'I come peacefully!' But he slid a hand over the smooth comfort of his pistol butt even as he spoke. A man could never be too careful.

He waited several long moments before the farmhouse door opened and a man emerged, lamp in hand. 'Please, help us. He's hurt badly. I need to stitch him up.' Liam struggled to keep the panic out of his voice. Preston Worth would not die on him. But if he was going to be any help to Preston, he had to remain calm, had to take charge. People didn't question authority, they responded to it. The man hurried forward, calling for others to come and help. Two tall, gangly boys spilled out of the house behind him, followed by a woman who came and silently held the lamp.

Hands reached for Preston as Liam eased him down. 'Careful, he's been stabbed,' Liam ordered more sharply than necessary, but the family took it in their stride. His best friend was bleeding out right before his eyes and he'd never felt so helpless. What if his skill wasn't enough? What if he should risk a doctor after all? Liam swung off the horse and tossed the reins to the other boy. 'Take care of him, I'll need him rested.' The movement, the command, was enough to regain his focus. He couldn't think about what he couldn't do. He had to focus on what he *could* do. That was the trick to surviving disaster. He'd survived enough of those to know. *Just think about the next thing that needs to happen.*

He caught the woman's eye and issued another set of instructions. 'I need compresses, bandages and hot water heating.' She gave a sharp nod and led everyone inside.

Liam scanned the room. 'Clear the table and let's get him laid out.' It would be the best place to work, near the fire with plenty of heat and light. Liam took off his coat and rolled up his sleeves, finding a basin of hot water ready at his elbow.

'Leftover from cooking dinner,' the woman explained with a kind smile. 'It will do until fresh is ready and you'll be wanting these.' She produced a needle and thread.

'And a candle, some whisky, too, if you have it.' Liam pulled back Preston's shirt, able to see the wound clearly for the first time.

'You're a doctor, then?' The woman passed him a brown bottle.

'Something like that.' What he did could hardly be called doctoring. Doctors were wealthy men who went to schools and universities and had white lace-curtained offices. The only schooling Liam had was what Preston had given him and the only doctoring he'd acquired was on a Serbian battlefield. He prayed tonight it would be enough.

Liam pulled out the stopper, taking a deep sniff. It was good whisky, strong whisky, and it was going to hurt like hell. He nodded to the older boy. 'Take him by the shoulders and hold him firm. He's going to want to jerk when this firewater hits him.' The boy was pale, but he did what he was told.

Liam bent over Preston and offered the explanation out of habit, the words more for himself than Preston, who remained unconscious. 'I'm sorry to do it, old friend, but it'll clean out the wound and cut down your chances of inflammation.' He poured the whisky on Preston's chest, lending his own weight when Preston roared and bucked. Good, good, Liam thought. Preston could still be roused, he still had some strength. 'Be still, Pres, we're at the farmhouse and I'm stitching you up just like you wanted,' he murmured the reassuring words.

'No doctors.' Preston's voice was hoarse and insistent.

'No doctors.' Liam smiled, his face close

to his friend's so Preston could see his eyes. 'We're safe here.' He hoped that was true. He hoped Roan's men wouldn't come barging through the door any minute. He hoped they wouldn't come and harass this kind family tomorrow. He'd been careful with his trail even in the dark, but there was only so much care one could take with a wounded man who needed speed more than he needed discretion. Discretion took time and Preston hadn't any of that to spare.

'Here's the items you wanted.' The woman held up a needle, already threaded. She offered a friendly smile. 'I have to be prepared with these three around. There's always cuts and bruises on a farm.' She sobered. 'How bad is it?'

Liam stepped aside, letting her look as he held the needle in the flame. 'I don't think anything vital was hit, but he's lost a lot of blood.' He nodded his head towards the whisky bottle. 'Give him some to drink now, he'll need it once this needle goes in him.' With luck, Preston would pass out after the first couple of stitches. But first, he had to bathe the wound. He wanted a clean working surface. The fresh hot water was ready now and he dipped a cloth in it. Washing away the blood made it look better, better being a relative term. The bleeding had stopped, he could see that now, and he could put aside his worry that the knife had punctured a lung. But the gash was long and it was ugly, made by a jagged blade. Preston wasn't going to get out of this without a scar.

The farmer took up a position at Preston's head with one of his sons. 'You'll probably need two of us. Your friend looks like quite the fighter.' The woman and the other son each grabbed a leg. Liam drew a deep breath, prayed for steady hands, crossed himself and began to sew.

It was over in a matter of minutes although it felt like hours. Liam was exhausted. He looked at his handiwork. Would it be enough? Had his precautions been enough to ward off inflammation? He'd been in enough battles to know it wasn't the wound that killed a soldier. More often than not, it was the swelling that followed, or the poor medical work, lace-curtained training or not. He couldn't bring himself to think of being the agent of Preston's demise instead of his salvation. If it hadn't been for Preston, he would still be scrambling for work and living hand to mouth in the streets.

The farmer slipped an arm about his shoulders, drawing him back from the table. 'My boys will watch him while the wife cleans up. Let's go and have something to drink. You've had a hell of a night.'

And it wasn't even over. The farmer pressed a glass of whisky into his hand. 'We'll make up a pallet for you in front of the fire. You can be near your friend.'

'No, I have to push on.' Liam swallowed the whisky, letting the gulp burn down his throat and warm his belly. The illusion of warmth gave him the strength he needed to resist the offer. He wanted nothing more than to sleep and stay near, but he had promised Preston. He had miles to go before he could rest. The more distance between him and Cabot Roan, the better. 'You've already done so much, but I have one more favour to ask.'

'Consider it done,' the farmer interrupted. 'We'll watch over your friend as best we can and hope no fever sets in.' Preston was stitched, but that wasn't a miracle cure-all.

'I can pay you. He'll need food, meat to build back the blood he's lost.' Liam reached in his pocket for a bag of coins and pressed it into the farmer's hand.

'It's not necessary.' The farmer tried to give back the bag.

'It is, I assure you. You have done a greater good tonight than you realise.' Liam furrowed his brow. 'You've done so much and I don't know your name.'

'It's Taylor. Tom Taylor. And yours?'

Liam grinned. 'My friends call me Case.' The farmer nodded sagely, understanding the protection Liam had offered him. Sometimes names could be dangerous. Better that this good family not know too much. Liam did not want them harmed in return for their generosity.

The farmer jerked his head towards the inside. 'Do you think anyone will come looking for him?' He'd want to know, would want to protect his family.

'Maybe.' Liam wouldn't lie to them. He hoped not. Preston would need a couple of weeks to recover, a month even to be back to full strength. He glanced inside at Preston's prone figure. He didn't want to leave, but he couldn't wait. Edinburgh was a long way from where he was. He'd need a head start if he was going to reach May in time, assuming Cabot Roan even knew to look there. Liam hoped he didn't. He wanted to gamble that May's remote and unexpected location would protect her. Then he could stay until Preston was in the clear.

The farmer looked to the sky. 'There will be rain tonight. A lot of it. Are you sure you want to go?'

He wasn't sure at all. He didn't want to go, but he'd given Preston his word. He had to go to May whether she needed protection or not, never mind she'd be about as pleased to see him as he was pleased to be there.

Liam didn't bother to go back inside. His resolve was weak enough. The offer of a fire and a hot meal would do him in. He shook the farmer's hand, thanked him once more and mounted up with a wary eye skyward. Maybe the rain would hold off, he was due some luck. Two miles down the road the clouds broke in a soaking deluge. Whoever said the Irish were lucky definitely hadn't met Liam Casek.

Chapter Two

Village on the Firth of Forth, Scotland—
November 1821

'A penny and nothing more,' May Worth argued, facing down Farmer Sinclair and his carrots in the market. Farmer Sinclair didn't want to sell her carrots any more than she wanted to buy them from him, not at that price. 'Three pennies for a bundle of carrots is highway robbery.'

'A man's got to feed his family.' Sinclair rubbed his stubbly chin with a weathered hand. He gave her a steady look. 'What do you care if they're one penny or three, you can afford it either way.'

'Being of means, as *modest* as they are,' May emphasised, 'doesn't mean I squander them unnecessarily.' In the four months she and Bea had been in residence, they'd tried to live frugally in an attempt to call the least amount of attention to themselves as possible. Still, despite their best efforts, there were some like Farmer Sinclair who'd concluded they were ladies of independent means.

Sinclair grumbled, 'Two and a half. These are fine carrots, the best in the village, and the last fresh you're likely to get until spring.' It was hard to argue with that. Sinclair's produce was always reliable. The carrots were likely worth two and a half this late into autumn, but May didn't like losing. At anything. Now that she'd engaged in battle she couldn't back down.

'Two.' Sinclair would lord it over her if she gave in too easily and so would Bea when she told her. Bea would laugh and that was worth something. These last few weeks had been hard on Bea. She was in the last month of her pregnancy, large and constantly uncomfortable. She was unable to walk as far as the market these days without her feet swelling. 'Two. For Beatrice and the baby,' May added for pathos.

That did the trick. 'Two,' Sinclair agreed. 'Tell Mistress Fields I send my regards.' He handed her the orange bunch and she tucked them victoriously into her market basket. But it was only a partial win and Sinclair knew it as well as she did. Bea would have got a better price *without* haggling. Everyone in the village *liked* Beatrice. It wasn't that they *didn't* like her, it *was* possible to like more than one person at a time. Liking wasn't exclusive, but they were definitely wary of her.

The carrots were the last of the items on her list. It was time to head home. She didn't like being away from Beatrice for too long with the baby due soon and she had letters to read— one in particular from her brother that she was eager to read. She knew Bea would be eager for it, too. News from home was sparse these days. The other was from her parents, which she was less eager to read. That one, she would read in private later. Besides, without Bea at the market, her own socialising opportunities were more 'limited'.

May understood quite plainly she was tolerated because of Bea and she understood why. She was too blunt for some of the ladies and too pretty for some of the wives who worried she'd steal their men. If only they understood she wasn't interested in men. She'd come here to escape them. So far, that part was working out splendidly. The men hadn't any more idea what to do with her forthright behaviour than the women did. No one knew what to make of her, no one ever had, except Beatrice and Claire and Evie.

Her friends had never tried to make her fit a mould. They'd simply accepted her as she was, something her own parents had not succeeded in doing. Instead, they'd threatened to marry her off to the local vicar back home if she didn't find a husband by next spring. She didn't really think they'd do it, they were just trying so hard to make sure she was betrothed before spring. She highly suspected the second letter in her basket was a long-distance attempt to reintroduce the theme as they had done this past summer.

They'd made countless attempts, some subtle, some less so, during the Season to throw eligible men her direction. She'd thrown them all back and her parents were definitely frustrated. One more Season had passed and she still hadn't become the dutiful daughter. Here she was, nearly twenty-two, with three Seasons behind her and no suitor in sight, all because of one man.

She'd loved deeply once, although she'd been warned against it. She was too young, he was too 'dangerous' in the way unsuitable men are for well-bred girls who are restless and fresh out of the schoolroom. But she had done it anyway and now she was paying. She couldn't have him. Their harsh parting had seen to that. There could be no going back from the words and betrayal they'd flung at one other. But that didn't stop her from measuring all others against him and no one could possibly measure up. Her father called it disobedient, outright rebellious. Her mother called it a shame.

Perhaps they were right. Maybe she was rebellious. Maybe she was a shame to the family. There was certainly argument for that. For all outward appearances, she had everything a successful debutante could want: she was pretty, her family was respectable, her father the second son of a viscount, a valued member of Parliament, and she had a dowry that more than adequately reflected all that respectability. What was not to like? She should have been an open-and-shut case, a prime piece of merchandise snatched off the marriage mart after two Seasons.

Although, to her benefit, all that parental frustration had probably been the reason her parents had let her accompany Beatrice into Scottish exile while she waited out her pregnancy: the errant daughter would be out of sight, out of mind. Perhaps her parents hoped a few months in Scotland would change her mind, show her what life was like alone and isolated from society. A spinster could expect nothing more.

May smiled to herself and gave a little skip along the dirt road. If that's what her parents hoped for, they couldn't be more wrong. She loved it here. Never mind the villagers didn't know what to make of her. That could change in time. Even if it didn't, she liked being on her own, just her and Beatrice. She liked doing for herself. She'd discovered she had a talent for cooking, for shopping for their small household, for growing things. She and Bea had the most spectacular greenhouse where they would be able to grow vegetables year-round—not enough to live on, not yet. They would still be reliant on the Farmer Sinclairs of the world for a while. But come spring... That put a stop to her skipping.

Would they still be here in the spring? She hoped so, but Beatrice's parents might call her home after the baby was born. Her own parents certainly would want her back at some point. This had become an anxiety point for both of them over the last few weeks. The baby coming changed everything and 'everything' was uncertain. Beatrice feared someone would come and take the baby away. She was unwed after all, never mind that the village called her Mistress Fields and thought Mr Fields was a small merchant explorer away at sea, a fiction they had liberally borrowed and enhanced from one of Bea's favourite romance novels. The truth was, Beatrice had been indiscreet last winter and now she was paying for it. When this was over, Beatrice didn't want to go home any more than May did.

'We simply won't go.' May had told her just last night when Bea had been up worrying again. 'They can't make us.' That was only partly true. Their parents *could* make them. Their parents could cut off the allowance that let them keep the spacious cottage and buy food. Maybe Preston would stand up for them. Preston always did. He was the best of brothers. He was what May missed most about being away from home.

But she couldn't rely on Preston for this. This was her decision alone to make, hers and Bea's. They had to rely on themselves. They were already saving part of their allowances in case they were cut off. They had the greenhouse. They'd have their garden in the spring, they could make preserves, maybe enough to sell in the market or to trade. They had the clothes they'd come with and the horses too, although horses needed hay. If they economised, they could be countrywomen in truth. It was a daring plan to be sure and not without some risk. They would be giving up life as they knew it, but they would have their freedom in exchange.

Nothing changed until you did. That was the motto of the Left Behind Girls Club, of which there remained only two members now, her and Bea. Claire and Evie had both married. She'd gone to Evie's wedding in October. Evie had been a radiant autumn bride, proud to stand beside her handsome husband, a royal prince of Kuban who'd given up his title for her and become a country gentleman in Sussex. If Dimitri Petrovich could do it, perhaps she and Bea could do it, too. They had to be the agents of their own change. They had to stand up for what they wanted, even if they had to fight for it.

The heavy weight in May's skirt pocket reminded her of how literal that fight might be. *Promise me you won't let anyone take the baby,* Beatrice had pleaded tearfully with her. If anyone came, they wouldn't stop at an argument, something May could win. They would resort to physical force. It was a sad truth that men could simply overpower women to take what they wanted when reason failed, but guns were great equalisers; Preston had taught her that. She had one now in her skirt pocket, just in case. She'd promised Bea no one would take the baby as long as she had one good shot. A Worth's word was golden.

The hairs on the back of her neck prickled as she approached their cottage. Usually the sight of their neat brick home with its steep slate roof brought her a sense of comfort. Today, she felt unease. Perhaps all this thinking about someone taking the baby had put her imagination on edge. The baby wasn't even born yet. May tried to talk herself out of the premonition. Her mind was playing games. But it was no use. Something was wrong. There was mud tracked up the porch steps to the door, the way boots tracked mud. Boots meant men. Men meant trouble. It was market day, no one would make a special trip out. If there was business to be dealt with, she would have taken care of it in town.

May set down her basket and scanned the yard, her eye catching the anomaly. There! A horse, not one of their own; an animal too sleek to be a farmer's. This was the kind of horse owned by someone who rode. Horses meant money and this one looked vaguely familiar. Her mouth went dry. Had Bea's family come already? May slipped her hand into her pocket and slowly pulled out the pistol, letting calm slide over her. *Just think about the next step.* It was a trick Preston had taught her, something he'd learned from his work for the government.

Through the window, she could see the top of a man's head. Someone was sitting in the front parlour's spare chair. Good. Whoever it was couldn't see her. *Take them by surprise. Don't give them a chance to think. The only one thinking should be you.* Preston had taught her that, too. She'd know where to turn once she came through the door; she'd know where to aim her gun. She wouldn't waste a moment learning the layout of the room and who was where.

May drew a breath and threw open the front door with her shoulder, using more force than necessary. It banged against the wall, making noise and startling the room's occupants. She whirled towards the chair at the window, the pistol trained on the man. The light from the window might obscure the details of his face, but she could see enough to hit him. She would aim for his shoulder. 'Get out, we don't want you here.' She let the ominous cock of the pistol fill the stunned silence of the room, a silence that didn't last nearly as long as it should have.

Most people took guns seriously. Not the man in the chair. He laughed! The sound of it sent a shudder of recognition down her spine as he drawled, 'Hello, Maylark. It's nice to see you, too.' With those words, the element of surprise was neatly turned on her.

May froze. Liam Casek was here? She blinked against the light from the window, against the improbability, trying to digest the reality. Liam Casek—her brother's work partner, her one great moment of foolishness, the man against whom she measured all other men and found them lacking—was sitting in her front parlour in the middle-of-nowhere Scotland, the last person she'd ever have expected to see. In truth, he was the last person she *wanted* to see here. He could only bring her trouble as he'd so aptly demonstrated on earlier occasions. How would she ever explain him to Beatrice? She lowered the gun, her arm suddenly heavy from the weight, and his eyes flickered towards the motion.

'How like you to greet gentlemen with pistols.' It was an insult if ever there was one. The last time she'd seen him had been five years ago, a mere seventeen-year-old girl. She was far more grown up now. She should say something witty, one of her famed biting retorts, but all she could do was stare.

He was much as she remembered him: blue Irish eyes that sparkled in the face of danger—she didn't know many men who would take a pistol aimed at them sitting down—untrimmed hair falling over his shoulders in a tangle of dark waves that rebelled against any attempt at convention, a body that dwarfed anything in a room. Tall and lean, Liam Casek had always known how to take up space, only there was so much *more* of him now. There were new things about him, too: the tiny curving scar high on his cheek near his left eye, the long, refined cheekbones that gave his face its sharpness. Its shrewd intelligence was new, too—signs of the man that had been carved from the boy she'd once known.

But, oh, his mouth was the same. He had the mouth of a gentleman; thin on top and falsely hinting at aristocracy, full on the bottom suggesting sensuality. That mouth was the merest suggestion of softness set above the square jut of a rugged chin, to remind a woman that any pretence to tenderness was illusion only. That mouth knew how to tease a woman, to lead her on, intimating that other mysteries might lurk beneath the rugged façade should that woman dare to look. She'd been that bold once, that naïve. She'd thought to discover those mysteries once upon a time. Back then, she'd been on the brink of womanhood, and he on the brink of manhood at twenty-one, still not quite full come into the man who now stood before her. They had been reckless, she most of all. He was not for her. They both knew it with a certainty which made it inconceivable that he was sitting before her now.

May's mind started to work again. 'What are you doing here?' He wasn't here for her. They'd parted badly. But if not for her, then who? Preston? No! Her thoughts became a whirlwind driven by not a little panic. The letter she'd picked up at the market! It was at the bottom of her basket.

May darted to the yard where she'd dropped the basket, her mind working at full speed. She grabbed the letter and raced back inside, firing off questions. 'What's happened to Preston? Where is he? Is he with you?' It wasn't beyond possibility he had come with Liam, and was off on an errand. She tore into the letter. Two loose pages fell out. She was not interested in them, only in the bold scrawl of Preston's handwriting. She scanned the letter, trying to assimilate the information. May glared at Liam. 'Tell me. What, *exactly,* has happened to my brother?'

'He's been stabbed, May,' Liam began evenly, perhaps in the hope of not panicking her. But there was no way the word 'stabbed' could be received with bland reaction. There was a gasp behind her, a reminder that Bea was still in the room, silently watching this unexpected reunion play out.

May took a step backwards and sank next to Bea on the little sofa, vaguely aware of Bea taking her hand in support. She would not panic. She would not go to pieces in front of him. 'When did this happen? Tell me everything.'

'Six days ago.' Liam flicked a questioning glance Beatrice's way and May's stomach knotted. He would only tell her part of the truth without knowing Beatrice's full measure. It worried her greatly if Liam was considering mincing words. What needed to be hidden? May picked up the papers from the floor. She studied the sheets. She could see now that they were ledger pages recording expenditures and funds received. There were names and amounts, very condemning proof indeed for whatever had happened and Preston had sent it to her. It spoke volumes about his injury.

'Is he going to pull through?' They were hard words to utter. She had to presume the wound had been dangerous enough to warrant Liam coming to her. For the sake of her own sanity, she had to also assume Preston was alive, at least six days ago. Bea's grip tightened around her hand and she was grateful for her friend's support.

Liam hesitated. 'I stitched him up as best I could. I took him to a remote farmhouse.' He answered her next question before she could ask it. He'd always been good at that—knowing her thoughts before she did. It was a damn annoying habit when it wasn't being useful. 'Preston wouldn't let me send for a doctor.' Of course not. Her brother would be concerned for the safety of anyone he implicated. Whoever the villain in this mission was would seek out doctors in his search to find a wounded man. 'Preston made me promise to come straight to you.'

'To me or to the letter?' May queried, but Preston's actions already indicated the gravity of the situation. He had sent her information that needed protecting by someone whom her brother would trust with his life.

'Do you even need to ask?' Liam scolded her. 'Your safety was Preston's first thought as he lay bleeding in the road.'

His words shamed her. She'd known better than to assume otherwise. They also frightened her. She heard the unspoken message. Preston had thought there was the possibility he might die if he'd sent Liam as his proxy. An idea struck her. 'You can take me to him.' He would know where Preston was. She half-rose from the sofa, plans coming rapidly. She would pack, they would go by horseback for faster time. 'We can leave today.' Within the hour.

That got a literal rise out of him. The very idea of travelling any distance with her accomplished what the explosive end of a pistol had not. Liam was out of his chair in an instant. 'And take you in to the lion's den with the very evidence your brother risked his life to get?' His incredulity was obvious. 'What kind of fool-brained idea is that? Your brother sent me to protect you, not to expose you.'

Expose her to whom? She wanted details, but she wasn't going to get them with Beatrice in the room. 'I can protect myself just fine. I will shoot anyone who crosses that threshold uninvited, as you are very well aware.'

'It is irrelevant.' Liam's reply was sanguine. 'I am sure you can shoot *one* man. I recall you have excellent aim. There are men's lives at stake, shooting one won't be enough.' Again the vagaries. She had no choice but to get Liam alone if she wanted more information. 'If the man in question is caught, he faces treason and the noose. He will not send one man. He did not send one man against your brother and me on the road. He will not send one man against you. He will not care there is a pregnant woman in the house or a baby.' What had Preston got himself involved in now? She knew his work was more than what it appeared on the surface, but tracking treasonous individuals? That was far more than she'd anticipated.

May tried not to look affected with the dire picture he painted. Her desire for details warred with her concern for Beatrice. She didn't want Liam upsetting Beatrice who had enough to deal with. 'Whoever this new enemy is has to find me first.'

'He's desperate. He will find you. He's a man with resources and you were just in Sussex for a friend's wedding. Your family knows. Presumably they will have mentioned it to someone, perhaps several people. Someone, somewhere, will know you're here.'

'Surely you're not suggesting we leave.' Suddenly the thought was appalling, although it had been her very thought just moments ago. This cottage, this village, had become her world. This was where she was free. To leave would be to march straight back into society's silk-and-lace prison. While she would have given up the cottage to go to Preston in his need, she would not give up this cottage on the outside chance she would be discovered. They couldn't possibly take Beatrice with them in her condition and yet Beatrice couldn't stay. If anyone was looking for her, the trail would lead here. Beatrice wouldn't be safe.

Liam leaned back in his chair, hands laced over the flat of his stomach, his eyes skimming hers. 'Not at all, Maylark. *We* stay here and wait it out.'

'You're going to stay here?' It was her turn to be incredulous. In this small cottage? With her? Cosy was already becoming cramped. How would they ever manage to share this space?

Liam grinned, an irritatingly devilish smile full of smugness. She hated having risen to the bait. The dratted man had known how much that idea would irk her. 'That is exactly what I'm suggesting. I can sleep in the barn.'

'No, we have a spare room.' Bea put in quickly. 'The barn is too cold in winter.' May shot her a hard look. When had Bea turned traitor? Couldn't Bea see she didn't want him here? Maybe not, to be fair. Bea didn't know

Liam Casek. May had told no one, not even her close friends, about that summer at the lakes, the summer Jonathon Lashley hadn't come on holiday with the Worths and her brother had brought this friend instead.

Liam nodded gratefully at Bea. 'I appreciate it, Mistress Fields.' Bea actually blushed. May rolled her eyes. He'd already got to Beatrice with his rough brand of gallantry. She'd forgive her friend. She knew how easy it was to fall for that charm.

'I'll go ready the room, Mr Casek. May can show you around our little place.' May stifled a groan. Mister this, and mistress that. Good heavens, all this polite formality was going to kill her if showing Liam around didn't do it first.

'How long do you suppose you'll be here?' May asked bluntly.

Liam's blue eyes narrowed to dancing flints. 'As long as it takes to keep you safe. Until the new year, I imagine.' He shot Bea a considerate glance. 'I'll be sure to make myself useful. Looks like that barn roof could use a little work and you'll need an extra set of hands once the bairn gets here.' That was his breeding showing or lack of it. No *gentleman* friend of Preston's would have considered the impact of one more mouth to feed and care for. Neither would a gentleman have mentioned a pregnancy even if a nine-month belly was staring him rather obviously in the face. Liam Casek might have a gentleman's mouth, but he'd been raised working poor. Life held no secrets for him.

'It will be good to have a man around the house,' Beatrice acceded with another smile. Not that man, though. The last thing May wanted was to be alone with him, and now she would be for months, not because she felt threatened by him but because of who she was when she was with him. *That* frightened her a great deal even as it thrilled her.

Chapter Three

Liam stepped outdoors and scanned the yard, looking for a destination. The stone fence to his left seemed as good a place as any to have this conversation. He strode towards it, aware of May behind him. He'd give her five strides before her patience broke and she started demanding information.

One… May Worth could still frighten the living daylights out of him. That hadn't changed in five years. He would have thought a man who'd been to war, a man who'd seen men die, who'd often delivered that death personally and intimately on behalf of the Crown, would not be so easily frightened by a single female. But logic failed to account for May Worth. There was so much to be frightened by: her beauty, her intelligence, her overwhelming confidence in the rightness of her opinion, but it was her stubbornness that frightened him the most, not because she intimidated him but because he revelled in her fearlessness.

Two... He'd once found her fearlessness so intoxicating he'd believed he could change the world for her. He'd been drawn to it like an addict to opium. He was a stronger man now, his own ideals and expectations better tempered by reality. Was she? He feared that reckless stubborn streak would be the author of her demise someday.

Three... Look where it had led already today: it had her pulling a pistol on a guest and demanding safe passage to her brother's side, then refusing to leave the cottage. Very shortly it was going to prompt her to ask for every ounce of information he possessed regarding Preston and she was not going to like what he had to say.

Four...

'Tell me everything,' May blurted out, catching up to him. Five strides had been too optimistic. 'We're alone now, there's no reason not to.' There was a scold in there somewhere for him. She was angry he'd held back. She was anxious, which made her anger excusable, understandable even, but he still made her wait until they reached the stone fence. Someone had to teach May patience.

He leaned his elbows on the rough surface of the stone and looked out over the expanse of green field. It was far less disconcerting than looking at her and seeing those beautiful green eyes that could stalk a man like a tiger or burn with emerald passion, the rich walnut sheen of her hair, the elegant sweep of her jaw, the defiant point of her chin, the delicate, straight length of her nose set to perfection on her face, all of which informed a man without asking that this was a lady born to wealth and luxury. And then there was that skin, so perfectly translucent it called to mind every cliché he'd ever heard about silk and pearls and alabaster. It was indeed hard to speak when one could choose to look at May Worth instead. He'd learned to cultivate the skill, however. His sanity and male pride had depended on it.

'The Home and Foreign Offices sent your brother to track down a man named Cabot Roan.' He began in low tones, glancing around out of habit. They were in the middle of nowhere, but he couldn't help it. One could never be too cautious. 'Roan is suspected of leading an arms cartel whose interests do not always parallel Britain's.' He would not patronise May with an elementary explanation. She was intelligent. She would understand the implications.

'Apparently my brother found him,' May said drily.

'Yes, and then they found us, on the road out of town at dark.' Liam paused, letting her digest the information. She knew the rest from what he'd told her inside. 'Roan will come looking for you. If he can't find Preston, he will want to use you as leverage to get to him. The protection I offer is real, as is your need for it.'

May scoffed and repeated her earlier argument. 'Hardly anyone knows I'm in Scotland. I rather think my location is my best protection.'

'You've already heard my answer to that. Roan is very resourceful. He will find the people who know. Now that his life is on the line, he will be even more redoubtable. We must proceed as if he will find out.'

May was instantly wary. 'Does this process involve more than sleeping in my cottage and repairing my barn roof?' He could feel her eyes on him, probably narrowed to emerald slits of consideration.

Liam mentally braced himself for the storm. She wouldn't like this next part. May did not tolerate being told what to do under the best of circumstances. 'I am to be with you at all times and, if not, I need to know where you'll be, when you'll be there and who you'll be with.' He had to look at her now. The temptation was too great.

She shook her head and the storm broke. 'I will *not* be treated like a small child who can't be out of her mother's sight on the off chance this Cabot Roan *might* come looking for me. So if you'll excuse me, I have vegetables to put away before they wilt.' May's eyes flashed and she turned on her heel, presuming to walk away.

Liam reached for her, grabbing her arm, forcing his body to absorb the shock of touching her again after so long. 'This is not the time to be stubborn, May,' he growled, determined to make her see reason.

Her gaze went to his grip on her arm, her voice sharp. 'Take your hand off me. I will not allow you to be my gaoler.'

'Not your gaoler, May, your bodyguard. Please, May. This is not about what you want or even what I want. This is about Preston, about keeping Mistress Fields and the baby safe.' It was his best argument, this appeal to pathos. May would do anything for the ones she loved, the ones who needed her protection. It was yet another way she was like her brother.

Some of the fire went out of her eyes and she relented. 'How long before we know if Roan is coming?'

Liam shook his head. 'We don't know. He could come tomorrow, perhaps he is just a day or two behind me. Perhaps it will be a couple of weeks or months depending on how long it takes Roan to discover where you are.'

'Perhaps he'll never come.'

'We can hope for that.' The odds weren't convincing. He knew Roan. The man was tenacious.

May wrapped her arms about herself and shivered in spite of the wool shawl she wore. It was cold out, the day brisk even for November, but he thought the shiver was from something more than the weather. 'We'll have to tell Beatrice.' She shot him an accusing glance. 'You could have told her inside.' Now that she had her information, she could indulge in the scold he'd sensed was brewing earlier. 'You didn't have to hold back. You can trust Beatrice.'

It was his turn to go on the defensive. 'How was I to know if I could trust her or if it would be too upsetting in her condition?' He had his suspicions about Mistress Fields and her seafaring husband, but he wasn't going to voice them out loud and risk alienating May. He had more important battles to win today.

'I had only an acquaintance of minutes to rely on for my judgement. I erred on the side of discretion for the sake of the baby.' If Beatrice Fields had secrets, it was hardly any of his concern. In his line of work, he'd learned women had secrets just like men, and like men, they, too, could be dangerous creatures. He wasn't going to underestimate anyone simply because they were female. At the moment, his only interest in Beatrice Fields was her connection to why May was in godforsaken Scotland.

'I've told you what I know, now it's your turn. What are you doing here? Why didn't you stay in Sussex with the family after the wedding?'

'That should be obvious. Beatrice needs me. She can't deliver a baby on her own.' May fidgeted a little and looked past his shoulder out to the field. There was more to this than the loyalty of friendship.

'That's what doctors and midwives are for. Have *you* delivered many babies in the last five years, then? With a gun in one hand, none the less?' Liam pressed. May wasn't lying—May never lied, not even to spare a man's feelings, so he had learned. But she wasn't telling him quite the truth either.

'This is the wilds of Scotland. Two women on their own can't be too careful. I wasn't expecting company, that's all,' May snapped. He realised it was as close to an apology as he was going to get for being greeted with a pistol.

He arched a dark brow. 'I disagree. No one carries a pistol when they're *not* expecting anything. I think you *were* expecting something— trouble, perhaps?'

'Trouble doesn't follow me everywhere,' she began.

'No, it doesn't. *You* follow it, as I recall. There was that incident with the oak tree, the rowboat, the cigars—need I go on?'

'I was precocious in my younger years.' Her cheeks burned with the admission. He shouldn't have teased her. She would hate having her adolescence thrown in her face as much as he would.

'I'd wager you are still precocious.' His tone softened and he allowed himself a smile. It was dangerous to let himself entertain even a moment of nostalgia where May was concerned. 'I always liked that about you, May. Never afraid of a challenge, which leads me to conclude that's really why you're here. You've followed your friend into exile perhaps, as you say, to help her birth this whelp, perhaps to thumb your nose at your parents and society. Perhaps a little of both. But, there is something more. Neither of those are a particular challenge to you.' He was quiet for a minute, studying her, searching for the answer. He hadn't ferreted out the real reason she was here. 'What is Mistress Fields going to do with the child?'

'Raise it. It's what you do with children,' May said too sharply. He'd hit pay dirt.

'Hence the need for the pistol,' Liam surmised with no lack of sarcasm. 'She's afraid her family will come and take the child from the home of a woman with only an errant husband to provide for her.' With no man in the house, a protective, financially secure family would want to see a child raised in far safer circumstances. Assuming there was a husband at all—he had his doubts there, but no proof.

'No one will take it,' May said firmly, her eyes locking on Liam's, her reckless stubbornness in full bloom. May thought she could hold off Beatrice's family with a gun and the two of them could play house and raise the baby on their own. It was an admirable goal even if it was a bit over-innocent in its assumptions. Two women alone would be prey to all sorts of mischief. May didn't know true danger. He never wanted her to know it.

Something protective stirred in him, something he didn't want to acknowledge. There'd been only trouble down that path last time he trod it. May Worth wasn't for him. She was beautiful and headstrong, naïvely confident that she could overcome anything. That was what money and a good family could do for a person—create the innate belief that you were as close to immortal as one could get. There wasn't anything you couldn't conquer. He didn't want the world to crush that out of May.

They stood in silence, the wind picking up around them. May shielded her eyes and looked towards the empty road, Beatrice and her dubious husband forgotten. 'You think he'll come.' She let out a deep breath.

'Yes, I do. But I'll be here, May. You needn't worry.' In that moment he wished it were all different; that he hadn't been born a poor, Irish street rat, the unwanted son of a St Giles whore, or that he hadn't aspired above his station, that Cabot Roan didn't pose a threat to her, that he hadn't had to come here and endure the exquisite torture of being in her presence. It was a moment's whimsy only. All he had to do was remember how they parted and the anger would come rushing back, the resentment. In the end, class and wealth and privilege had all proven too big of a chasm to cross. When it had counted, she hadn't wanted him. Even five years later, she still looked at him as if he was the biggest mistake she'd ever made.

'I wouldn't have come if it hadn't been for Preston.' Perhaps if he defined the rules out loud they would serve as a clarification of the boundaries for both of them; a clarification they both needed if there was to be no repeat of their previous foolishness. That might be excused as the folly of the youth. But now? Now, there would be no excuse. They both knew better. 'This is strictly business, May.'

She glared. 'I know. You've made that *abundantly* clear.' She turned towards the cottage and this time, he let her go, pretending the rules would indeed succeed in preventing disaster from striking twice.

Who was he kidding? The rules had never held any power over him, not where May was concerned. After all, despite her protests to the contrary, he'd seen her pulse beat fast at his nearness and his own thoughts had wandered towards nostalgia more than once. They were both in jeopardy here, rules or not. All it would take to shatter their fragile restraint would be for him to decide he wanted to try on that brand of foolishness one more time, just to be sure it didn't fit.

Chapter Four

He'd looked at her like she was the biggest mistake he'd ever made! He wouldn't have come if it hadn't been for Preston! He had made his feelings perfectly clear. May hacked at the feathery green tops of the carrots and began slicing with more ferocity than finesse. She threw the carrot pieces into the stewpot.

'Toss, May.' Beatrice leaned across the worktable in the kitchen and put a restraining hand on her arm. 'We *toss* the carrots into the pot. We don't hurl them. Especially when they're Farmer Sinclair's carrots,' she added with a wry smile. May smiled back, apologetically.

'Good. Now that I have your attention, tell me what's wrong. Is this pique of yours entirely about Preston or is it something more?'

'Something more?' May snapped, reaching for another carrot to dismember. 'Isn't it enough my brother is lying wounded in an obscure farmhouse at the mercy of a treasonous villain and no one will take me to him?'

Beatrice smiled patiently, years of experience in dealing with May's hot temper and outbursts behind her. 'It is enough. I am worried sick for him myself.' Her hand went unconsciously to her stomach and rubbed it in a soothing, settling gesture. 'I think the baby is worried about him, too.'

She laughed a little, but May frowned. 'Are you all right, Bea?' Bea had struggled the last two weeks with swollen feet and the occasional contraction, and she was *huge*.

Bea waved a dismissive hand. 'We were talking about *you*. Don't try to change the subject. You have a bad habit of doing that whenever the subject gets too hot.' Bea reached for the mallet to hammer out meat for the stew. 'Speaking of hot, May, Liam Casek is no iceberg.' May didn't miss the sly look Bea gave her. 'Do you know him? I don't recall Preston ever bringing him around.'

'Bea! Shame on you for noticing. You're about to give birth.' May opted for a teasing scold.

Bea gave her a sly smile. 'It doesn't mean I don't notice a handsome man.'

May finished putting the ingredients in the stewpot and lifted it, trudging over to the large arched brick hearth and hanging the heavy pot over the fire. She wiped her hands on her apron before responding. 'He's not the sort to be brought around.' How did one explain Liam Casek and how he'd somehow risen from a pickpocket to being one of the Home Office's most prized agents. She wasn't sure exactly what he did, but he worked with Preston and that carried some weight. Preston did important and apparently dangerous work that could only be entrusted to the best.

'But obviously Preston brought him home at least once.' Bea was persistent, studying May with an intensity that boded no good. Suddenly, Beatrice snapped her fingers. 'I know when it was! The summer of 1816, the summer you went to the lakes and Jonathon Lashley was home recovering from his wounds.' May watched in dismay as the wheels of Beatrice's sharp mind began to turn. 'Preston always took Jonathon on holiday with your family, but that year he was unable to go.'

It had been a terrible year. Jonathon's brother had gone missing in action and Jonathon had come home near death after Waterloo, something no one had expected. He was an heir. He was supposed to have been kept safe delivering dispatches behind friendly lines. May remembered hearing the news. Jonathon was one of her brother's closest friends. The family had gathered in the drawing room, quiet and sombre. Her indomitable mother had been pale and her father had taken her grown brother in his arms and held him tight as if to convince himself *his* son was alive and healthy. They'd gone to the lakes that summer and Liam Casek had come in Jonathon's place. Her father hadn't entirely approved of Liam in the beginning. Her father had liked him a lot less by the end.

'It's funny you never mentioned him.' Bea cocked her head to one side, considering. The next moment she let out a pained gasp, one hand on her belly, the other on the worktable to steady herself.

May was instantly beside her. 'What is it, Bea?' Beatrice had gone white.

'I don't know. Oh!' Another pain took her and May got an awkward arm about her waist.

'Let's get you to your bed. You can lie down.' It was all May could think of to do. It was hard work moving Bea from the kitchen to the downstairs bedroom. May was thankful they didn't have to go upstairs. But Bea wouldn't lie down. She held on to May's arm.

'You need to go for the doctor, May,' she said softly. 'I think I'm bleeding.'

'I'll go.' Liam's voice in the doorway made May jump. She'd have to get used to him being around all over again.

'I'll go, I won't get lost. You don't know where he lives,' May insisted. If he was out seeing patients, Liam would never find him.

'Then give me his direction,' Liam insisted, his eyes hard as they squared off. 'We can hardly have you out riding willy-nilly over the countryside presenting an easy target and we can't both go.'

'Just *someone* go!' Bea said through clenched teeth, doubling over as another sharp pain took her, her grip on May tight.

May relented at the sight of her friend's agony. 'He keeps an office in the High Street next to the solicitor's.'

'Ah, so you can sue him if you don't like his remedies.' Liam chuckled. 'Very nice arrangement.' Even Bea smiled a little at the jest.

Liam was fast in bringing Dr Stimson, a tall, sombre man whose face showed no emotion. He wasn't the friendly encouraging sort, but he'd been educated in Edinburgh. May didn't especially care for him under the best circumstances. Today, she had no use for him at all.

He examined Beatrice, suggested she was likely experiencing false labour which was entirely normal and which seemed to have stopped once she lay down. He prescribed bed rest until the babe was born and pocketed a little more of their coin.

'I could have done as much!' May challenged, following him out to his horse. 'It has to be more than false labour. How do you explain the blood?'

The man didn't even glance at her as he mounted up. 'All babies come into this world in their own way.' His voice was weary. 'When you have birthed as many children as I have, you can tell me how to do my job, Miss Worth.'

May grabbed the bridle of the big horse. 'She will not be one of the twenty per cent, sir.'

That got a response. He cast her a condescending look down the long pike of his nose. 'What does that mean?'

'Twenty per cent of women die in childbirth. She will not be one of them.' It was a recent great fear of hers since Beatrice had got so big. What if there was no one around to help when the baby came? What if they didn't have enough skill if the birth was difficult?

She knew Bea worried, too, and all she could give her friend were empty promises she didn't know if she could keep.

'May, let the good man go. I had to call him away from his supper.' Liam was behind her, his hand over hers, removing it from the bridle, his touch, no matter how perfunctory, sending sharp pricks of awareness up her arm. He was too close. She had nowhere to go that didn't involve backing into his chest.

It was too close for the doctor, too. 'Are you her husband?' Dr Stimson's eyes slid between them.

'No, sir, I'm a friend of her brother who has come to watch over them,' Liam offered and May bristled. He made it sound like they were children who needed a nursemaid.

The doctor shrugged, ignoring her entirely. 'Too bad. That one needs taking in hand, a strong hand.'

'Duly noted, sir.' Liam nodded and May stepped on his foot. How dare he engage in a conversation about her when she was right there?

'Ouch! What did you do that for?' Liam scowled once the doctor had ridden away.

'Why didn't you defend me?' May railed. 'I despise that man and you kowtowed to him. "Duly noted, sir,"' she mimicked.

Liam laughed. 'You don't need defending, May. You can handle yourself perfectly well when you want to. But you have to learn not to alienate the entire neighbourhood. Don't you know you catch more flies with sugar than vinegar?'

May folded her arms across her chest, studying him. 'Is that what you've been doing these past years? Catching flies with sugar?' There'd been nothing but vinegar about him when she'd first met him, this glorious, angry young man who rebelled at everything, who was fiercely proud of being from the streets. He'd been rebellious in ways she couldn't be or didn't dare to be. She'd admired what she thought of as his courage.

'When it suits me, yes.' The rebel was still there in his long tangle of hair, the rough-hewn planes of his face and the hard muscles of a man who knew how to labour. But the rebel shared space now with a man who carried intelligence behind his blue eyes alongside his anger. This was a man who knew how to control himself, whose anger was no longer tossed about indiscriminately. She wasn't sure if she resented him for that or if she envied him that control. 'It's important to be nice, May, until it's time to be something less...nice.'

'You sound like Preston.'

'Maybe because that's where I learned it.' That gorgeous mouth of his smiled at her as winter dusk fell about them. Her knees wanted to go weak. This was the real danger, not the elusive Cabot Roan, but these moments when she could forget the past, forget the problems of the present and lose herself in him. She didn't want to succumb to his rough charm again. One disaster was enough.

Disaster seemed to be the theme of the day. May sat on the edge of her bed, unopened letter in hand, staring at it. It was going to be bad news, she just knew it, but there was no sense in waiting. If she didn't know what was in the letter, she couldn't begin to plan against it. She drew a fortifying breath and slid a thumb beneath the seal. Her mother's flowery script always looked so innocent. But she'd learned long ago that doom lurked in those elegantly cultivated letters. May skimmed the opening paragraphs, confirming they were her mother's standard opening gambit: news about town, friendly gossip to soften the reader up so when the real punch came, it would blindside you.

There it was, four paragraphs in. May re-read it slowly.

We will be in Edinburgh for the holidays in order to conduct some business of your father's regarding shipping and manufacturing that I don't pretend to understand. We would kindly request your presence.

We've taken a town house in New Town, the address is at the bottom of the page. I'll pack your gowns since you'll have nothing suitable with you to wear. We are looking forward to spending the holidays together even if we are not able to spend them in London.

I have heard Edinburgh is quite festive this time of year and there will be plenty of entertainment. We'll expect you December first. Several of your father's business associates will be in town as well with their families.

Families. May crumpled the paper. She knew what that meant. Sons. Sons who had been groomed to run wealthy, productive businesses, who were ready to take their place in society as wealthy men. Some of them would probably have titles, all of them would have connections to some sort of nobility—perhaps their grandfathers if they were in business and allowed to make money, but still acceptable for the daughter of a second son like herself, still well placed enough in society to rise above the stigma of trade if need be.

She'd been so sure she'd run far enough that her parents couldn't get to her here, that she'd be safe from their matchmaking efforts. All along she'd been worrying over the summons home. But they'd proven her wrong. If they couldn't bring her home, they'd simply come to her and they had. Suddenly Scotland didn't seem so big any more. Edinburgh was just a ferry's ride away from their village on the firth and she didn't think her mother's letter was as harmless as it sounded. Her mother likely had a suitor picked out, or two or three.

She would not panic. She still had some time and she had Liam Casek under her roof, the one man in all of England her father truly despised. She could only imagine the look on her parents' faces when she showed up on their doorstep with him. There was no question of him allowing her to travel without him, he'd made that plain today. Of course, that was assuming she went to Edinburgh at all.

She had almost a month. Anything could happen. There could be a storm. The Forth could be too choppy to cross, the alternate road route impaired from winter weather. Perhaps Cabot Roan would actually kidnap her! Her parents could learn of Preston's injury and cancel their journey. Maybe they already had. This letter would have been posted before they'd have had news of Preston. Then again, if Preston was working secretly, they wouldn't know at all. Still, it was possible one disaster could play against another to her benefit.

The news would devastate Beatrice. May wouldn't say anything until she had to. If she actually left, it would most likely mean she wasn't coming back. She didn't see how she'd escape Edinburgh. The baby would be born by then and her original argument for coming here would be gone. Her parents would insist she'd done what she'd come to do and make her go home with them, back to 'real' life.

May folded the letter into squares. Just this afternoon, she'd been looking ahead to spring, making plans for the greenhouse, imagining raising a baby here. In a matter of hours, that fantasy had been shot to hell. She fought back tears. The past was closing in on her from all sides. She couldn't go to Edinburgh. It would be the end of her life as she knew it. There was only one solution. She just wouldn't go. One disaster was enough.

* * *

One disaster was one too many as far as Cabot Roan was concerned. He drummed his fingers on the polished surface of his desk and stared down the two men standing before him, caps twisting in their hands nervously. 'How is it that you cannot find Preston Worth? He is severely wounded, likely suffering from loss of blood and unable to travel. He's a rabbit gone to ground, and you two…' he made an up-and-down gesture with his hand '…you two are certainly more than rabbits. You are foxes! You are hounds to the hunt. Surely you should be able to find one wounded man.' No one who knew him would be fooled by the incredulity in his voice. It was done with the intent of overt sarcasm.

The taller of the two ventured to speak. 'With all due respect, we questioned the local doctors in every town within a five-mile radius, sir. We offered gold for information. We asked innkeepers, we asked patrons at coaching inns if anyone had passed through.'

Cabot Roan nodded. Preston Worth was a slippery customer. He had managed to disappear and it didn't matter whether he'd done it with or without help. It only mattered that Preston was gone and he'd ripped sheets out of his ledger. In the hands of the wrong people—Worth's people—the information on those sheets would lead to unearthing his entire operation.

Under other circumstances he and Worth would have been friends. Worth's break-in had been simple but bold. The man had wanted the information so he'd come and taken it. Few men would dare to invade his well-guarded domain. But Worth had braved the fences and the dogs and the guards. His window with its long crack and the broken lock still bore the mark of Worth's presence. Cabot admired the man's skill and his bravery. But that skill was going to put his head in a noose if Worth wasn't caught before the information reached its destination.

Roan reached into his desk drawer and threw two pages on the desk. 'Do you see these? They were "recovered" from the mail bag before it left on the mail coach.' He'd paid a handsome fee to the postmaster for the right to look through the mail. Only a man as bold as Worth would trust damning evidence to the London mail coach. Hiding in plain sight as it were. That had been three days ago.

'You have the proof back, then. It doesn't matter if we find Worth,' the shorter man said cheerily.

Roan slammed a hand down on the desk and half-rose. 'No, you fool, it matters more than ever. Can't you see, these are copies? The originals are still out there.' With luck they were on Worth himself and his need to convalesce would slow down their arrival in London, but Roan didn't feel that lucky. Worth would want the papers to travel with all haste even if he couldn't. He would not hesitate to separate himself from the ledger sheets as his attempt at the London mails indicated.

'Pack your bags, gentlemen. You are going to London.'

'But the papers are here.' The short one still didn't quite comprehend.

Roan smiled tightly. 'You're not going for the papers. You're going for his sister. If we can't go to Worth, we'll just have to bring him to us. I have it on good authority the family lives nearly year-round in the city and should be in residence.'

The short one knit his brow. 'Forgive me, sir, but how will Worth know we kidnapped his sister if we don't know where to send the ransom note?'

Heaven save him from fools, but apparently this man was the best at his job that could be found. Roan scowled. 'The family will know how to reach him. Send the ransom note to them. They'll set our little game in motion.' He blew out a breath and silenced any further questions. 'How hard can it be, gentlemen, to kidnap one spoiled debutante when she goes out shopping?'

Chapter Five

She had gone shopping. And she hadn't told him. Of course she hadn't. She was mad at him; mad at him for showing up, mad at him because she couldn't be mad at Preston for getting hurt, for putting her in this situation, mad at having her freedom curtailed, at being told what to do after running wild for months with no one to answer to but herself. He understood this was no more than a knee-jerk reaction to having her freedom limited by him, of all people. But understanding her reasons didn't make the situation better. Anger was no excuse for irresponsible behaviour. This kind of action put everything in danger!

Liam pounded his fist in frustration against the side of the barn. The stubborn little fool! Didn't she understand this wasn't a game? What if Roan was out there right now? That man was a real foe who would do her real harm. Roan would not be intimidated by May's sharp tongue or her pistol. Liam scanned the horizon. May was out there, somewhere, on foot, exposed to whoever might happen along. He had to think along those dangerous lines even if May wouldn't. She'd made it clear last night she was willing to believe the remote location would protect her. He could not afford that luxury. He had to see danger everywhere.

He strode into the stable to saddle his black. He had to go after her, there was no choice. He'd promised Preston. Even if he hadn't, his own conscience demanded it. He'd been here a scant twenty-four hours and he already knew May Worth was going to be the death of him. That hadn't changed, although much else had. May had grown up from a seventeen-year-old on the verge of wild beauty into her full potential. She'd been stunning in the front parlour yesterday, dark hair down about her shoulders, eyes blazing as she aimed a gun at his chest.

Liam swung up on Charon and set off down the road. Presumably, he'd find her in town. It would be best for her if he did. He couldn't scold her publicly there. That would have to wait until they were alone and, if she was lucky, his anger would have cooled into something more rational. But heaven help her if he overtook her on the road with his temper still seething.

Liam pushed Charon into a fast canter, hoping his estimates were accurate and there was no way Cabot Roan could be in Scotland yet. By his calculations, he had approximately a two-week margin give or take a few days before the threat became real; five of those days were already spent in travel. He was banking on London. Roan would look for May there first, which would slow him down, but which would also ultimately reveal her location. Someone in London would know where she was. Despite what May believed, Roan *was* coming, it was just a matter of when. If his calculations were wrong, however, Roan and his men could be here any day.

He wasn't willing to chance it by letting May roam free and unprotected. It infuriated him she was willing to take that chance. She had blatantly chosen to ignore him just for spite. He knew very well why she'd done it; to prove to him she didn't need him, had never needed him, that he hadn't hurt her, that indeed, he had been nothing more than a speck of dust on her noble sleeve, easily brushed off and forgotten.

But that wasn't quite the truth. He had hurt her, just as she had hurt him. They were both realising the past wasn't buried as deeply as either of them hoped.

To get through the next few weeks or months they would have to confront that past and find a way to truly put it behind them if they had any chance of having an objective association. The task would not be an easy one. Their minds might wish it, but their bodies had other ideas. He'd seen the stunned response in her eyes yesterday when she'd recognised him, the leap of her pulse at her neck even as she demanded he take his hand off her. Not, perhaps, because he repulsed her, but because he didn't.

Goodness knew his body had reacted, too. His body hadn't forgotten what it was to touch her, to feel her. Standing behind her in the yard, watching the doctor leave had been enlightening in that regard. He wasn't immune. He hadn't thought he was. He had known how difficult this assignment would be. His anger this morning at finding her gone proved it.

Anger. Lust. Want. These emotions couldn't last. A bodyguard, a man who did dirty things for the Crown, couldn't afford feelings. Emotions would ruin him. Once he started to care, deeply and personally, it would all be over. He thought about the rules he'd attempted to put in place, definitely fragile and already under attack. He chastised himself for making basic, careless mistakes. He'd charged out of the stables, thinking only to get to May as soon as possible. He'd not taken time to consider the road where the land was hidden from view behind tall bushes or around corners or up an incline.

If anyone had been lying in ambush, he would have been an easy target. The man on the passing wagon could have simply picked him off. If he was going to be successful, he had to treat May as he would any other assignment and that meant with a firm hand and objective detachment. She was a job, nothing more, not his past, not his future. Just his job.

The village was busy, considering today was not market day. Liam would have preferred it to be less so. People milled in and out of shops, or stopped to stand in front of a window and admire a display. Liam quartered all the busyness with his gaze, taking the street in section by section. He was familiar with it now, having travelled it to retrieve the doctor yesterday. His professional's eye saw the alleys between buildings where someone might lurk undetected. He saw a heavy dray moving down the street slowly and obtrusively, blocking traffic. On purpose? his expert's mind wondered and his pulse quickened, alert to trouble. Then he saw her.

To the casual observer, she looked like any other countrywoman, dressed as she was in a forest-green wool, a blue-and-green plaid shawl wrapped about her, a basket on her arm, a bonnet on her head. It was remarkable, really, how well she blended in. Who would guess she was the daughter of Albermarle Worth, granddaughter to an earl on her father's side? But Liam would never take her for just another pretty country miss. The way she walked was unmistakably May. May moved with purpose, with confidence, a step faster than other women.

With grim determination, he strode stealthily through the crowd. At the corner, he made his move, coming up behind her, a strong hand about her waist, trapping her against him, his grip steering her into the dim privacy of the alley. In two steps, before she could even think to scream, he had her alone up against the alley wall, a hand over her mouth, their bodies pressed together. Closeness was a matter of protection for him. The closer May was, the less she could hurt him. May wanted to fight, he could feel her body primed for it. She was furious, wanting to strike out with her fists against his chest, a kick to his knee, but at this distance there was no chance.

'What are you doing? You scared me!' To her credit, May was a pale virago. He had succeeded in frightening her and that had been his intention.

'I'm showing you how easy it would have been to have stolen you away, with no one on the street any the wiser,' he growled into her face. 'Did you see how none of your fine villagers noticed you slipped off the street? How none of them thought to come to your assistance?' He let her go and stepped back out of range.

May glared. 'How dare you pull such a stunt after everything that has happened? I have my brother on my mind and Beatrice, too.'

'All the more reason you need me. You're distracted.' He would not let her push the blame in his direction. 'I'm not the one pulling the stunt, May. I'm not the one who left home without an escort.' Perhaps his lesson was harsh, but it was needed. Mixed with his anger over her disobedience had been a certain amount of fear. 'What were you thinking to leave without me?'

She didn't need to answer. He knew what she'd been thinking. Liam took her arm and pulled her out of the alley. 'Walk with me. We can finish your errands, *together.*'

Back on the street, Liam inclined his head discreetly towards a man leaning against the wall of the inn. 'Do you see that man over there, the one with the hat pulled low over his face?'

He felt May stiffen beside him. 'Is he...?' She couldn't bring herself to say the words. But she *was* worried. Good. He needed her scared. He needed this to become real for her.

'No, he's not, but how would you know? Did you even notice him?' Liam went on, 'Most people don't notice anyone out of place until it's too late.'

'Most people don't need to notice,' May retorted.

Liam slid a sharp glance her direction. 'Do you think you're most people, May? Because if you do, that is your first mistake. You are the granddaughter of an earl, the daughter of a wealthy and powerful man in Parliament. Your father is deep in the government with opinions that some men find unpopular at best, dangerous to their own livelihoods at worst. You are in constant threat of being made a target for other men's ambitions. You cannot afford to think of yourself as "most people".' Neither could he. That had been his mistake back when he'd been barely out of adolescence. He'd seen plenty of the world in those days, a slum-raised kid couldn't help but see it in all its roughness, all its darkness. But he'd never seen a world like hers. Despite what reality had taught him about the gulf between people like the Worths and people like him, he'd been ill-equipped for it and for her. He'd been cocky, full of his street smarts and he'd reached so far above himself he hadn't even understood how far it was.

May gave a toss of her head. 'I refuse to live life gaoled by my fears. I cannot spend my days second-guessing the motives of everyone I meet, or seeing danger around every corner.' Like he did, that was quite obviously implied, just as it was implied that such behaviour was a slur on one's character.

'Thank goodness you don't have to, then. That's what people like you hire people like me to do for them.' The careless words slipped out.

May stopped, hands on hips and faced him, studying him until he couldn't take the silence. 'What?'

'I'm just wondering how you can walk at all.

Must be difficult to move while carrying something so heavy around with you all the time. Big chip on the shoulder and all that. Must weigh you down something fierce.'

He probably deserved that. This had always been the sticking point between them, this issue of birth and class and social status, something she had argued didn't matter...until the end when it suddenly had. Liam said nothing. He reached for her basket and she raised a brow as if to say 'now you choose to play the gentleman?' They finished her errands in terse silence and made their way to where Charon was tethered. He cupped his hands, ready to toss her up. But May hesitated.

'C'mon, May.' He gave her a grin, daring her, even though it broke his personal promise to remain objective. *She was just a job these days.* But if that was true, why did he keep tempting himself with pleasurable reminders that it hadn't always been this way. 'Surely you remember how well we rode together?'

'I remember,' May said tersely, her chin set stubbornly. He could see she wanted to refuse, but she put her foot in his hands and hauled herself up anyway, refusing to be outdared. Liam wisely made no comment and swung up behind her.

* * *

She hated how he could do that. How did he know? Of all the memories she had of him, how was it he could hone in on one of her favourites? May felt him settle into the saddle, his strong legs encasing her in the vee of his thighs. She should have argued to ride behind him. Then she'd be the one wrapping arms around his waist. Now he was the one doing the wrapping with his one arm about her as he held the reins, his thighs about her, her body drawn against him, back to chest, buttocks to groin. Riding before him was far too intimate, although once she'd revelled in stealing such intimacy. It had been her first taste of a man. She didn't want to remember. She pulled her shawl more tightly about her. It had been summer then, a day far warmer than this chilly November afternoon...

'Faster!' she had cried, throwing her arms wide and lifting her face to the sun as they raced across the meadow, Liam's arm tight about her as the dark stallion surged beneath them.

'Hold on, May!' Liam's voice warned in her ear, but she didn't care. She was safe with him. He would never let her fall. She had a fast horse beneath her and Liam Casek mounted

behind her, what more did she need? This was heaven.

At the edge of the meadow where the flat run gave out to a copse of tall oaks, Liam swung down and held his arms up for her, his hands strong and steady at her waist. May knew what she wanted. She'd barely touched the ground before she grabbed him by the hand, dragging him into the little woods behind her, but it was he who pressed her against the trunk of a sturdy oak and kissed her, hard and open-mouthed, his body pressed to hers, pulsing with life.

She'd not imagined a kiss could be so full-bodied, that it could make a person feel immortal, as though they could take on the world, do anything. Now that she knew, she wanted to feel that way again and again. Her arms were about his neck, holding him close, her hands in his long dark hair, the hair her father hated and had offered to have his valet cut. She was glad Liam had refused. She loved Liam's hair, loved dragging her hands through it, anchoring her fingers in it as he took her mouth.

His hips moved against her in honest suggestion, the hardness of him evident through breeches and skirts. There was no reason to hide anything they felt from one another, not their feelings, not their bodies. They were one in this burning, consuming passion that made life so much brighter—that brought the edges of slow, lazy summer days into sharper relief. Her hand dropped between them to the source of his hardness, tracing it through his breeches, cupping it in her hand until he groaned.

'If you keep that up, May, you'll bring me off in my trousers.' His mouth was at her neck, his breath coming hard between his words.

She was powerful and coy in her response. 'I'd like to do that.' She laughed. He bit her neck in playful retaliation and she yelped.

'And I'd like to bite you some more, but we don't dare leave any marks your father will see,' Liam cautioned with a wicked smile before stealing a short kiss from her lips. 'One more kiss, May, and then we have to go. The others will be looking for us.' Only Preston had seen them slip away from the picnic. Her father had settled into a post-picnic nap and her mother and the neighbour's wife had wandered down to the lake.

'Only one more?' Her arms were back around his neck, her tone teasing and light. 'Make it a good one, then.' She cocked her head, her tone slightly more serious. 'Or maybe I should? This time, let me kiss you.'

Liam gave a throaty chuckle. 'I thought that's what you had been doing.'

She dropped half-lidded eyes to his mouth. 'You know what I mean. Let me start it this time. I want to kiss you.' She brushed her mouth across his, slowly at first, letting her tongue trace the contours of his lips, coaxing his mouth to open. They'd got much better at this since that first kiss in the stables. She liked this slow, languorous kissing as much as she liked the heated madness of the others, the sensual exploration of being in his mouth, of tasting the sweet remnants of lemonade on his tongue. She let her mouth say all the things she didn't have words for yet in this new heady world of Liam Casek and stolen kisses. Forbidden kisses.

May was not oblivious. If there was one blight in May's perfect world it was that this had to be hidden. Her father could never know about this. He tolerated Preston bringing this friend along. He even understood this was an opportunity to do some good for a young man with potential who'd been born into poverty. However, he would never condone that young man kissing his daughter, no matter how much potential he had and heaven forbid he find out

his daughter had put her hand on an Irishman.
She was meant for far greater men...

In retrospect, the beginning had been quite nearly the end as well. Maybe there had never been any hope, their passion ill fated from the start, only they'd been too naïve to see it. But for a while the illusion had been nice. More than nice. There were still nights when she lay awake, wanting to feel that way again, free and immortal, even knowing those feelings were part of an illusion, part of something unsustainable. In the end, he had left her.

Liam brought the horse to a halt in front of the cottage and leapt off, taking her perfunctorily by the waist to help her down. There was no boyish exuberance on his part and there was no grabbing of his hand and dragging him off for a kiss on hers, further proof the wounds they'd given one another had been deep and lasting.

'I need to check on Beatrice and get supper started or we won't eat until nine o'clock,' May excused herself and hurried inside. Those wounds would never go away. They were scabbed over, a thick outer layer of protection. But scabs could be picked, if they weren't careful, and those wounds could be exposed. The wisest course of action here would be to tread carefully. The afternoon had shown her that much.

Being close to him had conjured up memories best left undisturbed and, oh, how easily they'd been conjured! It was as if they lay just beneath the surface instead of buried deep down. May tied on her apron and reached determinedly for the round of bread dough. She gave it a thorough punch and began kneading. If she was going to survive the next two months, avoidance would be her best policy.

Chapter Six

That night he dreamed of her. He couldn't avoid her, not even in his sleep. A mental flashback come to life: May with her hair down, her face shining with mischief, her features softer and more innocent than they were now, before the world had disappointed her for the first time. Or perhaps it was only he who had disappointed her? In the dream, it didn't matter. The dream was before all of that...

She was tugging him, half-running, half-walking, down the wide aisle of Worth's summer stables, dust motes dancing in the shafts of sunlight as she laughed over her shoulder. There was something she wanted to show him and apparently it was at the back of the stable—the immaculate stable—Liam noted. There wasn't a single errant stick of straw about the place. Of course not. Worth hired a boy just for that purpose. Liam caught sight of a young boy with a broom in hand out of the corner of his eye as he and May ducked around a dark corner to her destination.

May leaned against the wall, looking up at him with her dancing eyes. Good lord, those eyes were going to be the undoing of him. They made him want things he had no right to want. 'I envy him.' Liam jerked his head towards the sweeping boy moving away from them with his rhythmic push and glide of broom against floor.

'I don't,' May answered bluntly. 'Doing the same thing every day.' She shuddered her distaste. And why wouldn't she? She had access to so much more. 'He sweeps all day, every day. How boring is that?' If there was one thing May Worth despised, it was being bored. Preston's sister was a wild handful. She'd dogged their steps since their arrival, riding with them, fishing, even swimming although he was fairly sure her parents hadn't known she'd come along.

Liam leaned an arm against the wall just over her head, suddenly aware of how close they were to one another and how alone. 'I think he's quite lucky. I've done much worse than sweep for a fraction of what he receives in return.'

'What he receives?' May queried with an interested cock of her head. 'A few pennies?'

Liam chuckled. 'Oh, May, he gets more than pennies from this. He gets good clothes, a warm place to sleep, three meals a day and, yes, a few pennies in his pocket. Then there's his future and he gets that here, too. He's not just sweeping. He's learning about the stables every day, learning the care of horses simply by being around them. He'll move up the ranks when he's of age. He won't sweep for ever. He'll be a groom. If he reaches high enough, he could be master of horse eventually. He'll be able to tell his bride he has an honourable, reliable living they can raise a family on. He can build his whole life from this. He'll never need to worry.'

That silenced her, pretty May Worth in her pale pale blue summer riding habit, who wanted for nothing, who couldn't begin to imagine what it meant to live in constant need. 'I will never look at a sweeper the same,' she said with quiet sincerity, not necessarily because of what he'd said—although that had clearly made some impact—but because he'd shown too much of himself and she'd seen it— the wistfulness that he'd once dreamed such a position might be available to him.

Her green-eyed gaze turned contemplative, her voice soft. 'What's the worst thing you've ever done?'

She was dangerous to his senses like this, an unbridled threat to a reality that said he could not have a girl like her—beautiful and spoiled beyond measure. In these moments, rich and poor didn't matter, didn't exist. Maybe that was why he told her the truth. *'I worked for a doctor in the slums. After his, ah, surgeries, I disposed of the waste, the remains.'* It was the most delicate way he could describe what he'd done for the doctor who visited the St Giles whores.

May put a hand against his chest, the first time she'd ever deliberately, voluntarily touched him. Could she feel his pulse speed up? *'That's why you do it, then,'* she said it almost more to herself.

'Do what?' he asked cautiously.

'Add things up with your eyes. When you look around a room, it's like you're estimating the value of its contents.' Thinking about money was one thing a gentleman was definitely not supposed to do. Price was to be no obstacle and yet surrounded by all this opulence, Liam couldn't stop thinking of the cost of it all and not merely the financial expense, but the social

expense it took to sustain all this. A gentleman never counted costs—of any kind.

'I'll have to work on that.' Perhaps gentlemen were born, not made, after all. It was a hypothesis Preston was working on—could a man become a gentleman? Or was it something a man was born with, some indefinable quality passed through the genes?

'How old were you?' May wasn't done with her gentle interrogation.

'Nine,' he answered, aware this was becoming far too personal. 'But I don't think that has anything to do with what you wanted to show me when you dragged me out here.'

She slanted him a coy glance that spoke of trouble, her eyes starting to sparkle again. 'No, it isn't.' May stood on her tip toes, twining her arms about his neck. 'This is.'

'May, what are you doing?' But he knew. His hands were already at her waist as if they had always belonged there.

'A girl only gets one first kiss and I've decided, Liam Casek, mine should be with you...'

Liam woke, almost able to feel the press of her lips as if it had only just happened. He'd never forgotten that kiss, long and slow like a lazy summer afternoon, as if they'd had all the time in the world. He'd had a lot of kisses since then—five years' worth of kisses, some more tumultuous, others more passionate, but he still remembered that one, would always remember that one. That kiss had lit a spark of hope, misguided as it turned out to be. There were days he thought it might have been better if that spark had burnt down the barn instead.

It was some comfort to note he wasn't suffering alone. May felt the tension, too. By noon the next day, it was clear May was trying to avoid him. It wasn't even very subtle. She simply endeavoured to be wherever he wasn't. And she wasn't being entirely successful. He was making it difficult on purpose. If she was going to haunt his dreams, he was damned well going to haunt her days. He wasn't going to suffer alone. Misery loved company, after all. At least there were no more unaccompanied jaunts to town.

He wasn't gullible enough to believe it was because he'd succeeded in knocking any sense into her about the gravity of her situation. It was more likely because she didn't want him to come after her. Whatever the reason, he'd take it if it kept May safe. The road that passed the cottage was not terribly busy, only a few wagons went by and he'd learned their patterns, just as he'd learned May's and the days took on a shape of their own.

Between them, they implicitly claimed their own spheres of influence. They divided up the labour of running a small holding. He took the outdoors, spending his days repairing fences and the barn roof in anticipation of the snow and sleet to come. She stayed near the house, busy with laundry, with cooking, with turning mundane domestic chores into a subtle siege against his rules of restraint. He wasn't even sure she intended it to be an assault as much as she intended it to be revenge for hot words spoken years earlier: *you're nothing but a spoiled princess. You could never survive in my world. That's why you're afraid. You're a coward and a hypocrite.* Regardless of what the ploy was, it *was* working.

It was a dangerous domesticity to look over from his work and see her outside, in the cold November weather, washing his shirt, or to lie down at night on freshly ironed sheets sprinkled with lavender and to know that the shirt, the sheets, had all been done with her hand. Every careful crease had been her doing. For him. Another man would be flattered. He was too smart to be that man, even if he had to admit he wasn't entirely immune to her efforts.

The kitchen door opened and May came out, wrapped in a warm shawl, a mug of something hot cradled in her hands as she moved towards him, likely oblivious to the sway of her hips. 'I thought you might like something to drink. I made hot cider. It's cold today.'

Liam took the mug. He welcomed the warmth and the drink, but with scepticism. 'What are you playing at, May? If you think I'll let you go into town because you made me cider, you're wrong. It's far too dangerous.'

Her eyes flashed for a second and he wasn't fooled by the demure words. 'Do I have to want something?'

'Yes,' he said boldly. 'You've been doing your best to avoid me and now suddenly you've voluntarily brought me a hot drink. Forgive me my penchant for suspicion.' He chuckled, breathing in the warm steam. 'Have you decided to stop avoiding me, May?' Not that avoidance had been very successful to start with, as they were both well aware. No matter how hard she tried for distance in the day, there was always supper at the end of it and neither of them could escape that. They started their days together with breakfast and finished them together with supper. Company was unavoidable on those occasions, especially now that Beatrice was confined to her bed. Quite frankly, avoidance had only served to make them more aware of one another when they were together. He was sure *that* aspect had definitely not been part of May's plan.

'I'm not avoiding you.' May's determined point of a chin went up.

'Not me, perhaps, but what I stand for—a past you'd rather forget, a past that is awkward to remember let alone face.' He eyed her over the rim of the mug, watching her for any telltale signs of the truth. 'Or is it that you've come to gloat? To lord the past over me? Have you come to collect my surrender, May?'

She looked frustrated. 'Whatever are you talking about?'

Liam leaned on the shovel. 'You've been making your case all week with your laundry and sheets, your perfectly cooked meals and...' his gaze slid down to the mug of cider in his hands '...hot drinks delivered to a hardworking man in the cold. You want to prove I was wrong about your ability to make it in the real world.'

'I dare say most men would be appreciative of my attentions,' May argued, refusing to acknowledge the old quarrel, the hard words that had been spoken between them. But it was acknowledged in other ways: the flush of her cheeks, her breath coming in visible huffs in the cold. She'd not forgotten that quarrel any more than he had.

'Other men don't know you like I do.' May was not flaunting her rather impressive domestic skills for the reason other women might: to catch a husband. A husband was the last thing May wanted. No, May was attempting to prove she wasn't the spoiled rich girl he'd once accused her of being. 'So which is it, Maylark? Why did you come out here? As a bribe or to start an argument?' That got a rise out of her. How he did love nettling her! She was never more herself than when she was mad.

'You're the only one that calls me that and the answer is neither. You are an insufferable man who greatly overestimates his appeal. Maybe I just came out to tell you supper is in two hours.'

Liam watched her go with a chuckle. Maybe it was worth being here just to fight with her again. Nobody he'd ever met fought quite like May; honest and bold and sharp. That didn't mean he wasn't paying for the pleasure of her company. He had two hours to work off his own heat, two hours to wonder if their little quarrel left her feeling as dissatisfied as it did him. Maintaining his sense of professional detachment was deuced hard when he'd been damned tempted to settle this quarrel the way they'd settled their quarrels in the past...

'We could go away, May, maybe to America. There's opportunity for anyone who is willing to work for it.' She was in his arms, in the grass beneath a tall, shady tree, her hair falling against his arm, her hand tracing idle patterns on his chest. They'd not talked of plans or futures, but the summer was coming to an end. They had a week or two at most before the Worths would go back to London, Preston back to Oxford and he would go...well, back to earth after this idyll in heaven, unless...

'America? What would we do there? What opportunities would there be for us?' May questioned, her response not as positive as he'd hoped for. He'd lain awake nights thinking this through.

'I could work on the docks. Boston is becoming a big port, or we could go south to the port of Charleston. I hear the weather is warm. That would be nice for a change. No more cold winters.'

'As a clerk?' May murmured.

'Um, no, as a dockhand at first,' Liam hedged. His reading and penmanship proba-

bly weren't up to the standards necessary for a clerk. Not yet, anyway. He was making progress, a lot of it, in fact, for a man who'd been illiterate until last year.

'*How would we live?*' *May persisted.*

'*I will work, you could work maybe in a dress shop, or taking in laundry.*' *He knew they were the wrong words as soon as he said them. No one expected the regal May Worth to work. She probably didn't even know how to do laundry, another blatant reminder of how different their lives truly were. She would expect a decent home in a decent neighbourhood. He'd never had a home, not even growing up. He had slept on whatever beds were vacant at the whorehouse and here was May expecting more than a bed, a whole house.*

'*I suppose I could,*' *May hedged. She didn't sound convincing.*

'*You're afraid,*' *Liam accused, angry at her, but mostly angry at himself for suggesting it, for not having a better plan, for not being more.*

May sat up, eyes flashing. '*I'm not scared, it's just that I'm not stupid. We can't go haring off halfway around the world on a whim and hope everything will work out.*'

Her honest words cut. In a few sentences, she'd managed to destroy his plan. '*Then what*

*do you think happens when summer is over?'
Liam challenged.*

*'I don't know.' He saw the sadness in her
eyes. So she had thought about it, too—all of
this glorious passion coming to an end. They
were silent for a long moment, grappling with
their thoughts, eyes holding.*

*He broke the quiet, reaching for her. 'I don't
know what happens next week, but I know what
happens now. I don't want to waste the time we
have left quarrelling with you, May. I'd rather
spend it loving you.' He kissed her hard on the
mouth, taking her back down to the ground,
rolling her beneath him. At least on this score,
they could agree.*

Chapter Seven

Liam put away his tools for the day and washed up at the pump outside in spite of the cold. He'd need all the cold he could get. The cottage would be warm in all ways. Dinners were the best and the worst part of the day, the one time they couldn't avoid each other.

He stepped inside the cottage, the smells of fresh bread and stew reminding him how hungry he was, how demanding a day of manual labour could be on a man's appetite. He smiled to himself. He was getting soft on all the good living that had come his way since he'd met Preston. That day, nine, almost ten years ago, had changed everything for him. One day he'd been running errands for a merchant who delivered supplies to one of the dons at Oxford and the next he'd been sitting down to dinner with an earl's grandson and learning the elementary aspects of chess.

The table was set for them in the kitchen. May liked to eat by the fire at the worktable. As usual, the worktable had been laid with a clean blue-and-white checked cloth, and the pewter plates and bowls had been set out, a loaf of bread and a pitcher between them. Liam knew many men who would delight in coming home to such a setting. A hot meal made all the difference at the end of a hard day.

'Dinner smells good.' He wasn't going to let a quarrel get between him and hot food. Although the St Giles slums and starving days were years behind him, he'd never forgotten what a luxurious commodity hot food was. There'd been a time when he'd gone months without hot food, living off bread crusts and meat scraps from tavern dumpsters.

May untied her apron, trying to ignore his smile, trying to ignore *him* which she hadn't yet been able to do, he had made sure of that. Maybe that was *his* revenge. Maybe she wasn't the only one who wanted to prove the other wrong. Maybe he wanted to prove to May *he* could change. At least a little. He would never be a gentleman-born, but he'd certainly become more than a street rat. Still, there were some things he wasn't willing to change, not even for her. He would never forget where he was from. He didn't want to, it kept him honest about the world and it was part of him. Anyone who accepted him had to accept the entirety of him, history and all.

'How was Beatrice today?' Liam pulled his customary high stool up to the table and sliced the bread, offering her a piece. Small talk and mundane actions could go a long way in creating the illusion of normalcy.

'Fine. The same.' May took the bread and spread butter on it, butter she'd traded for in the market. May hadn't mastered the art of butter churning. It was good to see there was one domestic skill she hadn't acquired. It meant he didn't have to admit he was wrong just yet. 'I don't think there will be much change until the baby comes, which should be any day now.' She ladled stew into his bowl and passed it to him, fingers brushing his. Normalcy was going well if one didn't count the way his blood heated when she touched him, or when she reached for something on the table, drawing the bodice of her gown tight against her breasts with the movement.

'Then perhaps we should go into town tomorrow,' Liam suggested, ignoring the beginnings of an arousal he'd barely subdued in the yard with cold, hard work. The food, the firelight, the company in the warm kitchen seemed hell-bent on destroying those efforts. 'We might not get another chance and it's already been several days since our last visit.' While he liked the stationary nature of the past week, he was growing agitated with the lack of information that came with such stagnation. 'I was thinking there might be some news from Preston.'

At the admission, May's eyes met his. Whatever bad blood lay between them, they both loved Preston. They were united on that at least. It was a start. 'Do you think he might find a way to send news?'

'There are ways to disguise a missive and Preston knows them all.' Liam smiled, enjoying for a moment that May's guard was partially down. 'A letter could be addressed to Beatrice Fields. It could be signed from a fictional sender,' he offered. 'No one would suspect it.'

May set down her spoon and fixed him with a considering stare. 'What exactly do you and my brother do for the government that demands such secrecy? That has people knifing my brother on dark roads?'

Liam shrugged as if he hadn't inadvertently opened himself up for an inquisition. 'Your brother protects the coast against smugglers. You know that. Not all smugglers deal in brandy and not all smuggling takes place during war time. Just because the war is over, doesn't mean there's nothing to do.'

'And yourself? What have you spent the last five years doing?' May didn't miss the fact that he hadn't answered the last part of her question. Maybe he'd been wrong and it wasn't her guard that was down, but his.

How to answer? 'I've spent the last five years proving to you that I can rise above my birth?' or 'I've spent the years trying to earn your father's respect', or 'I've been proving to myself that I am worthy, that I'm more than a street rat.' All of it? None of it? If he said the words, the old wounds would open. It would make confronting the past and their choices inevitable, something they'd barely skirted this afternoon. He'd not come up here for that. Liam groped for his professional detachment. Disclosing details about where he'd been, what he'd done, wasn't part of the job. Liam opted for something far more neutral. 'I've been working with your brother.' True. 'It's my job to watch his back and right now that includes you.'

May gave him a cold smile and tore her slice

of bread in half. 'I'm a job. What a positively lovely way to think of oneself.'

'Yes, isn't it?' Liam didn't back down although the comment drew them ever closer to more dangerous subjects. Her father had viewed him as a job, a piece of *noblesse oblige* to be satisfied with crumbs from the high table. 'It really provides perspective when one understands their place.' His sarcasm was sharply evident.

'Stop it.' May's eyes fired, her hands braced on the table.

'Stop what? Stop reminding you that we have a history? That we have some difficult truths between us? Stop reminding you you're my job? Hurts, doesn't it?' He half-rose and leaned over the table, the frustration of the last week coming to full boil. 'Would you prefer I remind you that you were once my lover instead?'

'Keep your voice down!' May hissed. 'Do you want Beatrice to hear you?'

He gave her a wicked grin. 'I don't care who knows, May. But apparently you do.' He felt the grin slip off his face at what that meant and his anger pitched. 'You little hypocrite. You're still too embarrassed to acknowledge me, to stand up for me. Your friends don't know what you got up to that summer at the lake, do they? They don't know the pristine Miss May Worth went slumming for some hot Irish c—'

'Stop it!' she yelled, hurling her stew bowl at him in a lightning move that surprised them both. Only his street-honed, battle-tested reflexes saved him. The bowl sailed across the table, barely missing him and finding the wall instead. Meat chunks and carrots slid ignominiously down the wall. Better the wall than him. Crockery was hell on the skull.

May covered her mouth and staggered back, anger evaporating in the wake of her shock. She couldn't complete a sentence. He could see her playing the scene again in her mind, horrified at her knee-jerk reaction. 'I'm sorry. Oh, my... I can't believe... I didn't mean to...' But of course she did and maybe he had meant to do it, too. He'd made her mad, perhaps on purpose. She had a temper. He could always bring out the best and worst in her. He knew it and he'd done it anyway. In his book, that made him culpable, too.

'Don't lie, May. You're not any good at it. You wanted to hit me.' Liam snatched up a rag from the counter and bent to clean the wall. She was beside him on her knees, tugging the rag from his hand.

'Let me. It's my fault.' She was quietly apologetic. He should have accepted what passed as an apology with May, but he was feeling penitent, too. He'd taken his frustration out on her by provoking her. So much for his vaunted objectivity, hardly the behaviour of a trained professional with his impeccable record.

He clenched his hand around the rag, not giving it up. 'It's not entirely your fault, May. Maybe I wanted you to throw that bowl.'

She pulled at the rag again with no success. 'That's just like you. You can't even let me take the blame without wanting to one-up me. *This* is my fault. I could have hurt you.' She paused, her grip on the rag going slack as she studied him. 'You *are* all right?' Her gaze searched his face for signs of a cut, of a bruise and the concern that flitted across her own face was more dangerous than any harsh words. He was always ready for her sharp tongue, always prepared. But he was not ready for kneeling together on the kitchen floor, the firelight and evening about them, those words of concern as heady as fine brandy as she looked at him. How many nights had he lain awake wanting this? Or worse, dreaming of this? Of her touch on his body again?

With one hand she traced the small curving

scar high on his cheek, the delicate tracing of her finger raising goose bumps on his flesh. 'How did you get this?' Her voice was quiet in the fire-lit darkness of the kitchen.

'Carelessness.' His old protectiveness surged, the protectiveness that didn't want to burden May with anything unpleasant. 'I was sloppy and a man got too close with a knife.'

'You are too hard on yourself, I think,' May said with a soft smile. For a moment it was easy to believe he had his May back, that they were both young again and anything was possible as long as they were together. 'Someday you'll realise you aren't invincible.'

'I hope not,' Liam breathed. It was his worst fear: that his strength and skill would fail when he needed them most. They had to last at least until after Cabot Roan was brought to justice and May was safe.

He shouldn't have done it, but the night was already so full of things he shouldn't have done, shouldn't have said, that one more hardly seemed to make a difference. *Carpe diem* was what Preston called it. Seize the day, or at the very least the rag. Would that be *pannum* or *linteum*? he wondered vaguely. Those Latin lessons of Preston's had been ages ago. Liam tightened his grip on the rag, taking advantage of May's inattention to it and pulled at the cloth until she was in his arms, until her body was up against his, and his mouth was on hers in a kiss that claimed and kindled, the old ways alight at last. Now *this* was how to settle a fight.

It was not a gentle kiss, there was no need to play the courteous swain. There was only need and it sprang like a wildfire from him to her, her mouth open to him, her tongue hungry for a taste as it sought him, her teeth biting greedily into his lower lip, sucking hard as he pressed her to the wall, their arms and legs starting to grip one another in an attempt to find equilibrium. Her arms were around his neck as if they remembered where they belonged, holding on to him as if he were a rock, an anchor that would keep her steady. His hands were at her skirts, tugging them out from where they were trapped under her knees. He wanted to slide his hands beneath them, up her legs, to her wet core. He wanted to touch her, wanted to remind her, wanted to remind himself.

His hand was halfway up her thigh when she shoved at him, eyes blazing with a thousand emotions: want, need, anger, betrayal. She was no fool. She'd gone to him willingly and now she was angry with herself for letting it go this far, for liking it. He was no fool either.

He was going to pay for her anger. 'What the hell do you want from me?' she snapped, her breath coming hard.

His voice was a fierce growl. He gripped her arms. 'I want you to admit you didn't always hate me.' That even now after throwing a bowl at his head, she didn't hate him.

She wrenched herself away, getting to her feet, her chin coming up in a mimicry of the defiance she'd displayed in the yard. 'That's something you'll never hear from me, Liam Casek.'

His own defiance couldn't resist a parting shot as she stormed out of the kitchen. 'Too late.' He had what he wanted. May Worth still burned for him. She'd just proven it far beyond words. But like most ill-conceived wishes, it brought more questions than it answered. Now that he knew, what did he do with it? What *could* he do with it?

In many ways, his hands were just as tied as they'd been years ago. Perhaps more so. The things that kept them apart once were still there and now there were new burdens—burdens he'd ironically acquired in an attempt to improve himself. He'd made his way in the world, become successful at what he did, but at what cost? What would May think if she knew? She had once understood the boy who disposed of remains for the doctor. Would she understand the man who occasionally disposed of British difficulties? She thought she knew what he did, but his life was far darker than her brother's. With so much of the unknown stacked against him, he began to question what he'd done tonight. Why had he done it? What did he hope for?

What had she done? May stumbled down the short dark hall towards the two bedrooms in the back of the cottage. There was no sense in a composed, elegant departure now that she was out of sight, no sense in hiding just how much Liam had got to her. Sweet heavens, she'd nearly lost herself right there on the kitchen floor. Was that what she wanted? To have her lover again despite everything? She'd had her hands all over him; around his neck, in his hair, and that wasn't even everywhere she'd liked to have had them. It had taken his hand up her skirts to bring her to her senses. Oh, she hadn't minded that hand at all. She had to be brutally honest with herself.

She'd plenty well *liked* everything that had happened on the kitchen floor. It was the motives she questioned. The physical game had never been their problem. It was the mental one. How dare he profess to be here only out of loyalty to Preston? How dare he tell her she was nothing more than a job and then act entirely to the contrary? He couldn't waltz in here and pretend he hadn't failed her at the critical moment, or pretend a five-year absence was akin to an apology, that there was a statute of limitations on betrayal and all was now forgiven. But she wasn't sure his was the worst crime of the night. That honour was quite possibly hers. She'd *let* herself enjoy the interlude, if only briefly. Perhaps he could assume such pretensions, after all. Her response to him certainly indicated as much.

Even now, with her anger still simmering over his parting shot, her mind was contemplating the possibilities of forgiving—or at the very least dismissing—the past, as long as she didn't forget it. For her own sanity she had to remember that Liam Casek was no gentleman. He ascribed to none of the honour codes that defined a gentleman. Liam Casek was a product of the streets and had his own code: see to thyself first.

She had not understood that before. But now that she did, perhaps it was possible to enjoy the earthy pleasures he provided without encountering the hurt. That was the improbable thought running through her head—a wicked compromise to the emotions he stirred in her. Tonight had been proof that those earthy pleasures still existed between them. Time had done nothing to wear down the edge of their physical attraction. If anything, it had ratcheted that attraction up a notch. He'd been no green boy kissing her tonight, but a man who knew full well what he was about, what he wanted and how to get it. That kiss had told her something else, too. She wasn't alone in the frustration. He felt it as well. Tonight, it had been as if a dam had finally broken, burst apart by the tension between them. What if he felt the same way: that they might be able to assuage those physical needs without addressing the emotional ones? It was a dangerous thought.

Her shin knocked into a small console set in the narrow hall. 'Damn it!' she swore, remembering at the last moment to keep her voice down. She didn't want to wake Beatrice.

'May? Are you all right? You can swear out loud. I'm not asleep.' There was the rustle of covers from Beatrice's room.

'I'm fine, don't get up,' May called out softly. But it was too late. Beatrice, lamp in hand, stood at the door of her room.

'You don't look fine. Unless I miss my guess, you've been quarrelling with our house guest, again.' Beatrice paused, fixing her with a stern stare, but her voice was soft and inviting. 'Don't you think it's time you told me all about it? All about *him*?'

Chapter Eight

May entered the little room with a tentative step. This was a conversation she'd hoped to avoid from the moment Liam had shown up. 'There's nothing to tell. Yes, I knew him from before. He's a friend of Preston's who came to the lakes with us.' May shrugged, trying to make light of it in the hope Beatrice would stop prying, convinced there was nothing to it.

'I've never known you to throw crockery at any other of Preston's friends,' Beatrice said mildly. 'In fact, I don't recall you ever threw anything at Jonathon.'

May winced. 'You heard?'

Beatrice gave a soft laugh. 'Yes, I heard. How could I not? This isn't Worth House in London with its twenty rooms and four floors. Now, you can either take a seat and keep a pregnant woman company, or you can let me imagine the lurid worst.' That was the problem, May thought. The lurid worst might not be that far from the actual truth. Still, she opted to sit. If Bea wasn't going to be dissuaded, she might as well get this over with.

'Are you sure you want to hear? Wouldn't you rather sleep?' Bea looked tired. Even in the dim lamplight, May could make out dark smudges under her friend's eyes. Bed 'rest' didn't seem to be all the restful.

'I lie around all day and all night with nothing to do but worry. I am so uncomfortable I can barely sleep more than two hours at a time. You aren't keeping me from anything but my own thoughts, which I desperately need a break from. I'd love a chance to worry about something else.'

May reached for her hand. 'Bea, what's wrong?' She heard the frustration in her friend's voice.

Bea shook her head resolutely. 'Oh, no, you don't. We are going to talk about you and Mr Casek. I believe you said it was the summer at the lake?'

'Yes. The summer of 1816, the year after the war ended.' She was stalling now, playing the coward. Bea didn't want facts, she already had most of those worked out. 'We were both very young and we became infatuated with one another...' Or at least the idea of one another. The memory of her first sight of him was clear: he'd come striding into the drawing room of the big house they'd rented, dressed for dinner country style; buff breeches, polished boots, a bottle-green coat that had done devilishly handsome things for his eyes, dark hair slicked back in a queue. She'd never seen long hair like that on a man before. He'd bent over her hand and kissed it.

It had all been a game to him and to Preston, to see if they could pass off a street rat as a gentleman. They'd apparently met at Oxford—although she hadn't been quite sure in what capacity until much later—and Preston had decided to befriend him, to see if he could be polished up.

She could have told them it wouldn't work. There'd been an undeniably rugged air about him, something unfinished that was as appealing as it was obvious. It wasn't something a Weston coat and Hoby boots could hide or change. She'd known immediately here was something wild, something that could not, should not, be changed.

But they'd all tampered with it, with him.

Preston with his Pygmalion game, her father with his sense of *noblesse oblige*, had found Preston's efforts worthy and joined in. Perhaps she'd even contributed, too, tempting Liam to look beyond his station.

'We spent time together and, the more time we spent, the more infatuated we became.' She'd liked the wildness in him. It had matched her own restless, seventeen-year-old spirit, and she had liked the rebellion in him, the idea that he thumbed his nose at society even as he ate off its plates, rode its horses and lived in its fine houses. Much like her. Her debut had been approaching within the year and she'd rather have done anything than give in to the seamstresses and the parties and balls all designed to sell her to the highest bidder. And yet, without all that propping her up, what was she? It was a profound and unsettling question for a girl who had never questioned her identity. That summer, in Liam Casek, she had seen what she thought of as the answer: that she could be whatever she wanted, as long as she was willing to pay the price.

'How infatuated?' Bea asked when she'd finished.

'Very. I had never met anyone like him,' May said with a strong hint of finality in her tone.

'You never said a word when you came back,' Bea mused. 'Do the others know? Did you tell Evie or Claire?'

'No, Bea. I didn't tell anyone. What was the point? The summer was over and he was gone.' May rose, signalling the conversation was over. She wasn't ready to disclose any more.

Bea sat up higher against her pillows. 'Didn't you see him London? You came out the following year.' May could see she was searching her memory for any remembrance of Liam from the balls and debuts. If he was Preston's friend, surely he'd been among the young men Preston had cajoled into dancing with her and her friends.

'No,' May said quietly. 'He wasn't of the right calibre. My father didn't want him around.' There were other reasons her father had banished Liam from the high society circles Preston associated with in London, but she didn't want to go into that tonight.

Bea seemed to accept her answer. She pulled her blanket up and snuggled in with a pleasant smile on her face. 'Thank you for telling me. It's a good story to fall asleep to on a cold winter night: summer love, young love.' She knit her brow. 'You'll have to tell me the ending, though, another time. No sadness tonight.'

'How do you know the ending is sad?' May was surprised by her own defensiveness.

Bea laughed. 'You threw a bowl at him tonight. That isn't exactly a sign of a happy ending. But...' She paused. 'One must always remember that love and hate are merely different sides of the same coin. They're not that different. Maybe your story isn't over yet.'

'Good night, Bea.' May laughed. She didn't want to contradict her dear friend. She didn't miss the wistful undertones behind Bea's words. Bea had never given up on her lover, not even at this late date. If anyone knew about the fine line between love and hate, it was Beatrice. She'd not been able to bring herself to hate him for disappearing and leaving her to face her pregnancy alone.

'May, a good man isn't always a gentleman.' Bea's voice trailed softly after her into the hallway. *And a gentleman isn't always a good man*, May thought conversely, as Bea's case proved. That particular gentleman had left her pregnant and alone. She couldn't bring herself to disagree with Bea's line of reasoning. Liam Casek for all his rough background *was* a good man. That was part of the problem. If he'd been a bounder, she could have dismissed him out of hand and that had made all the difference—

a difference that had her hurtling stew bowls at him one moment and kissing him on the kitchen floor the next.

What could possibly go wrong next? Cabot Roan crumpled the note in his hand. May Worth was gone and her elusive brother had not yet surfaced. Neither had the documents. Roan took a swallow of ale, grimaced over its poor quality and sat back in the shadows of the inn to think. What did he know without doubt? What could he only speculate about?

He started with Preston. The man hadn't surfaced after being knifed and the wound had been significant. That was fact. What was not fact but likely, was that he'd lost a lot blood. He shouldn't have been able to travel far. But apparently he'd either been hidden extraordinarily well or he'd crawled under a bush and died, the body yet to be found. If Worth was dead, no one knew it. Roan had scanned the papers looking for obituaries. He wasn't sure the absence of such news was a sure indicator Worth was alive. There was always the chance the family and the government had chosen to keep that news quiet for the sole purpose of making him sweat. It was a valid strategy. As long as Worth was presumed alive and at large,

Roan *did* have to worry. Just as he was worrying now.

Roan tapped his fingers on the rough surface of the table. It was killing him that he couldn't go charging into London and see the situation for himself.

The other man. His men had reported a second fighter in the road, a man who'd been with Worth before the ambush. The man had been skilled with a knife. Those two clues didn't create fact, but a fairly stable assumption. Roan would bet half his fortune the second man was Liam Casek, Worth's long-time friend and sometimes partner. Worth hunted down the crime. Casek disposed of the perpetrator.

Roan swallowed hard at the thought, his hand reflexively massaging his throat as if he could already feel the rough hemp burn of a noose. There was nothing like facing one's own mortality. Perhaps he should be honoured the government had sent Casek. It would be a simple elimination: no trial, no public scandal, no waiting around for days, weeks, months in a cell building false hope, none of the indignities of publicly dangling from a rope.

Sending Casek might mean something else, though. Maybe the government was unsure of its proof. Maybe they weren't sure of winning a charge of treason? After all, a private businessman is just that—private. He could conduct business with whomever he liked. Roan smiled. That was conjecture only.

The other consideration was that Casek wasn't after him at all, that he'd merely been with Worth out of friendship. Casek was dog-loyal to Worth and Worth trusted Casek with his life.

Apparently with his sister's life, too. Roan stopped drumming, another scenario taking shape. Who better to have at one's side when wounded than a best friend? Who better to entrust the original ledger pages to than a best friend? That wasn't too big a leap of logic. If Casek had been with Worth, Worth was alive and well hidden as he recovered. That made reasonable sense. Find Casek, find the originals. The larger leap of logic was this: May Worth wasn't in London, although her parents were, his men had seen them on several occasions leaving the town house for the evening. Was it possible that she was with Casek in an undisclosed location?

Roan worked through the probability. Who better to protect one's sister than Liam Casek, a man known for his successful protection of key individuals during critical times, as well as his ability to eliminate those who disturbed the great balance of British power? It was like a giant chess game, a game he happened to play very well. But he couldn't take the next step until he had a location. All the suppositions in the world wouldn't matter if he couldn't find her. She wasn't in London. She wasn't in Sussex. It was like looking for a needle in a haystack. But he'd found harder men than one pretty, outspoken debutante.

The door of the inn opened and two of his foxes entered, shaking droplets of rain off the shoulders of their coats. He smiled expansively at them and gestured them over. He tried to gauge the quality of their news by the speed of their stride. They were walking quickly, it might be good news at last.

'Well?' he prompted without preamble.

'We know where the girl is,' the taller one began. Good news indeed. This was going well. He could finally take some action.

'Where?' The hesitancy that followed dimmed his sense of relief.

'She's in Scotland, sir.'

Roan narrowed his eyes. 'Where in Scotland? It's a rather big country.' Somewhat undeveloped, too. There were a lot places someone could hide and be unnoticed.

Their eyes dropped. 'The best we can gather is a village near the Firth of Forth.' This was both good news and bad. The bad was that it would take time to make the journey. He could reach the border in three days and then who knew how long it would take to reach the firth and comb the villages. The task was not impossible, but it would take time and that was something of a dubious commodity. He didn't know how much time he had. The good news was that a rich debutante would stand out. People would know if she was among them. Scotland wasn't for those used to soft town living.

Roan nodded, taking it all in. He would go after the girl himself. He might be safer in Scotland than hiding out on the outskirts of London anyway. The sooner he had the girl, the sooner he could draw Worth out of hiding and continue this rather elaborate chess game. He slapped a palm on the table, decision made. 'All right. Pack your bags, gentlemen, and find five men to bring with you. We leave this afternoon.'

Chapter Nine

By the next afternoon, May could add slapping to the list of things she wanted to do to Liam Casek. Liam had managed to turn going into the village into a social occasion with his insistence on meeting everyone. 'I thought we wanted to keep a low profile,' May scolded as they exited the little dry goods shop, leaving a gaggle of interested women behind them, although a few of the more intrepid sorts discreetly followed them out into the street.

'It's easier to know who is out of place if you know everyone,' Liam replied with a seriousness that reminded her sharply how dedicated he was to his job, to his protection of her. It reminded her, too, that in order to acquire these skills, he'd been to dark places, perhaps done dark things. What experiences had taught him such vigilance? 'I want to know everyone. Men especially in this case.'

'Men? It was hard to tell in there. The women seem interested enough though.' May slid a sly glance his way. The women had been ogling him since he'd stepped into the shop. And why wouldn't they? He was exactly their type: a strong, rugged man unafraid of hard work. He was dressed like them, too, decent, clean clothes, nothing near fancy enough for London. No one would guess he had the ability to run in higher circles. Perhaps Preston's game years ago had been a success. After all, that had been the point of it—to create a man who could pass himself off as a beggar or a gentleman depending on what the circumstances required.

'Anyone catch your eye? I could make an introduction.' It was a cold joke designed to prove to him that last night had affected her not at all, merely a lapse in judgement caused by heightened emotions. Never mind it was a blatant lie. It *had* affected her.

'I'll make my own introductions to the ladies if I need anything.' His own terse reply suggested he didn't find the issue amusing.

'Would you?' May felt an unbidden twinge of jealousy. She didn't want to think of Liam with any of these women. She had no claim on him. He was perfectly able to seek out any company he liked. Or was he? A horrible thought came to her. 'Or are you committed elsewhere?' Surely there'd been women over the years. He wasn't the sort to embrace celibacy. A man of his intensity would need an outlet for all that emotion. Besides, celibacy wasn't required of him, certainly not by her.

He gave her a harsh look, his voice dropping. 'Do you think I would kiss you if my affections were engaged elsewhere? Is that the kind of man you think I am?'

'I think you're a man who takes what he wants. You always have been.' They were fighting words the moment they left her mouth.

'I did not take anything you weren't willing to give,' Liam growled, herding her away from his growing trail of admirers. May was spoiling for a fight and he damn well wasn't going to give it to her here in the middle of the street with an audience. But restraint was hardly May's strong suit. He steered her into a side street. 'Even a cat knows when to retract her claws. You're lucky I can't haul you into an alley and spank some sense into you.'

It was a poor choice of words, evidenced by

the furious blush racing up May's cheeks, proof that his threat had not conjured up images of corporal discipline, but images that ran akin to his rather wayward mind: of her across his lap, her skirts up, her bottom displayed, bare and white, and deliciously round.

'How dare you!' May spat, but she wasn't mad, not really.

'How dare *you*? You insult my honour by suggesting I would take liberties with you while committed to another.' His body was close to her now, close enough to smell the scent of rosewater on her skin, the scent of a lady. It was one of the first things he'd ever noticed about her since the moment he'd bent over her hand in the drawing room. She knew how to take care of herself. He'd never known women like that until he'd met May. Once, he'd been easily impressed by the cheap perfume of the St Giles whores, but May had changed that. May, who always kept herself neat and clean, had shown him even at seventeen what a real woman could be.

'Your honour—' May began and he cut her off, stepping back, his hands out to his sides in a gesture of surrender.

'I'm not going to have this discussion with you here in the middle of the village. I did not come here to dredge up the past. We made mistakes. We can't undo them. Fighting over them can't fix them or change them. I came to the village to meet people. You came to check your mail. I suggest we do that before one of us says too much.' Or before the fight turned into a public repeat of last night's outcome. Quarrelling with May was disturbingly arousing. Even now, he felt the beginnings of want start to stir. He wanted to push her up against the wall and kiss her hard, he wanted to yank up her skirts and finish what his hand had started last night, he wanted to bury his cock in her and hear her scream his name as if those cries alone could shatter the walls between them like the trumpets at Jericho. Oh, yes, all kinds of want were starting to surge through him. 'I'll meet you at the gig in a half hour.' That should be enough time to meet a few more people and get his 'want' under control.

A half hour was just long enough. Work had a way of re-establishing his equilibrium. Liam sauntered towards the gig, a whistle on his lips. Aside from quarrelling with May, the afternoon had been a good piece of work. He'd walked the village, studied its layout, met its people. If he couldn't whisk her away to the protection of

a city like Edinburgh with its watch and con-
stables, this village would have to do. It was
small and that suited him well. There were few
places to hide and escape routes were obvious.
Options were limited. There was just one road
and the sea. Anyone coming into the village
couldn't help but be noticed.

Liam ticked off time on his fingers. He'd
been here twelve days. Almost two weeks,
plus the five days it had taken him to travel
here. Seventeen days in total. Preston would,
God willing, be on the road to recovery now.
More worrisome though was that the window
he'd estimated before Roan could reach them
had nearly passed. The honeymoon, as it were,
was over. If Roan was looking for May, he'd
have discovered by now she wasn't in London. He would have had time to learn where
she was and make the journey. He would be
flying over the roads once he had the destination. He wouldn't let early winter roads slow
him down when there was lost time to make
up. Roan could be here any day.

He'd done all he could given the circumstances. He'd kept May close, much to her chagrin. He'd worked outside at the cottage to keep
an eye on the road. He'd made a reconnoitre of
the village and the places she frequented. He'd

met the village people, as many as he could. He knew it didn't account for people living in the countryside. Those he could meet, he'd tried to ingratiate himself with in case the time came when he needed their help. But it wasn't enough. He was still blind.

Liam would feel better if he had news. There was so much he didn't know. Was Preston recovering? Was Roan actually looking for May or were these efforts and worries for nought? Perhaps Preston's ledger copies had made it safely to London and even now officials had Roan well in hand?

A lack of information made him feel impotent. Out here, miles from an effective postal service, he was blind. And he was alone. More than ever, he wished he could take May to a city. He felt exposed in their isolation. If Roan did come, there was only himself to stand between May and harm. If they were still safe after Beatrice's baby was born, he wanted to move May to Edinburgh whether she willed it or not. Perhaps if she understood how much danger she put Beatrice in, she might reconsider. A move to Edinburgh was a good idea. It would keep Roan guessing and it would lead him away from Beatrice. Perhaps by then, the errant Mr Fields would endeavour to make his way home to see his new child. Mr Fields was a long shot, but anything could happen. He knew just how fast a world could change. It only took days, hours, a few words.

Liam leaned against the gig, watching the little street, his gaze landing on a man coming out of the inn not far from him. Inns were important places to watch and he'd chosen to park the gig there for just that reason. Inns were gathering places for travellers, people passing through. In short, the inn represented people he hadn't met yet and didn't know, making all of them potential harbingers of disaster. The stranger leaned against the exterior wall of the inn, eyes giving the street rather alert attention.

Across from the inn, May came out of a shop, chatting with another woman. The man's eyes followed her. Liam counted the seconds in his head. One, two, three. The man's gaze was more than just a casual perusal of something that had caught his attention. His gaze lingered and a finger of fear touched Liam. Was Cabot Roan here already? It wasn't impossible. May was only twenty-five feet from him, just across the street and walking towards him, but it seemed like a far larger distance with this man suddenly eyeing her. Liam edged closer to the man at the inn wall until just the corner of the building separated them. He wanted to call out to May, but he didn't dare. The last thing he needed to do was confirm to the man she was indeed May Worth, just in case the man wasn't sure of his mark.

May was in the middle of the street when the man moved a hand inside his coat. That was all the sign Liam needed. He rounded the corner and took the man from behind in a strangling bear hug that froze the man's arms into place. He shoved the man up against the wall, face first, a hand at his neck, another running down the man's body looking for a weapon. 'What were you doing, staring at the lady?' He kept his voice loud and gruff. Volume intimidated and it gave the guilty less time to think of an alibi.

'N-nothing,' the man stammered. 'I didn't mean nothing by it.'

Liam gave him a frustrated shake. 'Where's your weapon?' He hadn't found one. Perhaps it was concealed, but that didn't make sense. Hidden away in a secret pocket would prohibit the man from easily drawing it.

'I ain't got one. I'm a farmer, sir. What would I be carrying a weapon for?' The man was starting to squirm, the rough side of the inn wall digging into his cheek. 'Please, sir, I didn't mean nothing by it, honest. I'm sorry I looked at your lady.'

'Liam!' He was aware of May coming up behind him.

'Get in the gig,' he growled. The last thing he needed was for her to put herself within arm's reach of an attacker.

'Liam, let him go!' May stood her ground, refusing to budge. Had she no sense? 'This is Evert Shambless, a sheep farmer. He lives a few miles out.' She tugged at his arm.

Reluctantly, Liam stepped back, releasing the man. 'My pardon. I misunderstood the situation.' He gave a curt nod. There was nothing else to say to the poor farmer. He'd apologised, but that was all he could do without explaining why he'd done it. He could feel May bristling beside him and he wanted to be far away from the centre of the village before her anger broke. He put a hand at May's back. 'Get in the gig. We need to go.' He could imagine all too well the scolding May would heap on his head. She'd say he'd acted impulsively, that he was over-protective, paranoid. He picked up the reins and called to the horse, enjoying what remained of May's silence.

The silence lasted far longer than he thought it would. She sat beside him all the way home on the driver's bench, her shoulders square, her head up, looking so collected, so refined. She was Damascus steel, beauty pounded into lethal perfection, and like steel, forged from heat and fire. He loved her for that. He hated her for that.

The silence was becoming untenable. Perhaps that was what she wanted—for him to start the conversation that would most assuredly become an enormous row. He pulled the gig into the yard of her little house. May didn't wait for him to help her down. She climbed out under her own power and followed him into the barn as he unhitched the horse.

'Everyone will think you're my lover.' Her voice was stern and quiet in the interior of the barn. This was not what he'd expected when he'd anticipated her anger—not the quiet of her tone, nor the topic. He saw to the horse, waiting for May to continue. 'You assaulted a man because he looked at me.' May grabbed a brush and began to curry one side of the horse with short, furious strokes.

'A gentleman can protect a lady's honour without such aspersions being cast,' Liam offered, studying her carefully. She had him off guard here. He needed a moment to anticipate where she was headed with this.

'No one would mistake you for a gentleman. Not after that display today,' May said crossly. She gave up on the horse, which was probably best, Liam mused. Being hacked away at with a curry brush probably wasn't that enjoyable.

'I am well aware of that.' He put the horse in a stall and forked in some hay, trying to ignore the dig, trying to ignore the twinge that perhaps it mattered to May that he hadn't pulled off the illusion.

'Besides, even if *that* were up for discussion,' May went on, 'a gentleman doesn't live in the same cottage with the object of his affections. It was one thing to have you here when it was put about you were sent to watch out for us as a friend of my brother's. But now, who will believe that's all it is?'

Liam folded his arms and faced her. It was time to remind her what her priorities should be right now. 'Concern over what the neighbours think about your chastity should be the least of your worries.' He advanced on her, desperate to make her understand. He'd seen Cabot Roan cold-bloodedly execute a man in front of his family for double-crossing him. 'Cabot Roan is likely after you. He and his men could already be in Scotland. You have no idea what that means. He is a dangerous man, not just because he sells arms to countries England doesn't support. You do not want to be under his control, May. He's not particularly kind to women, especially not the kind who fight him.'

May took a step back, her chin jutting defiantly. 'You're trying to scare me.'

'Yes, I damn well am. I want you scared.' He kept coming. If she wouldn't respect her lover, perhaps she'd respect her bodyguard. 'I'm trying to provide you with some perspective. And, yes, you should be scared. You should have let me take you to Edinburgh straight away.'

'No!' May spat out immediately. There was so much vehemence in that one word. He wondered what the source of such resistance was? It was the same tone Preston had used when he'd begged for no doctors. Preston had been protecting others. What was May protecting? 'No Edinburgh and you have to stop going about the village punching men who simply look suspicious.'

'I can't promise that, May. I have a job to do and that's to protect you. If that means a few jaws get roughed up, then that's what it means. I will not compromise on that. Your safety is not negotiable.'

'Apparently, neither is my reputation. Is that expendable, too?' They were standing toe to toe now. Her back was against the wall, there was no place for her to go. He could see her pupils widen with her emotion. May was never more delightful than when she was cornered.

'And I have to protect you! That man had his hand inside his coat. He could have been reaching for a gun, May! I was wrong today, but I'd rather be wrong a hundred times than see you dead.'

'Oh, yes, that would mar your perfect record. You must be successful at your job! And that's what I am. A job you can't afford to fail at. What would happen to your reputation?' May's voice had risen, her anger, her frustration, both of which had been mounting since his arrival, broke free of their tethers as she railed at him. 'Well, I'm sorry you had to come here. I am sorry you have to protect me. I know I am the last person in the world you ever wanted to see. I am sorry that you hate me. I didn't ask for this to happen any more than you did. But I would appreciate it if you'd stop playing the scowling martyr!'

Is that what she thought? The words struck him with force. 'I don't hate you, May.' He heard the resignation in his own tone. He'd accepted that years ago. He couldn't hate her. She'd not chosen him. She'd simply acted according to her nature and the life she'd been raised to when she'd rejected him. He couldn't hate someone for being who they were born to be. He might hate the situation, might hate how their past had gone down, but he didn't hate *her*. Deep in his bones, he knew he never could. He would carry May Worth with him for the rest of his life, just like the scar on his cheek.

He watched her raise a dark brow in doubting question. 'You've given a good impression of it since you've been here.'

'Then you've got the wrong impression.' Wanted her, lusted for her, understood he had to impose some limits on their association in order to keep the past from repeating itself: those were all things he'd admit to since he'd been here. But not hating her.

Something dangerous glittered in her eyes. Her pulse was starting to race at the base of her neck as her breath caught. 'Then prove it.'

That was when the leash of *his* restraint broke. 'Damn right I'll prove it.' He took a half step, made a slight turn of his body and pinned her to the wall, obliterating two weeks of hard-won discipline.

Chapter Ten

She'd done it now. She'd poked the dragon and now it was awake, wide awake, and bent on ravaging. Her body thrilled to the roughness of him, the intensity of him. Her mouth opened to him, all too eager to let the dragon plunder. Her senses were on high alert; she could feel the crudeness of the wood at her back, smell the scent of hay and horses mixed with the scent of her man, soap and leather mingled with sweat, a reminder that Liam Casek was no pampered dandy. In this regard, Preston's experiment had failed.

No gentleman would take a lady like this, against a wall in a barn with no prelude. She arched her neck, giving him access to her throat. A little moan escaped her; a mewl of desperation mixed with abdication. She couldn't fight her want today, couldn't seek to understand it, not after what he'd done for her in the village. He'd risked his body for her and, when that had proven to be unnecessary, he'd risked embarrassment. Everyone had seen what he'd done and ostensibly why he'd done it. For the sake of her safety, he hadn't bothered to explain the real reason for his actions. He could have exonerated himself in a single sentence. *I'm her bodyguard.* For that matter, he could have exonerated her. But at what cost? Perhaps more than exoneration was worth. She could see that now when it was too late. She'd already scolded him, accused him of squandering her reputation only to recognise his choice had not been made out of malicious intention. The fierceness of his words still resonated. *I don't hate you.* What did those words mean?

'It's not a lie, May. I am your lover, whether you want anyone to know or not.' The stubble of his beard rasped against her cheek, his body hard against her, his hand rucking up her skirts, pressing against her, cupping her. This time she didn't stop him. The passion between them had always been beyond words, beyond reason. Her body wanted this, wanted *him*. She could construct her explanations later.

She hitched a leg about his waist and he

lifted her, she encircled his waist with both legs as he settled her against the wall, his voice a soft growl at her ear. 'Say you want me, May.'

'I want you.' The words escaped her in a strangled whisper before she could call them back, before she could think about them too much. She thought she'd say anything in these moments to calm her body. Desire and remembrance coursed through her until she was wet with it, until her pulse thrummed with it, proof that Liam Casek was in her blood.

How had she thought she didn't need this? Didn't need him? Her hand was between them, reaching for him, fumbling for him at the fastenings of his trousers until his hand closed over hers, working the flies with her. Then, he was free and hot in her hand at last and she cried out with the joy of it. She ran her hand down the long length of him, feeling unbridled life running through him as she edged him towards her entrance, to the place that ached for him.

'Easy, May. I know where it goes.' His voice was warm at her ear, his body pressed against hers, the tightness of his muscles a testament to his own eagerness. She was not alone in this. His hand slipped between them, testing her readiness beyond words. 'Good heavens,

May, you'll drive a man crazy with that kind of wanting.'

She answered with a fierce kiss. 'Only you.' She felt him push inside then, her body stretching to accommodate, stretching with memories. They'd done this before, years ago. But memories had soft edges. Not even memories had prepared her for this: for the powerful thrust of his body, for the spasms of pleasure that took her and teased her with each stroke of more pleasure to come. She was helpless against the onslaught. All she could do was hold him tight, keep him deep inside her as the pleasure grew. Towards the end, she heard herself cry out, her head thrown back against the wall in abandon, her body vaguely aware of how the ultimate pleasure was achieved. Liam had taken her all the way and seen to her deliverance first before he spilled himself against her leg, protecting her to the very last.

She dreamed of him that night; of the first time they'd come together towards the end of that magical summer when touching and petting, lying in the grass, holding one another so close their bodies shared no secrets and such intimacy was no longer enough to express or suppress the wildfire that raged through them.

It had been the day after he'd asked her to run away to America with him and they had fought. Desperation had driven them, both of them seeing the end nearing.

He'd been rugged even then, dark hair falling into his face, eyes mischievous and laughing as he dared her to challenge convention. She remembered those moments with shocking clarity; the sky had been blue like his eyes, the sun over his shoulder as she looked up into those laughing eyes, the young muscles of his arms straining as he rose up over her, a defiant god and she his goddess. The dare had been to convention, not to love him. Loving had never been part of the challenge. She did not have to be dared to love him. She would have loved him regardless. He made her feel immortal, especially when he was inside her. They'd been immortal together in those days, daring to fly so close to the sun. They'd not been careful in those days like they had been earlier in the barn. In those days, they laughed at risk, they played the odds, vowing whatever came they'd face it together. They were Romeo and Juliet, only smarter. No one and nothing could come between them. Until, of course, someone, something, had.

May was glad she woke when she did, the

dream ending with the two of them walking back towards home, hand in hand, the sun setting behind them. It was easier to remember the pleasant memories. But not safer. Oh, no. Waking only brought questions and what ifs. What if she'd gone with him when he'd asked? What if she'd stood up to her father at the critical moment?

I don't hate you. He should have, though. Heavens knew she would hate her if their places had been reversed. She'd denied him. In one single choice, she'd betrayed their young love. *Liam should never have put you in that position!* came the old familiar rebuttal, tired and perhaps true. He'd discussed none of it with her, had never told her what he was planning and then when the moment came, he'd put her on the spot and forced her to choose without warning.

May squeezed her eyes shut and hugged her pillow tight. She didn't want to remember *that* day. That day had changed her. That had been the day she'd sworn to herself that no man would ever hurt her like that again; not her father, not a lover and certainly not a husband. She would not give any man *carte blanche* over her life. If her parents wanted to know why she was still on the market after three Seasons, that was a large part of it, the other part being Liam himself. He'd proven more than the non-existence of his hatred in the barn today. He'd proven that she'd been right—no other man could possibly measure up. But that didn't change the fact that what they had was ruined and she'd ruined it, years ago.

The past couldn't be changed. Perhaps the only question that mattered was how it affected the present. If he didn't hate her, did that mean he loved her? Or could love her? Had never stopped loving her? Or had he simply resigned himself to more neutral feelings that were neither love nor hate? Was such neutrality even possible after what had passed between them this afternoon? A man who was ambivalent didn't love a woman like that; hard and rough with everything he possessed up against a barn wall until she screamed, and even in the throes of passion had forsaken his own complete release to keep her safe.

It made her wonder, as late-night thoughts were wont to do, if there was a chance for them. But a chance for what? A grand fairy-tale romance that defied convention and succeeded? They'd already done the defied-convention piece. It was the success part that had eluded them and might elude them yet. A happy ending seemed unlikely. However, could there be a chance to recapture the passion for a short time? Possibly. Her body began to hum at such a prospect while her mind counselled caution. Anything was possible in the dark, after all. The night was notorious for breeding impossible dreams. It was what happened in the morning when those dreams met their tests that counted. In their naïve hopefulness, those dreams hadn't fared well.

Perhaps this time it could be different. Perhaps with the worldliness that came with age and the wisdom of hindsight, they could simply enjoy one another's bodies without the emotional commitment and the expectations that commitment led to. Was that what the barn had been about? A first step towards a temporary affair? Would she truly settle for that with Liam simply to let him go again? Could she engage in a physical affair and not want more from him than the prowess of his body? It had never just been sex with him, there'd always been so much more. This time around, she'd be settling for less. *In exchange for protecting yourself? You can't get your heart broken if you don't engage it.* But she had an answer for that, too. Perhaps something was better than nothing and she'd never know if she didn't ask.

The next move had to come from her. He'd quite firmly established that today. He'd made his overture in the barn. Now, she had to respond and that response had the power to set the tone for what happened next.

May was no coward. She woke the next morning, fully determined to take matters into her own hands and put the proposition to Liam. It might go a long way in dispersing the unresolved tension between them. Apparently, it was on his mind as well. He was already out of the house by the time she made it to the kitchen. May smiled to herself as she set out the breakfast dishes. Liam had been here. She could always tell when he was up because he started the fire—a thoughtful gesture and another reminder that he was no gentleman in the best of ways. She put the iron pot on for porridge, saving the eggs for Bea. She'd get Liam's breakfast started and then take breakfast in to Bea.

At eight, Liam came into the kitchen, carefully stomping his boots against the step to rid the soles of dirt. 'Breakfast smells good.'

'It's just porridge.' May offered him a smile

and set down a bowl in front of him. 'You always say that.'

'It *always* smells good,' he said, but his words were remote. He wasn't entirely engaged in the moment. He was wary and reserved.

'Is everything all right?' Her mind began to go over all the possibilities of what might be wrong. Had he seen signs of Cabot Roan? Despite what he believed, he had succeeded in scaring her yesterday. Liam hadn't been the only thing on her mind last night as she'd lain awake pondering the future—a future that by necessity had to include consideration of Roan's danger. This man had tried to kill her brother and he would keep coming until he had what he wanted.

'*Is* everything all right?' He paused and set down his spoon. 'Perhaps we should talk about yesterday, May. It was precipitous on both of our parts. I don't think it was something either of us intended to happen.'

'But it did.' Some of her earlier hopefulness began to carefully retreat. 'You are not suggesting it was a mistake, are you?' She dared him to deny it with her eyes, her gaze holding his across the worktable.

'I am suggesting that we both know how this turns out if we continue down this path.'

'And what path is that?' May glared.

'A path that leads nowhere beyond bed, May.'

Hadn't she just reasoned that out herself? Wasn't that the conclusion she'd drawn in the small hours of the night? Then why did she want to argue that conclusion? She had the perverse desire to disagree with him.

'So, that's what "I don't hate you" means. I was wondering. Now I know it means "I like you enough to have sex with you but nothing more. Keep your hands on me, but keep your heart to yourself, please."'

'May, be reasonable. What did you think would come of it? That your father would suddenly change his opinion of me? That society would accept me? That *you* would suddenly accept me? I know it bothers you I'm not a true gentleman. You and me together, is not the way the world works. I'm lucky to have come as far as I have, but I've reached the top of my ladder. Did you think everything would change and we'd live happily ever after?'

'I think *we* are in charge of our own happily-ever-afters. I decide for me and I used to think you decided for yourself, too.' There were so many grounds on which to challenge him, she could hardly grab at all the arguments. 'I'm not looking for happily-ever-after, I'm looking for happy-right-now, and you're wrong. I do accept you just as you are. I'm not a spoiled little rich girl. Just look around here. Would a spoiled little rich girl be able to do all this?'

Liam waved an arm to indicate the kitchen. 'Is that what this is? Living in a cottage, learning to cook and manage a budget is "deciding for yourself"? Your parents are still providing for you. They send you an allowance every month that enables you to pursue this rustic, domestic fantasy, and when you get tired of it, you can go home to your big town house and your country estate, your silks and satins, and eight-course meals. You're not in charge any more than you were five years ago. You are lying to yourself if you think you are.'

She took a deep breath and placed her hands flat on the worktable. 'No. I won't do it, Liam. It's not going to work this time. You want me to fight with you, so *you* don't have to make a decision, so you can walk away and try to blame it all on me. Well, I'm not going to fight back. What can I say, anyway? You already know I disagree with you on all fronts and you continue to hold me accountable for what happened years ago. It was your fault, too. You weren't there when I came after you. You left as soon as you could.'

'Now, listen here, May—' Liam began, but he never finished.

There was a shuffle of feet behind her and May turned to see Beatrice waddling towards them, her nightgown gathered against her, her hand shaking as she clutched the doorjamb. 'May, my waters have broken. The baby's coming.'

Chapter Eleven

It was happening! The moment she and Beatrice had waited for, prepared for over the last four months and still May felt inadequate for the task. May pasted on a smile, all thoughts of the unfinished business with Liam shoved aside. Don't panic! Remember the plan. All she needed to do was send for Dr Stimson and support Bea.

'I'll go for the doctor.' Liam was halfway out through the door before she could act.

'He'll be fast,' May assured Bea. 'Let's get you into a clean night-rail and get fresh sheets on the bed.' She kept the chatter up as she helped Bea. She could see Bea was nervous, scared, Bea who was always so confident and in charge. 'This is exciting, Bea. In a few hours, we'll meet the little prince or princess we've been loving for months.' She could not let Bea see that she was nervous, too. 'All the reading we've done will pay off very shortly,' she tried to joke. She and Beatrice had spent countless hours reading whatever they could lay their hands on about childbirth, which had been shockingly difficult. Apparently, women were just supposed to *give* birth intuitively, not study it or understand it in any scientific fashion. They had found a couple of tomes, though, and a few pamphlets they'd gone to no small lengths to attain. Getting them had delayed their departure from London earlier this summer.

'How are you feeling, otherwise?' May asked once she had Bea settled and her mind had got over the initial shock. It would probably help them both if they focused on the facts of the situation. 'Are you having any contractions?'

'Some, but they're fairly far apart and not terribly strong yet. They've been happening since daybreak.'

'You should have said something!' May scolded. She'd been wasting time on Liam when Bea had needed her.

'I wanted you to sleep as long as you could. Babies can take a long time.'

May reached for Bea's hand. 'Evie and

Claire will be so thrilled to hear the news. Everything is going to be fine. I have the herbs you put aside ready, I have hot water set to boil, plenty of towels, and best of all, I have the blanket we made ready to wrap the baby in the moment he or she appears. Everything will be fine,' she repeated, hoping if she said it enough it would be.

But everything wasn't fine. It had all gone wrong from the start. Liam was gone too long and when he came back no one was with him. May didn't let him deliver that news in front of Bea. She met him in the kitchen, arms folded, gaze fierce as if her countenance could persuade him to deliver different news, better news.

'The doctor has been called away to see to a family that might have measles a few hamlets over.' Liam told her in low tones. 'So, even if he returns in time...' His voice dropped off and May understood what he meant.

'There's no way I'd let him near May and the baby after treating measles,' she agreed. 'The midwife, then? Mrs Allen?'

'I went there, too. It's why I was gone so long. She's left to help her daughter with a birth. She's not expected back for a couple of weeks.'

'A couple of weeks?' May hissed. 'This will be over in a couple of hours!'

'A couple of hours? One can hope.' Liam chuckled. 'Most babies take slightly longer to make their appearance.'

May huffed. 'I know that. I was being facetious.'

Liam studied her with serious intent. 'What else do you know, May? How much do you know about birthing a bairn?'

'I've read a bit.' Liam's hand closed over her wrist in a gentle circle.

'It will have to do. Get the books, we might need them. She's big and in my experience that means two things: twins or trouble.' He nodded towards Bea's bedroom and drew a breath. 'Let's go break the news to her.'

Bea smiled when she saw them, looking relieved, her gaze going past them, searching for Dr Stimson. 'Is Stimson still outside?'

'Bea, we have to tell you something.' May knelt by her friend's side with another smile. 'The doctor can't come. He's attending a family with measles a few villages over.'

'Mrs Allen, then?' Bea said hopefully. It was exactly the same litany May had gone through just moments ago.

May shook her head. 'There's just us. But

don't worry,' she added quickly. 'Women have been having babies for thousands of years. How hard can it be? I am sure we'll do splendidly. We're smart women, we're prepared and we have our books. Do you remember the one with the chapter about birth? "Dr Jonson's guide to maternal care"?' It was just one chapter out of a huge tome devoted to medical practices, but it was the most any single book contained that was exclusively devoted to women.

Liam coughed discreetly in the doorway. 'I think you're forgetting something else. Me. You have me.' He entered the room then, filling the small space with his presence. 'You have May and me. Together, we are not going to let anything happen to you.'

He gave Bea a warm, encouraging look, but the gaze he gave May was warmer still and May felt all the stronger for it. She wasn't alone. She had Liam. Together, they'd once believed they could do anything. Suddenly, the unresolved issues of the barn, of their past, didn't seem important. It was only important that he was here with her, helping her face this bravely for her friend. 'I'm going to wash up with the hot water May has in the kitchen and then we'll see how this baby of yours is doing.'

It was impressive how Liam took charge so

effortlessly. He washed and rolled up his shirt-sleeves, and with gentle hands pressed down on Bea's belly, moving his hands here and there. 'Come, feel this, May,' he encouraged her. 'You can feel the baby's bottom here, his head here.'

'*Her* head,' May corrected. It was amazing to feel the baby and she couldn't help but smile and then worry, but she didn't dare ask Liam out loud in front of Bea.

'Bea,' Liam began, 'I think we have good news. There's only one baby. I was concerned there might be twins, but I can only find the one, just a big strapping baby waiting to be born.' He smiled broadly. 'But he *or* she has not turned yet, even though your waters have broken. Sometimes they don't, but they will eventually. We just need to wait.'

'How do you know so much about babies?' Bea asked. May fluffed her pillows and helped her sit up. They were going to be here a while.

'Yes, Liam.' May gave him a coy smile. 'Do tell us how you know so much about babies?' She perched beside Bea on the bed, letting him pull up the one chair in the room.

Liam grinned, looking ruggedly handsome, nothing at all like dour Dr Stimson with his medical theories. 'I ran errands for a doctor who did charity work in St Giles twice a week.

I followed him around like a puppy and he paid me a few coins for my efforts. I knew the streets better than any other kid in the neighbourhood and where to get things when he needed them.'

'St Giles?' Bea's brow knitted in confusion.

'I see May hasn't told you the story of my humble origins.' He cast her a scolding look.

'May hasn't told me much about you at all.' Now Bea was scolding her. She felt set upon by both sides, but she wasn't going to sit there and become the villain.

'Liam lived in St Giles during his childhood,' May said sharply, tossing Liam a 'there, are you happy now?' look. She'd prove to him once and for all she didn't care about his antecedents. To her credit, Bea did not disappoint. She simply nodded her head at the information and let Liam continue.

'The doctor treated everyone, but a lot of his work was with the…ah…' Liam hesitated.

'Prostitutes?' Bea supplied on a guess.

'You needn't be crass, Mrs Fields.' Liam winked playfully. 'I was going to say something more delicate like lightskirts, or ladies of the evening.' Liam raised an eyebrow in censure and the gesture made May stifle a laugh.

'Anyway, as you can imagine,' Liam went

on, 'there were some births and other *delicate* ladies' issues that came up.' He shot May a look, not wanting her to say more about his work with the doctor. It wouldn't help Bea any to hear it. 'Medicine fascinated me. I liked the idea of being able to help others in a significant way. When I was old enough to travel on my own, I went to Oxford. I wanted to be around all the learning I could and a university town seemed like the perfect place for me. That's where I met Preston.'

Bea brightened with a laugh. 'So you are a doctor! I should scold you for letting me think there was no one qualified to help me.'

May gave Liam a discreet look. Was he playing the old game or was he going to tell Bea the truth? She'd heard a variation of this story before. When told carefully, one could easily believe Liam had gone to Oxford, had met Preston as a fellow student and had studied medicine. Doctors were learned men, upper-middle-class sorts who were attached, even if loosely, to the family trees of nobility. Doctors were eminently respectable matches for daughters of baronets. The story, while true in essence but misleading in its conclusions, had been the one Liam and Preston had foisted on her father in their Pygmalion attempts. They'd nearly succeeded, except for one thing—Liam could barely read at the time. She wasn't sure now that she could let Liam mislead Bea, even if it was intended to put her at ease.

'Mrs Fields, I need to be honest with you. I am not a doctor. At best, I am a military surgeon's assistant.' Liam leaned forward, hands on knees, his blue eyes sincere. 'There was a time when I was pleased enough to let people believe what they would from my story, but no longer. I would pretend to be something I'm not to impress people, or to fit in. When I went to Oxford, I meant the city. I went to the city. I worked in taverns so I could listen to students talk. I drove delivery wagons to the colleges and the deans' houses so I could sneak into lecture halls and sit in the back. I couldn't read anything beyond my name when I met Preston. He taught me to read English and some Latin, because a doctor should read Latin, and Greek, but I'm no scholar and I'm not a certified doctor.'

May gave him a smile of appreciation. His admittance was bravely done. At the time, she'd thought the Pygmalion joke a wonderful prank to pull on her father and a way to rebel against the snobbery of society by passing Liam off as one of them. It had been entertaining to watch him in a room of guests at the summer house, fooling his betters into accepting him. But as entertaining as it had been, it had been wrong. Liam should never have had to pretend to be something he wasn't. He should have been acceptable as he was.

'A surgeon's assistant, though?' Bea pressed, shifting uncomfortably with a contraction that was too far apart to be a sign of hopeful progress.

Liam smiled. 'I went to Serbia with a private group of British mercenaries, for lack of a better word, although we were there with the government's blessing to ascertain the nature of the uprising. I spent two years in the Serbian army, as a result.' He tossed a glance at May. 'It was the first time I encountered Cabot Roan. He wasn't selling arms to the Serbians, but the Ottomans, in case you were wondering. Britain was not pleased but we couldn't prove anything at the time.'

May looked up, startled. She hadn't known. She'd only known that he was gone, beyond her reach. He'd stormed out of their house at the lake and disappeared. She had not seen or heard from him until he'd shown up in the cottage. Even Preston had stopped mentioning him. Now, she knew why. But as with most answers, other questions sparked. Had he gone to Serbia by choice or had her father arranged it purposely to get him as far from her as possible? And perhaps shot and killed in the process? Foreign wars weren't safe territory. Those were questions she didn't dare ask in front of Bea. It publicly exposed more of the story than she wanted when there was still so much between her and Liam that had to be addressed privately.

Liam was a good conversationalist. He kept Bea talking until afternoon, but by then the contractions were coming closer together and talking was difficult. This was a good sign, May assured Bea. It meant the baby was making progress. 'Look, it says so, right here on the page.' May triumphantly held the book up for Bea to see. When the contractions got stronger, she gave Bea the dittany 'tea' simmered in wine mixed with vervain and hyssop just as they had planned. It seemed the baby was cooperating at last. Liam's assessment confirmed it.

'The baby's turned,' he told Bea and May could see the relief on his face. Finally, something was going right. Only May wished it was going better, faster. Bea could no longer focus on conversation, so May read to her, grabbing the first book to hand, one of Bea's favourites: *The Pirate Rogue*. Liam took the opportunity to stretch and feed the animals in the barn.

'He's a good man, May.' Bea grabbed her wrist, straining through a contraction. Bea was starting to sweat, the dittany mixture no longer able to bring any comfort.

May smiled and reached for a rag to wipe Bea's face. 'He is. It's just never worked out for us.'

'Then make it work,' Bea replied earnestly and with no small amount of heat. 'He is worth fighting for, May. Whatever happened in the past, whatever his background, promise me, you find a way to keep to him.' She screamed then—it was the most sound she'd made all afternoon. 'May!'

This was it, truly it. After a day of waiting, everything happened in lightning speed. There was no time to panic, no time to worry, no time to go for Liam. There was only her and she was enough. May threw back the covers, all of the reading coming back to her as her mind sped through next steps. 'Yes, Bea, push! I think there's a head.' She was aware of Liam at the door—he'd come back inside and washed—but all of her attention was on Beatrice labouring hard to push this little creature into the world.

'When you can, May,' Liam instructed softly, coming to stand at Bea's head, 'take the baby by the shoulders to ease him out, not by the head, although that's tempting.' There was more screaming, more pushing and then suddenly it was over in a rush of baby and fluid and the babe was in her hands.

'Oh!' May gasped, tears of relief, of disbelief springing to her eyes. 'It's a boy, Bea, it's a boy! You did it, Bea.'

Liam was beside her, cutting the cord. 'Wash the babe and give him to Bea as soon as you can. I'll finish up here.'

An hour later, the house was at peace, as if the eventful day had never happened. Bea's room was clean, the baby snuggled against her, both of them sleeping. If it hadn't been for the presence of the babe in Bea's arms, May would have wondered if the whole surreal event had even occurred. All other signs of stress and worry had been obliterated. The baby stirred in Bea's sleeping arms and May went to take him. Bea needed to rest. There would be plenty of other nights when Bea would wake and care for him.

'You're my boy, too,' she whispered to the little bundle in her arms as she walked the quiet cottage. 'I delivered you, Matthew William.' She had not asked Beatrice why she'd chosen Matthew. William had been an addition. Bea had wanted the baby to have Liam's name in some discreet way, to honour him for his efforts today.

The warmth of the kitchen drew her. It was the cosiest place to be and her stomach was starting to rumble. She hadn't eaten all day. The porridge had only made it as far as the bowl and she'd been too worried about Beatrice to have an appetite later. Perhaps she should make something for Liam, too. She didn't think he'd eaten either.

She stepped into the kitchen only to discover Liam was already ahead of her. He looked up from the worktable where he was laying out a loaf of bread, cheese and cold meat. 'I was just about to come and get you,' he began, but his words caught as his eyes rested on the baby in her arms. His throat worked awkwardly. 'You look good with a baby, May.' That was when it hit her; she wasn't in danger of falling *in* love with Liam Casek again. She'd never fallen *out*.

Chapter Twelve

Goodness, it was hard to look at her with the baby in her arms and not think of the possibilities, his throat was thick with them, fantastical as they were. They might have had a child, they'd certainly been careless enough back then.

'The odds were on our side.' May smiled softly, reading his thoughts as she came to the table.

'Were they?' He busied himself with slicing bread, wanting to disguise the emotion that accompanied such thoughts. A baby would have changed everything. She would have had no choice but to walk out of the drawing room that day with him. They would have had no choice but to be together. Her father would have seen to it. No one would have been allowed to leave his precious daughter alone and with child.

May juggled the baby in one arm so she could eat with the other hand. 'A child would have forced our hand. We wanted to make our own choices in those days, not have them thrust upon us. That was the whole point of rebelling, to prove we weren't puppets to be controlled.'

Liam gave a quiet chuckle at her clumsy efforts to eat one-handed and came around the table. He took the bundle from her. 'Here, let me take him. You'll drop him at this rate. I'll hold him for you and then you can hold him for me. We'll take turns eating.' This was as close as they'd come to talking about what had happened between them at the end and it was enough to bring that horrible last day to life.

They were both thinking of it, both remembering it, here in the kitchen, a memory brought on by the events of the day; what might have been, what could have been, what wasn't and what was...

'I will marry her, Worth.'
Liam stood with straight shoulders, mustering all the dignity a young man could possess after being caught compromising a father's daughter. His trousers fastened, his shirt was tucked in, somewhat. The ache of incompletion ebbing from his body. It was a damna-

ble time to be hauled into account. There was no amount of decency that could rectify what Worth had seen and there was no explaining away what that was for anything else. But Worth was not interested in him, his offers or explanations. Worth's attention was fixed, blazing green eyes and all, on his daughter.

'Did he force you, May?' His voice was quiet, wrath simmering beneath the surface. A quiet, angry man was far more dangerous than a loud one. The loud ones forgot to think. Worth never forgot.

May's eyes, so much like her father's, fired with the same green temper, but her anger was far more rash. 'No!' She spat the word at him. 'You'd like to think that. You'd like to think that rape was the only way possible for a girl like me to be with a man like him.'

Rape. Liam fought the urge to cringe. Did she have to use such a strong, graphic word? Not even Worth had ventured to use it. He watched Worth's face colour at the mention. He wanted to caution May, wanted to go to her and squeeze her hand, but Worth stood between them, keeping May rooted in a chair by the window and he by the door. The closer to throw him out, was Liam's guess.

May wasn't done with her father yet. 'I love

*him. I love who he is, I love what he thinks,
what he stands for. I love how I am when
I'm with him.' The words made Liam proud.
His May was afraid of nothing. It gave him
strength. Even if they'd quarrelled over the
question of running away, she was still willing to fight with him for them.*

*'We will be married at once, as soon as the
banns are read,' Liam restated his offer.*

*A satisfied smile took Worth's mouth and
Liam felt as if he had just walked into a trap.
The right words had somehow become wrong.
'I am sure you would be pleased to marry my
daughter.' He waved a hand to indicate the
room. 'You think you'd have lifelong access to
all of this: summers at the lake, town houses
in London, country estates and hunting boxes
in the autumn, access to position and wealth.
Guess again. You marry her and I will cut her
off without a penny. There will be no dowry. A
man should take care of his wife, not the other
way around. If you were a real gentleman you
would have known that, just as you would have
known not to lay so much as a finger on her
until after the wedding. Real gentlemen marry
virgins.' Worth turned to May, who had paled
at the news. Liam's stomach clenched. She had
not expected to be cut off without a cent, with-*

out any recourse to the life she knew. Liam saw in her eyes that she'd wagered her family would support her if pushed. The pride he felt a moment ago wavered.

Her father read her shock, too, and his tone softened slightly as he turned towards his daughter. 'My apologies, May. You should go to your room. This discussion will be unpleasant and you need not be exposed to it. It is a matter to settle between men.'

Liam could have told Worth how that command was going to play out. May would have none of it. Her chin was up, her jaw was set. 'No, I will stay. This is my future. Who better to decide it than me?'

Did Worth not recognise his daughter's intractability when he saw it? It was so much like the man's own. Apparently he did. Worth merely nodded. 'All right then. You want to decide? Decide.'

'That is unfair!' Liam stepped forward, outraged beyond patience and frightened, if the truth be known. How could May possibly choose him in the face of her father's threat? He would lose her. 'She is seventeen. Why does it have to be either or?'

'That's right, she is seventeen.' Worth rounded on him. 'She hasn't even been out in society.

You should have thought of that before you bedded her.' Worth cocked a menacing eyebrow. 'Or maybe you did? Maybe you were counting on her naiveté. Consider this: what does she know of the world? How do you expect her to take care of you?' Worth snarled. If he hadn't been on the receiving end of his anger, Liam might have better appreciated the ferocity of his defence of his child. A lion could have done no better.

'She can't cook, she can't clean, she can't shop for food. She can, however, prepare menus for others to cook, she can arrange a seating chart, she can oversee the rotation of household chores, when to polish the silver, when to beat the rugs, how many times a year to polish the floors, she can fill out invitations and host teas with the help of her mother's guidance. In short, she is wasted on the likes of you. You haven't even one piece of silver to polish.'

'Father, that's enough,' May said quietly, her own anger fading. Liam stared at her, watching her wilt. Worth had humiliated them both with his last argument.

The man would not relent. He knew he had May backed into a corner and that Liam could do nothing, short of physically attacking him.

'*Then decide, May. Walk out of here now with him, or stay here with your mother and me and your brother, in the life you were born to live, the life you understand. We will sort out your mistake together.*'

The words gutted Liam. *Mistake.* He was to be classified as a mistake, something to be corrected, erased. He should never have come here, should never have let Preston talk him into the game. Mistakes were things like misspelling a word, or arriving late for a party. Minor oversights. Was he to be treated as nothing more than a small error?

He wanted May to fight, but he knew she wouldn't, she couldn't. She was trapped and he had no right to expect she would do other than what she did, no matter how much he wished otherwise. May looked down at her hands. '*Father, please, I love him. Isn't there another way?*'

'*I will not let him use you, May. It is my job to protect you and to protect this family.*' Her father deftly slipped into a gentler role, kneeling beside May and taking her hands.

'*I am not using you, May,*' Liam interjected from across the room, knowing the argument was already lost. Still, he had to try. '*I love you and I will provide for us.*' He tried to lend her *strength with his words. 'Do not be afraid to come with me.' He would prove himself. Somehow.*

'Even now, he's betting I will relent, that I will give in to your tears, May,' her father answered. 'Do not test my resolve. You know I mean what I say.'

Liam could see her eyes squeeze shut. She wouldn't look at him. He knew it was lost then, but that didn't stop the words from hurting. 'I will stay.'

Worth turned towards him now, the remainder of his wrath for Liam alone, his body shielding May from Liam's view. 'Go immediately. Do not stop to pack. I will have Preston send your things on. You may take the horse you've become fond of from the stable. That is all. Thompson will see you out.'

The butler already stood at the ready, his face impassive, showing neither anger nor sympathy. There were no arguments left to make...

The baby squirmed in his arms, starting to wake. The movement recalled Liam to the warm kitchen and the present. The little bundle would be hungry soon and wanting his mama. A thought occurred to Liam as he looked down at the little face. 'Was there ever a chance,

May?' Would anyone have told him if he was already gone? Would her father have given away the child as the most expedient solution to the lingering remnants of 'the mistake'?

May shook her head, too smart to pretend she didn't know what he asked. 'I was late, but that was all. Just a few weeks, which isn't all that unusual when there's undue stress.'

'I'm sorry, May.' Sorry there'd been no baby—because he heard the sadness behind her hurried justification and she had thought for a short while there might have been; sorry he'd left even if there hadn't been another choice for him.

'You would have lost your choices, too, if you'd stayed.' If there'd been a child, she meant. 'My father would have required you to marry me. More than that, he would have forced you to be the man you pretended to be among our guests. That could hardly be what you wanted.' There would have been no Serbia, no work for the government, no earning a place of his own as a highly trained agent provocateur, thanks to Preston's efforts on his behalf.

He would have had to pretend the rest of his life that he'd met Preston at Oxford as something more than a delivery driver. May's father would never have let him admit to being anything less, even if it was all a lie. There were those who would argue everything had worked out for the best. May had escaped a pregnancy and he'd escaped the shackles of matrimony that would have followed.

And yet, leaving her in tears, alone, to face the wrath of her parents in that great cavern of a drawing room had been counterintuitive to everything he knew about honour. He'd come to believe leaving hadn't been his choice, but May's choice for him. It was the only way he could justify leaving her behind: She'd been given the choice and she hadn't *wanted* to come. She'd made her choice. Leaving hadn't been his choice, it had been hers *for* him.

Over the years, he'd convinced himself he knew the reasons for it: he was too poor, too uneducated, too lacking in prospects. But he couldn't convince himself to hate her for it— although he tried. He really did try. He was more successful some days than others. Today was not one of those days.

'Why be sorry? It turned out well for you,' May said with a touch of steel to her tone. 'You got a fine horse out of it. You still have him. You kept Preston as a friend and you were able to advance your career.' She raised an eyebrow. 'Perhaps not a bad trade for a boy from the streets. You got Serbia, after all. I didn't know about *that*. Not until today when you told Beatrice.' There was hurt and practicality mixed with an odd sense of understanding. 'Perhaps if I had been in your position I would have done the same thing.'

'What did you want me to do, May?' There'd been only so much he *could* have done. He'd offered *for* her and *to* her and been refused on both accounts.

May came around and took the baby, fixing him with a penetrating stare. I think the question is: "What did you want *me* to do?"'

He gave the baby over to her reluctantly. They couldn't change the past. What was done was done. They'd parted, albeit at her father's direction. They'd spent years feeling betrayed by each other and that had left gaping wounds and unresolved, confusing feelings of love and hate. 'Maybe it only matters what we do now.' It was the sort of comment people made after a momentous day had successfully passed and they realised they'd survived it.

'Maybe.' Her gaze softened for an instant.

Maybe indeed. They were both changed. Had they changed enough or too much? He was twenty-six now. He had a career in the government, albeit a rather shadowy one with unsavoury aspects to it, especially for a man who had wanted to save lives instead of taking them. But one profession needed schooling, the other just needed good aim when it was required. It wasn't always required.

He wasn't the only one who had changed. May was different, too. He'd seen the difference in these weeks. The wild, unchannelled strength of her that had originally drawn him to her was now refined, sharply honed. She knew her strength, was experimenting in its use to be herself in a world that insisted she be otherwise. The image of her delivering a child, all cool competence when he'd come in from the barn, would always be one of his favourite mental pictures of her. Who would have guessed, May Worth, the coddled high-born daughter, would have had it in her to do *that*?

'You did well today, May,' he offered. Could these changes in them be enough to warrant trying again? They would be faced with the same obstacles, the same choices, but perhaps this time they'd make different decisions.

She paused at the door, the softness lingering in her gaze when she looked at him. 'So did you.'

He heard all the unspoken feelings in those words: *You let me deliver the baby, you didn't shove me aside as helpless, you didn't doubt my abilities, you didn't lie to my friend when you could have pretended otherwise. Thank you for being there for Beatrice and for me. I couldn't have done it without you.*

The words didn't answer the questions they'd posed. They were a three-word truce, nothing more, and that truce would hold until one of them broke it. Now that the baby was born, he needed to think about getting her to Edinburgh and safety, no matter what she wanted. He hated the thought of being the one who would take her away from the life she'd created here. Would she hate him for it, too?

Chapter Thirteen

Liam swung the axe hard, feeling the blade make a strong bite into the wood, the echo of that bite absorbed by his muscles. The physical work felt good. He was starting to sweat despite the cold weather. This morning, there'd been a heavy frost on the ground, which had prompted the need for more firewood. Liam set down his axe and cast an eye to the heavy grey sky. He didn't think it would snow. They were too close to the sea to see much of the white stuff and, fortunately, Edinburgh could be reached by ferry. Or unfortunately, if one wanted to be a pessimist.

Snow and poor roads would delay or prevent Roan from reaching them. But if Roan made it as far as Edinburgh, the ferry would help him, too. Neither of them needed to rely on the roads being clear when the time came.

That time would come, sooner rather than later. May needed to understand that.

May's stubbornness was fast becoming an issue. He picked up the axe and set back to work. That pile wasn't going to chop itself. He took a swing and then another, letting the rhythm free his mind to wander, to think. He was starting to figure some things out. There was a reason beyond the baby that May didn't want to go to Edinburgh and he was strongly beginning to believe there was no 'Mr Fields'. The number-one clue being that May wanted to avoid both of those topics whenever he brought them up.

There were so many topics to be avoid, it seemed. They'd never returned to their conversation in the kitchen the night Matthew was born, to the harsher conversation that had started their morning that day, they certainly hadn't revisited the 'barn incident' and he hadn't even dared to bring up Edinburgh. So much to talk about and *not* talk about, all hanging in the air between them. He supposed that was something else gentlemen did; they didn't talk about difficult issues for fear of creating more difficult issues. If that was the case, it was one more reason he'd never be a gentleman.

Liam reached for another piece of wood and stood it up. His shirt was starting to stick to his back. He took a hefty swing, letting the axe blade cleave the wood hard. He didn't think the 'barn incident' had been a mistake. What it had been was inevitable, like wildfire during a dry summer. He was sure what May thought. At the time, she'd enjoyed it. What she thought now was anyone's guess. There'd hardly been time to talk about it with the new baby to care for and Bea to look after. The delivery had been safe, but hard. Matty, as Liam liked to think of the wee man, had been a big baby. But Liam knew, too, just how much worse it could have been. They'd all been lucky, especially, Bea. But she wouldn't be able to do more than feed the baby and sleep for another few days.

Yet, despite the busyness of the last few days, Liam had a suspicion that May was up to something. He rested on the handle of the axe, staring at the cottage as if he could see through its walls and divine May's plan. It was early in the afternoon which meant she would be in the kitchen, chopping, slicing, dicing, baking—which meant punching bread. He imagined May liked that very much, especially when she was mad at him. She hadn't been mad at him for three days now. This was the indicator that suggested she was plotting: May was being nice.

Liam picked up a pile of wood and carried it closer to the house and stacked it in the little shed on the side of the kitchen. Of course, a nice May was delightful; she brought him hot coffee as he worked outside and quite often a little sweet something to go with it. She'd mastered the art of making shortbread biscuits. He sniffed the air near the kitchen. She might even be baking some now if his nose had the right of it. Almost done, too. He might get lucky.

He made another trip with the wood, letting the fantasy fill his mind. A man would consider himself lucky to have all this: a solid cottage for his family, a healthy babe in the cradle, a woman doing for him, keeping his house neat and clean, putting hot food on the table at night and hot coffee in his hands every morning. It only took the addition of a woman tucked close beside him beneath the quilts every night to complete the perfection of that fantasy—a woman with long dark hair, clever hands and an even cleverer mouth. Never mind that the fantasy was stretched a bit thin. The babe in the cradle wasn't his. But the rest of it could be. His groin started to stir. He had to give up carrying the wood for now and go back to chopping it if he was going to discourage any further arousal.

Never mind that what had started out as May's 'arguments' to prove to him that she was more than capable of a domestic life had now turned into May's seduction. The minx! She was luring him with the fantasy. She knew how potent it would be for him. How many times had they lain under the summer sky at the lakes, her head against his chest, his arm about her keeping her close, and drawn these very images?

'Liam, I would cook for you, bake for you, spread your bed with lavender-scented sheets perfectly ironed every night.' The more they discussed America, the more it became apparent she was afraid to keep house for him. Her concern was what sort of house that might be and how would she do both—keeping that house and finding work of her own. To a girl raised in luxury's lap, the prospect was overwhelming. She kissed him then, tenderly on the lips, before settling her head back in the hollow of his shoulder, her hair loose. He could smell the faintest hint of rosewater on those dark tresses. 'I'd be a good woman to you, Liam.' She ran her hand down him, finding him un-

erringly beneath his trousers, proudly ready for her touch.

He let her play before he rolled her beneath him, able to stare down at her from above so she could see the earnestness in his eyes, the heat she put in them. 'And I'll be a good man to you, May. I'll protect you, always, and I'll love you for ever. I already do.'

Naïve as the words were, he had managed to keep those promises, even if she didn't require it of him. Here he was in the far reaches of Scotland, protecting her and, heaven help him, loving her still. Those innocent words had been spoken by a young man who didn't know better—or rather who *did* know better and had conveniently forgotten the realities of the world for a while, a young man who'd got swept up in his own Pygmalion transformation and closed his eyes to the inevitable: he'd have to go back sometime.

Liam gave the axe a hearty swing, his shoulders starting to burn with the effort. He'd been chopping a long time. But he didn't dare stop now. He needed the clarity that came with hard work. He nearly had it all worked out when it came to May's secret plans. She meant to seduce him with the fantasy, meant to use it to convince him to stay here instead of going to

Edinburgh, even at the risk of Roan coming to them. And why not? He was just as likely to find them in Edinburgh. In her mind the odds weren't significantly different for her regardless of place. But here was safer for her in other ways that she felt *were* significant.

Did she want to avoid Edinburgh that badly? Badly enough to seduce him? The thought galled nearly as much as the knowledge that her plan had almost worked. But he was on to her now and forewarned was forearmed. He would not let May use the fantasy against him. Sometimes protecting someone meant protecting them from themselves. It wouldn't be fair to him *or* to her in the long run. She'd hate herself for it later if she let the fantasy go too far. It had already gone far enough. Why had it taken so long for him to see it?

The kitchen door opened and May stepped outside wrapped in her cloak, carrying a small plate in one hand and a mug in the other. He could see the enticing steam rising from here. Forearmed suddenly meant less than it had a few seconds ago. How was he supposed to fight this?

She was all smiles as she made her offering, the cold already turning her cheeks red. She'd made this a habit since he'd accused her the first time of trying to bribe him. If she thought regularity bred complacency, she'd be wrong. He was just as suspicious of her intentions now as he had been then, but no less appreciative. Whatever her intentions were, it was still cold outside.

'I thought you'd like something hot to drink. Your hands must be frozen. You've been out here for ever.' Her gaze drifted to his discarded coat hanging on a fence post. 'Maybe a hot bath? I'll need to start the water.'

'You've been awfully nice lately, May. Shortbread, coffee and cider while I work and now baths. It does make a man wonder.'

'So you've mentioned.' Her eyes narrowed with speculation of her own. He could almost see her mind working. 'Can I just be grateful for a service you've done my friend, one of my *best* friends?'

'You *can*.' He met her green-eyed gaze. 'But I still think it's more than that.' She needed to remember he wasn't a boy any more. He'd been trained by the government to think from others' perspectives, to see things people wanted to keep hidden. He and Preston had gone up against far greater strategists than May Worth. He drank from the mug, letting the coffee go down warm. 'Why don't you tell me the real reason I can't take you to Edinburgh?'

'We can't possibly leave Beatrice alone with the baby.' She didn't flinch, didn't hesitate with her answer; a sure sign it was a lie, or at least a half-truth, Liam thought. Lies came with all sorts of tells, one of which was answering too quickly. It indicated the presence of a rehearsed answer.

Liam pretended nonchalance and took another long swallow of coffee. 'Has she said anything more about when Fields will be home?' Beatrice talked about the man surprisingly little for a wife carrying her husband's child. He didn't even know the man's first name, although the last name was familiar enough. Where had he just heard it? *Fields* Something prodded his memory. It didn't surprise him. He'd be more surprised if the man existed at all, a hypothesis that was becoming more real to him by the day.

'No.' May shook her head with a sly smile. 'Roads can be difficult this time of year and the sea even more so. Travel is unpredictable. We may not see him until spring.' May was trying to buy time.

'He's at sea?' Liam asked, although he'd already been told before. 'His ship is the *Lillibeth*?' His memory was fully engaged now, the pieces falling into place. He'd heard these names before and quite recently.

'Yes.' May gave him a hesitant look, confirming what he suspected. Liam laughed heartily and loudly as the pieces came together, quite enjoying himself.

'You might as well admit it, May. There is no Mr Fields.' He held up a stalling finger when she would have protested. 'You've invented him.' Just as she'd invented everything else here. 'I recall that Fields is the Captain's name in *The Pirate Rogue*.' He was recalling a great deal more about the chapters May had read aloud when Bea was in labour. Fields had also been a merchant along with being an explorer, and given to long stretches of time away from land.

'Fields is a common enough name,' May argued, tenacious to the last. 'It's not unreasonable that a hero in a novel shares the name with any number of people in Britain.' He wished that were true. The absence of a real Mr Fields certainly complicated his position in regards to May and Edinburgh. It gave momentary credence to May's argument that they couldn't leave Beatrice. But he pushed on with his debunking. There was more to her reticence than Bea and the baby.

'And the *Lillibeth*? It seems unlikely there'd be a ship by that name captained by a man called Fields, even if every man in Britain bore that surname. I seem to remember the *Lillibeth* was featured in one of the chapters.' Liam gave her a soft smile. 'The defence of your friend is quite admirable, my dear, but it's time to give up the ship.'

May stood her ground, her chin starting to lift defiantly, daring him to contradict her. He should have known she'd try to salvage something useful from the wreck. 'So now you know. There is no father for the child.'

'Oh, there is a father,' Liam corrected. 'He's just not here, just not married to the mother, is that it?'

'Yes. Exactly so. We couldn't very well tell the villagers that and Beatrice is too young to be a widow. Preston says young widows are always suspect.' True enough. There'd been a young widow in Belgium who hadn't been a widow at all, merely lonely enough to lie about it. He'd nearly got a bullet in the buttocks for his troubles.

'What will you do when the village wonders why Mr Fields hasn't returned?'

'The sea is a rough place.' May shrugged. 'Our Mr Fields is a good captain. He'll go down with his ship.'

'As you are?' Liam raised an eyebrow, his

smile wry. His May was a cold-blooded minx. 'We'll just kill off Mr Fields? Is that it?' Then, to be perverse, he added. 'Bea will become a suspicious widow, after all.'

May gave him an impatient look as if he was an idiot who grasped none of the intricacies of their little plan. 'It won't be like that. He'll have died after the baby was born. No one will be suspicious then.' He understood their plan all too well, along with the two giant gaping holes in it. May would have to go home sometime. She was born to satins and luxury. Her parents would never tolerate her hiding away in a fishing village for ever. That was the first hole. The second hole was that May couldn't hold off Beatrice's family for ever if they came for the child, which seemed a more likely threat than it had in the beginning now that he understood all the details. If Beatrice was May's friend, she was likely high-born, too, and her parents would want her back as well once this birthing business was done with.

They were standing close together now and his heart ached for her. She was trying so very hard to avoid reality. 'You can't stay here for ever, May,' he said softly, perhaps as much for himself as for her, that this was a reminder she'd woven a fantasy for all of them at the cottage, but it could not hold.

Her own reply was quiet steel, her eyes meeting his. 'We'll stay as long as we can.'

Chapter Fourteen

May had never understood the phrase 'living on borrowed time' so completely or literally until now. She finished the dishes and took off her apron. The cottage was quiet. She could hear Liam upstairs in the loft, walking about as he settled for the night. Liam was restless and worried. She could see it in his face when she took coffee out to him in the yard. He was spending more time in the cold, his eyes glued to the road. They had enough firewood now to last for months.

She understood the reason for it: every day that passed brought the potential of Cabot Roan closer, just as every day brought Edinburgh closer. Staying as long as they could was getting shorter and shorter. She knew it even if they didn't talk about it. Never mind that she'd decided not to go. It didn't stop her from thinking about the deadline every time she looked at the calendar. Her parents would be arriving in the city, opening up the house they'd rented and expecting her. There'd been no news to the contrary. She couldn't risk a letter out any more than they could risk a letter in to her. Which meant either they hadn't heard about Preston, or that they had and Preston had counselled them not to send any further correspondence that would lead Cabot Roan to her.

Between the threat of Roan finding her here and facing the suitor her parents were eager to show off in Edinburgh, her time was most definitely running out and with it, all that time symbolised. Most importantly, it was running out on her freedom. That particular clock had started ticking the moment Liam had arrived.

Thinking of Liam was complicated. He represented both her freedom and the denial of it. He would drag her, although unwittingly, to Edinburgh and the prison that awaited her there. Another clock had been set with his arrival, too. This one far more personal. Did she use the anger of the past and her frustration with the present to sustain the wall between them, or did she use this precious time where there was no one to answer to, no society to stare in the face, to overcome the past and start anew? To what purpose? What did she *want* to come out of the new? *Maybe the question is what do we do now?* Liam had posed a bold question for which she had no answer, at least not one he would find acceptable. She wanted that answer to be: stay here and explore the possibilities. But they couldn't. Even if Liam was willing to sustain the fantasy, Cabot Roan was coming and he would chase them to Edinburgh if they hadn't left already. Borrowed time indeed.

May reached into the cupboard and rummaged until she found the bottle of brandy stored in the back. She would choose to stay until Roan's awful arrival happened. Just in case it didn't. But to do that, she'd first have to convince Liam it was a risk worth taking.

She pulled out the two 'good' glasses she and Beatrice had splurged on in the local shop, the memory of that decision making her smile. She put the bottle and glasses on a tray and drew a breath before heading up the stairs. What she intended was on the daring side, but desperate times called for desperate measures—desperate measures of brandy, that was. This afternoon in the yard had suggested to her rather blatantly that she needed a new plan of attack if she wanted to persuade Liam to give up on the idea of moving her to Edinburgh ahead of Roan.

At the top of the steps, she called out quietly to announce her presence. A lamp cast its soft light across the loft. Liam looked up from where he was stretched out on the bed with a book. 'Ever since I've known you, you've always had a book nearby.' May set the tray down on the little bedside table. The loft felt even smaller with Liam in it. 'What are you reading tonight?' She sat on the edge of the bed.

Liam marked the page with a thin ribbon and closed the book, showing her the cover. 'The *Odyssey*. I did the *Iliad* this summer. Took me three months.'

'You read too much.' May smiled and poured the brandy.

'I'm making up for lost time.' Liam chuckled. 'I spent the first nineteen years of my life without books. I don't plan to spend the rest of my life that way.'

'How is this one going?' May poured herself a glass.

Liam grinned. 'Slow, like Odysseus's journey. Only a daft fool takes ten years to get home to the wife he loves. He's with the sirens now. You can already tell that's going to go badly for him.'

May laughed and sipped her brandy, trying to ignore the little thrill of excitement that ran through her any time he was near, and the quiet evening ambiance of the room, and that he was studying his glass with quiet intent. 'Since when do you drink brandy?'

May laughed. 'I was drinking brandy months before I met you.' She crossed her legs on the bed and settled in with a wicked grin. 'Didn't I ever tell you about the time Beatrice and I got roaring drunk on my father's good stuff? Some of her father's stuff, too.'

Liam leaned back against the pillows, starting to relax. They'd talked like this in the old days, trading secrets. 'I don't believe you did, Maylark.'

May sipped some brandy, letting it burn down her throat, letting it embolden her. 'It was my seventeenth birthday and my parents were gone to London to celebrate something with Preston, graduation or his first appointment, I forget. But it was big and they left me at home because I wasn't out yet, even though it was my birthday.' It had hurt at the time. 'Preston was always the golden child. But I still loved him.' She took another swallow, a bigger one. 'I think my parents were afraid of all the trouble I'd get up to.'

Liam gave her a considering look of mock disbelief. 'Not you?'

May shrugged. 'Well, maybe they were right. Maybe I was a little too wild for London. I was certainly too wild to be left home. Beatrice came over to "celebrate" my birthday and we drank ourselves into a stupor and then got terribly sick.'

'And now, May? Are we going to get roaring drunk tonight?'

May gave a throaty laugh. 'Oh, no, I've become a much more responsible drinker since then.'

'Ah? Is that so? Are we celebrating then? You see, I'm trying to decide why you've come upstairs with brandy, May. I learned in the *Iliad* never to look a gift horse in the mouth. I thought we'd agreed this afternoon that your proverbial ship is sunk. You don't need to be nice, or grateful any more. I'm on to you, remember? And suddenly here you are, in my bedroom after dark, plying me with good brandy in the good glasses. You must want something badly.' His blue eyes were half-lidded as his gaze dropped meaningfully to her mouth, his voice low. Her breath caught at the attention. 'One might, in fact, think you've come up here to seduce me.'

His free hand cupped her cheek and stroked

the column of her neck, sending a delicious shiver down her spine. 'Do you know what seduce means, May? Have you ever looked it up in a dictionary? It means to "lead astray, to entice, to lure". Is that what you've come up here to do?'

May scooted back on the bed, taking a large swallow of brandy. 'I didn't want you here in the first place. Why would I suddenly want to entice you? Especially when you've pointed out that I have no need to play "nice" any more.' This was not going as well as she'd hoped. She'd *hoped* Liam would be a little less discerning than this and a lot more malleable. She took another sip. She was starting to feel warm and daring.

'Perhaps you've decided you don't hate me after all. You gave a pretty good impression of liking me in the barn the other night. Although, I take it we're not supposed to talk about that.' He gave her a cocky grin, the one that had always made her melt, even when they quarrelled. He swirled his brandy in the glass, holding it up to the light of the lamp thoughtfully.

'It might be that you're just after another tumble, in a bed this time, for old time's sake. Or, you might be after something much more important, important enough you'd be willing to seduce me for it.' His eyes glittered, sapphires in the dark. 'Since you've brought the good glasses, May, I'm inclined to think it's the latter. You think you can seduce me into letting you have your way about Edinburgh.' He got off the bed and paced the small room, careful to stay away from the sloping eaves where he couldn't stand upright. 'Tell me I'm wrong?'

When she said nothing, he laughed. 'You're a terrible liar.'

'You must be celibate,' May said coolly, 'if you talk to all the girls like this.' She'd rather not think of other girls, girls who'd replaced her in his bed.

'Only you, May,' he growled. 'Most women aren't as dangerous.'

'Dangerous, am I?' She wasn't ready to give up. She rose from the bed, joining him in the tiny space. She laid a hand on his chest, feeling his heart beat hard and strong. She gave him a tiny, teasing smile and looked up at him from under her lashes. 'Why?' She ran a nail down his chest, her gaze lifting to his. 'Is it because I make your heart beat faster?' Her hand dropped lower to boldly trace the rising length of him through his trousers, her voice a sultry whisper. 'Is it because you rouse to my touch?' Oh, how he did rouse! She loved the feel of him coming to life against her hand. She never tired of it, or of knowing *she* could coax such a response from him, this rugged, virile man who could charm any woman.

May circled him now, her hand trailing low to cup the firm round of his buttocks. She dropped a kiss on his shoulder. 'This would be so much better without your clothes on and mine.' She faced him again, keeping a little distance between them as she worked the laces of her dress. She wanted him to look at her, wanted him to see her undress, to become naked for him. 'Watch me, Liam.'

He did, those hot blue eyes of his riveted on her, making it a far more intense experience for both of them. She was supposed to be seducing him, but she felt as if he was seducing her, without a touch, without a word, with only his eyes. Her bodice went first, dropping to the floor. She felt need mingle with want, wetness gathering at her core as she let her skirt fall and she stood before him in her shift, the thin fabric catching the lamplight.

She took down her hair, unplaiting it with deft fingers, tossing him a coy glance, aware she had all of his attention now. She could see the attention in the glitter of his gaze, in the darkness of his eyes, nearly midnight with his desire. She slid her shift off one shoulder, her own hand trembling slightly at the gesture. She should have drunk more brandy for courage, but it was too late now. It had been a long time since she'd been nude with Liam. The barn had been a hurried interlude of clothes and coupling. But this, here in his loft, this was naked premeditation.

'May…' he stepped towards her, his hand staying hers, his voice harsh '…do not whore yourself for me. Do not dare to presume you can trade sex for anything with me, ever.'

'You want me.' She ploughed over his words, moving forward with her argument, her hand on him, closing over testament of that want. She was losing him, but not yet. His body wanted her, his body didn't make distinctions on what had caused the desire. For that matter, neither did her body. What had started as a predetermined ploy to seduce was rapidly becoming something else.

Apparently, Liam's mind was going to play hard to get. He pushed her hand away. 'Not like that I don't, May.' His voice was gruff now and not with desire alone. Losing him now was not an option. She could not go to bed with her desire unsatisfied.

She set her jaw. 'How do you want me, then?'

She moved her hips against him, her arms coming around his neck, drawing his head to her, taking his mouth in a kiss, her own desire rising. She wanted him with or without artifice. How did she convince him of that at this point after she'd already taken him down one road?

'The only way I've ever wanted you. Truthfully, honestly, fully.'

'All right, then we'll do it your way.' Her voice softened as she took his hand and drew it to her, placing it on the core of her heat, letting him feel the warm dampness beneath her shift, her evidence that this was not a ruse, no longer an item to be bartered between them.

'Good God, May!' he muttered the three-word surrender and she knew she'd won, for both of them. She stripped him in haste then, her desire starting to be more insistent than a pleasant warmth. She pulled his shirt over his head, she pushed trousers down past lean hips until his body was gloriously revealed. 'A warrior's body,' she whispered, trailing kisses down his breastbone. 'With a warrior's scars.' His was not a perfect chest, the smooth muscled planes and ridges she'd once known were marked with the occasional thin white line, remnants of a past she'd known nothing about until he'd told Beatrice.

She kissed each scar, kneeling as she went down his body. Her lips lingered over the last one, a long narrow strip at his left hip. 'This one is the worst, I think.' She feathered her words against his skin, her fingertips feeling the little rise of tiny goose bumps of desire at her touch. 'Serbia?' she whispered a guess. Or had he acquired it on one of his protective missions for the government? An injury he'd been paid to sustain so another might be safe?

'I don't want to talk about it now, May.' But she did. A part of her hungered for it. She wanted to know everything. She would wait and choose her moment. It would have to be soon. The gap between them had never seemed as real to her as it did tonight when they were so physically close.

He lifted her to her feet, pulling her shift over her head. 'Shame on you, you started first and you're the last to finish,' he scolded, tossing the shift away, his eyes never leaving her, not even to track where her clothes had landed. 'Come, lie down for me.'

He came to the bed with her, stretching his frame out alongside her. She was aware he was saying words, 'beautiful...exquisite...mine', but it was his touch that captured her, the feel of his hand at her breast, of his thumb running over her nipple until it ached, of his palm, warm and flat against her stomach.

Liam was not a rough lover necessarily, barn walls withstanding, but he was an earthy one, he loved with all his senses, shying away from nothing and his boldness made her brave, too, so when he slipped between her legs, his head at her core, her legs parted for him, welcomed him without hesitation or prudish thought for what he intended.

This was new, this was something they had not done before, but it felt right. Then his tongue moved against her and it felt more than right. It felt exquisite, and decadent, when he parted her folds and his tongue flicked across the tiny, secret nub within; the sensation was beyond pleasure, beyond description. May gasped, her body arching to accommodate this new pleasure. Her hands anchored in his hair, but an anchor for whom? For May to steady herself against these rising waves, or for him, so that he could not leave her in this sea of passion alone? When the final wave broke, she was ready for it, more than ready. The pleasure had become too much, like a swollen river that needed the release of a dam. She cried out once, twice, three times before the release was complete.

'Like that, did you?' Liam raised himself up with a smile, but she could see there'd been pleasure for him as well in the giving. To be sure, a different kind of pleasure than her experience. He'd need release, too, and she began to understand this had been a prelude. Her body quickened at the thought: *more to come. Soon.*

'Very much.' She gave him a come-hither smile and drew him to her, letting his body slide up the length of hers, letting his body cover hers until they were face-to-face, hip to hip, breast to chest, and he was nestled between her thighs. 'It's a fine opening course, to be sure.'

'This is why you're so dangerous, May.' Liam's eyes glittered with laughter. 'You'll use a man's body until he's drained.'

She answered him with a coy smile, 'Tell me when to stop.'

But it was he who bit her lightly on the neck with a possessive growl before sliding home. 'Never, never stop, May.'

Those became *her* words, *her* litany, moments later as her body picked up the rhythm of his, stretching, adjusting, conforming to the thrust and slide of his. This was honest lovemaking at its finest: fierce and open, without artifice. Liam was entirely hers in these intimate moments, there was no past, no agendas, no separation between duty and desire, nothing between them in this bed but pleasure mutually given and unabashedly shared. He strained above her, she felt the muscles of his body tense, felt his thrusts grow shorter, harder, quicker, felt her own body quicken in response, her fingers digging into his back, he locking her tight against him, as the pleasure took them, sweeping them away.

Chapter Fifteen

Swept away didn't even begin to cover it. His mind and body were full of contradictions. He was exhausted and exhilarated, careless and careful. He should have known. Loving May had always been like this. He wanted to protect her and yet he wanted to take great risks, many of them at her expense. He understood now as he hadn't fully understood before: she had more to lose than he.

Come away with me, let us go somewhere new and make a new beginning, let's remake ourselves, be whoever we want.

Those words had been his doom once before. He should know better than to repeat that mistake, but holding her in the dark, feeling the slow rise and fall of her body breathing against his, those were the very thoughts running through his mind. Only now, they were accompanied by another dangerous thread of argument: *This time it would be different.* They were older and wiser. He had something to offer May: a government job, savings, enough to get them a decent home.

This time *would* be different and in many ways it might even be *worse.* There was his position to consider now. Like anyone who was successful in their job, he had acquired enemies. Like anyone who had dedicated himself, immersed himself fully in his career, he carried the burden of that on his soul. He knew he was not unmarked. Constant vigilance on behalf of others had left him more cynical than he was already. The elimination of men who wished to harm the Crown had left him hardened, finishing the process the doctor had started so many years ago in his youth.

Perhaps all things happened for a reason. Even his abhorrent childhood. Without the harshness of his youth he might not have had the fortitude for his current position. As it was, he clung doggedly to the philosophies of Kant, that the ends justified the means. There was a tattered copy of the *Critique of Judgment* in his travelling bag to prove just how doggedly he held to those ideas, how hard he fought to justify his existence. May would have to share that existence. His enemies would become her enemies. Cabot Roan was just a taste of what that would be like. Could he wish that on her? In the case of May, would Kant's means justify the glorious end of loving her, having her? Would she agree?

May stirred beside him, looking up into his face with a sleepy gaze. 'You're awake and you're thinking,' she murmured. 'Should I ask?'

'Not thinking, I'm dreaming.' And, no, she shouldn't ask because he just might tell her and wreck everything. Maybe he didn't want to hear her answer. The old fear started to tug at its chains—that she'd merely used those arguments years ago to avoid telling him the truth; that he'd never be good enough for her in the long term. It was a fear he didn't visit too often and yet that fear had driven him for five years—driven him to read, to educate himself, to study anything Preston wanted to teach him, driven him to rise in his position, all in an attempt to prove himself to May whenever the time came, if ever it came. Even if it did, his efforts might not be enough. All of his efforts to 'improve' himself might push her away. She might run from the danger that loving him posed.

'Dreaming with your eyes open?' She gave him a low laugh and a smile. 'Those are the most dangerous sorts of dreams.'

Everything was dangerous with May. Being with her meant risking it all. He had to tell her. Not telling her was akin to deliberately misleading her, creating false hope. *If not now, when?* his conscience prompted. Perhaps now was the time, when she was sated and calm beside him. He combed a hand through her long hair, gently working some of the tangles. 'Shall I tell you, then?'

'Mmm-hmm. Tell me what goes on in that head of yours, Liam Casek, after you've made earth-shattering love to a woman.'

'Made earth-shattering love to *you*, May, not to *any* woman.' Heaven forbid *any* woman would provoke such hopes and fears. He'd be a wreck of a man if he was willing to forgo all he knew for any woman. She snuggled closer, liking the compliment. Her index finger drew idle circles on his chest.

He drew a deep breath. 'Cabot Roan gave me that scar on my hip, in Serbia.' The thin white line she'd caressed with her hand, kissed with her lips, would be the place he would start this conversation.

May looked up and there was no going back.

'Roan has more than one reason to come after you. We almost had him back in '17. He'd left Britain and I was sent to follow him, not officially. My job was to watch him, gather evidence and make a report to my superiors. To do that, I had to blend in. Like other mercenary soldiers for hire, I signed on to fight alongside Milos Obrenovic at Pozarevac and Dubjle when the Serbs drove the Ottomans from Belgrade. By the time Obrenovic negotiated his peace with Marashali Ali and it was clear the Ottomans wouldn't accept this defeat graciously, it also became obvious Cabot Roan was considering an arms deal with Marashali Ali. More arms would help the Pasha defeat Obrenovic.' He sighed. 'The Ottomans don't want to let Serbia go. I swear, May, that country is a powder keg and someday it's going to go off, maybe start something we can't contain.'

'It's not your job to save the world,' May murmured softly.

'Isn't it? What did Edmund Burke write? All it takes for evil to prevail…'

'Is for good men to do nothing.' May finished the sentence for him. 'My, you have become well read. I'm impressed.'

'It's more than an education, May. It's my armour. It's what keeps my soul together when

I have to do things that might otherwise be...
unthinkable.' How did he explain? How did he
make her understand the way he justified some
of his work? 'While I was in Serbia, Milos
Obrenovic was named leader of the country. He
brought back Karadorde, the leader of the first
uprising. He'd fled to Russia after its failure,'
Liam supplied, pausing thoughtfully.

How to say the next? He chose his words
carefully. 'Karadorde was assassinated after
his return. I am sure Roan had a hand in it.
The bastard would have loved nothing more
than inciting an internal Serbian conflict that
would have weakened the new state and opened
the door for the return of the Ottomans. War is
good for his business. He might not have fired
the shot, but he used his connections to sup-
ply the weapon and the opportunity. But because of my position, my orders at the time, I
couldn't do anything about it.' He let out a sigh
of regret. After all this time, he still wished that
could have turned out differently.

'Do you think you could have stopped it?'
May's question was quiet in the dark.

'Yes.' There was no doubt in his mind he
could have saved Karadorde. 'Obrenovic and
the Ottomans both feared him. Karadorde was
vastly popular. But he had no ambitions for

the new throne. Obrenovic didn't believe him, perhaps because of the poison Roan whispered in his ear about rebellions. Roan whispered that same poison to the Ottomans. It formed an odd alliance: the victor Obrenovic and the defeated Ottomans. Together, they sent men to kill Karadorde in the forest of Radovanjski Lug.' He and his men had been killed gruesomely, their heads sent to the Ottoman ruler to prove they were dead. He would not tell May that.

'I was too late to stop it. Roan delayed me quite deliberately on the road to Radovanjski. We fought, with blades, and I came out the worse for it. I wasn't nearly as skilled then as I am now.' A sword was a gentleman's weapon and he'd only had battlefield training where stabbing was more important than finesse. 'I swore that day I'd never be late again.'

'And so you became a bodyguard.' May brought the story full circle. 'So no one else would needlessly die.'

'Yes. And no one under my protection has.' He smiled in the dark, proud of that even if he wasn't always proud of the methods required to ensure that protection. Sometimes protection meant death to others, Kant's ends justifying the means, Burke's one good man preventing evil through his singular action.

May snuggled deeper into his arms. 'Thank you. I am glad you told me.'

'I *had* to tell you.' He played with her hair, checking his earlier work for tangles.

'Yes, of course.' May's tone was sleepy and light. 'You want me to accept that Roan is a real danger. I *do*. This is a man who tried to kill you and has tried to kill my brother. I do understand, truly.'

'No, it's more than that, May. Roan is but one of my enemies. I protect people in Britain's interest. There are those who would disagree, who would rather see me out of the way and those who just want revenge. Protecting others can be a dangerous business if one acquires a reputation.'

He could feel her still beside him, her thoughts grappling with the impact of his words. He had to give the rest of the truth to her now or he might never find the courage. 'The choice to join the Home Office has changed my life, May. Sometimes for better and sometimes for worse. It has also changed...me.' He kept his hand moving through her hair, not wanting to betray how much the next few words mattered to him. He didn't want May's pity, he didn't want her to be polite, and perhaps she would be if she sensed important feelings were at stake. Then again, maybe not. May wasn't one for sugar coating. 'I have enemies, May, and I have darkness. You should consider that when you wonder why you're in my bed.'

May started drawing again on his chest, a sign that she had her verdict. But it was too fast, too quick for the weighty insights he'd shared and it showed her desperation. 'All the more reason we should stay here.' It was such an obvious countermove. May would look for a way to turn this to her advantage. How could she get what she wanted? That would certainly be the best of both worlds for her; she could keep her cottage fantasy in Scotland and keep him with her. Perhaps he shouldn't be so cynical. She wanted him to stay. She'd said 'we'. *We could stay.* He said nothing. He waited. May was never good at silence.

'So many people are depending on us, just now,' she whispered her argument. 'Beatrice and the baby, Preston.'

'How long are you going to hide behind Beatrice? That baby will need you for ever, your friend will need you for ever if you allow it. Do you think Beatrice expects *you* to stay for ever?' In the weeks he'd known Beatrice, he didn't think she meant for May to share her exile on a permanent basis. Beatrice was strong, resourceful and, most of all, perceptive. Beatrice had allowed May to come this far with her because May needed it as much as she did.

'I'm not hiding. I'm trying to be a good friend, a loyal friend.' May's response was terse. 'I'm loyal to her, the way you are loyal to Preston. Surely you couldn't leave him just now?'

That was a sticking point, perhaps her most persuasive argument to date. They couldn't leave until they knew the ledger pages were safely in the hands of the government and that Preston was well. 'Cabot Roan won't be a threat for ever.' But he was for now. 'Then what, May? What happens after Roan?' He'd given her all the tools she needed to decide responsibly. 'What happens when Roan is caught and you're free? Do you go home to London and your family or do you tie yourself to a dangerous man who might put you in peril simply by association?'

May gave a hard laugh. 'Are there only two choices? Why can't staying here be a third option? Why does it always have to be my choice? Why does it have to be me having to choose what to give up?' He could feel her getting mad. 'What about you, Liam? What do you give up?' May sighed. 'Have you thought about that? You haven't got a family to risk. There's no one to risk but yourself, nothing to give up but your career. You could find another one. Preston could help you and you have credentials now. I am sure there's a safer occupation out there for you.'

She scooted away from him, propping herself up on one arm. He felt the loss immediately. He wanted her back in his arms. 'I want my freedom, Liam, but I love my family and it kills me that I can't have both. You were right. This cottage, this life I'm leading here, is not real independence. My father sends an allowance. Bea and I think we can make it on our own, but we don't really know. This is an experiment and if it fails, we can go back home. But it's the only kind of independence I can have that won't cost me my family. I resent my parents' determination that I marry appropriately, but I don't resent *them*. It's the only path they know.'

Liam rolled to his side and looked at her. This was a more mature May speaking, not the rebellious girl who had wanted to act out against her parents, who saw only that she was being denied what she wanted. This was a woman who had acquired perspective and it had tempered her. He respected that woman, he *loved* that woman. How could he stand to lose her again? 'Then tell me, May, what are we doing in this bed?'

May pushed at his shoulders with the flat of her hand and rolled over him, straddling him at his hips, her hair hanging forward over her breasts. 'We are doing the best we can.' She leaned forward and kissed him, letting those breasts brush against his chest in tempting promise. She reached between them, her hand grasping for him. 'We are together, right now. Let that be enough.' She kissed him again, letting her tongue run along the edges of his in a tantalising mirror of her hand below.

He didn't know what the future held, but he knew what it *should* hold. Every instinct in him told him Roan was coming, told him he should get May to Edinburgh as fast as possible. But here he was, on his back, letting May have her way with him, letting her refuse to directly answer his questions, letting himself pretend he had enough answers for now and that those answers symbolised progress. He'd told her his truths and May still wanted him, wanted the 'us' for as long as she could have it. Never mind—that was what she'd wanted once before.

May rode him with a slow, deliberate rock of her hips, his brain unable to concentrate on anything else but the sensation of his body in hers. Sweet heavens, three weeks of domestic life had made him soft. Well, not entirely soft. Parts of him were rock hard.

It occurred to him vaguely as May moved over him, taking him deep inside her, that maybe she'd got what she wanted. She'd come up here with her brandy and seduction in the hope of convincing him to buy into the fantasy—stay here in the little village on the Forth and live the pretence…the pretence that nothing would change, that Cabot Roan wouldn't find them and that somehow, miraculously, all would be well.

Chapter Sixteen

All would be well. Roan could feel it in his bones, along with the seeping cold and the wet damp of Scotland in November. But he'd take it. Cabot Roan slammed shut the articulating mast of his telescope with satisfaction. After days of racing over rutted roads and uncertain terrain that risked carriage wheels and horses alike, followed by days more of headquartering in an inn with a certain dubious 'rustic' charm, waiting for reports to trickle in, he had good news at last.

He'd found the sister and Liam Casek. Quite *together*, from the reports. One man had told him there was gossip circulating that Casek had thrown a man against a wall for looking at May Worth too long a few days back. If they were indeed *together* in that sense, it would make for an interesting dynamic when he took them. They were going to pay for this most uncomfortable trip. For a man with his fortune at his disposal, he resented not being able to spend it on good living. But high living also meant too much attention and he wanted the element of surprise on his side. Which explained why he was out on the road in the middle of the night.

In the dark, there were few details he could see about the cottage, but it meant he was invisible in the blackness. No one was out, there was no one to see him, no one to note that he wanted to take a closer look at the cottage rented by a Mrs Fields. His man had come back this afternoon, dripping wet and full of news. Two villages over in a fishing village on the Forth, there were two English ladies who'd taken a cottage at the end of summer, both of them dark haired, one of them expecting a baby and waiting for her husband to join them. That alone hadn't particularly interested Roan. Although, to be honest, his pulse had quickened at the news they were both dark haired, never mind half the female population of Britain had darkish hair. It had been the other bit of news accompanying it: a man, who was *not* the pregnant woman's husband, had joined them a few weeks ago. The clincher had been the story of beating up the farmer who had looked too long at the other woman.

That was a tip worth paying for. Liam Casek was here and Casek was edgy. Perhaps this delay had worked in his favour, Roan mused. Liam Casek would be restless, worried, searching for news, waiting for direction, his paranoia building. He'd see trouble everywhere and that had exposed him, exposed them.

Tomorrow, he would pay Mrs Fields a visit. It was market day and he was counting on Casek being out of the house for a bit. He'd walk up to her front door and ask about her house guest. He needed to decide how to do it. Roan wheeled his horse around, his mind filling with options. There were so many ways to terrify a person. Should he barge in, wielding a gun, and force a confession from her at pistol point? Should his men burn the barn and make her pay for harbouring Casek and the ledger evidence on her property? Should he play the gentleman and go to Mrs Fields with manners and flattery? He'd love to sit in her front parlour sipping tea, just waiting for Casek to walk in.

Better yet, perhaps he should leave Mrs Fields out of it altogether. He didn't think he'd hurt Mrs Fields. Harming mothers who'd just given birth and little babies made him look like a villain, not a businessman. He was only interested in extracting revenge from those who meddled in his affairs, although 'meddling' was putting it mildly compared to what Casek and Worth had done. Worth had broken into his home, his own private domain, and *stolen* from him. Casek had helped him get away. Roan was sure of that now. When a man interfered with Cabot Roan, he had to learn to pay the price— he *and* his family. But that was where Roan's vengeance ended.

That decided it. He would send one of his men to take the Worth chit in the village. Tomorrow was market day, a prime opportunity, and Casek would be with her, especially if he was growing paranoid. Roan smiled to himself. He felt much better about this plan. Mrs Fields needn't be implicated at all. He wasn't a bloodthirsty rogue, after all, but he was an exacting one especially when it was *his* neck on the line.

That neck was indeed on the line. Roan unconsciously massaged his throat, a gesture he was making too often these days. He was looking for Casek and those incriminating ledger papers. The names on those pages were looking for him. Coming to Scotland after May Worth was a convenient reason to get out of

England. It wasn't just the Crown looking to see him hanged. The people he did business with would not appreciate their names being made public, it made them just as guilty of treason as he. But perhaps not as tenacious. He'd survived this long because he was never ready to give up.

May wasn't ready to give up on her argument to stay put. Maybe Liam had it all wrong. Perhaps every day Roan didn't come should be viewed with hope—proof that he wasn't coming, couldn't find them, or didn't want to invest the time. Perhaps he'd decided as long as the papers were in Scotland they couldn't hurt him. Maybe he'd decided to wait for the pages in London and steal them back then when he was sure they posed a danger. Liam didn't agree. He would find such reasoning naïve. Every day Roan didn't come made Liam more nervous, more alert.

May slid a quiet look in Liam's direction as they rode into the village for the market. They kept the horses to a walk. There was no hurry today and the ride was mostly silent, as had been their breakfast. She was keenly aware that Liam had laid himself open for her last night. She was still trying to digest the magnitude of

everything that had been said and revealed.
He'd asked her about the possibility of a future
between them while at the same time seeming
to warn her away from it. As a result, she'd had
no ready answer to give and resentment lingered. How dared he make her choose?

Last night had not gone entirely to plan. The
sex, yes. The post-coital conversation, no. Her
plan had simply been to keep him here, to convince him Edinburgh was unnecessary without telling him why. She wasn't sure how he'd
respond to the truth about Edinburgh. There
was no love lost between him and her father.
That could possibly work in her favour. But if
there was a chance that Preston would be there,
too, Liam would tolerate no prevarication. They
would go even if he had to sling her over his
shoulder and carry her every step of the way.

With too many unknown reactions to factor
in, she hadn't dared to take her chances with
full disclosure. In the end she was glad she
hadn't. If she had told him a holiday season of
matchmaking awaited her, he would never have
asked her for a future, never have told her all
he had. He certainly would never have allowed
her to seduce him. Sometimes, too much of the
innate gentleman lurked beneath his rougher
exterior. It was complicated enough as it was,

just staying here. What *did* happen next? She knew her answer last night had not truly been an answer at all, only a delaying tactic.

'Perhaps there will be a letter today.' Liam broke into her thoughts as the village came into view. The ride had been good, exercise on a brisk, frosty day, a chance to be quiet with her thoughts, but now it was time to concentrate on the market and her tasks. She had a list from Beatrice.

May shook her head. 'You know there won't be any letter. It's too risky and Preston's too smart for that.' She refused to entertain other reasons Preston wouldn't write. Her parents wouldn't write, they were probably already in Edinburgh and expecting to see her shortly— too shortly—for a letter to be worthwhile. There was so much to think about, it made her head swim. She took a deep breath. She had to focus on one thing at a time. But it was hard to think about just the next thing when there were so many other larger issues pressing her attention: Roan, Preston, Edinburgh, all that Liam had revealed, her choices.

They stopped and dismounted, tethering the horses near the vendors' stalls. She just had to get through the market. Liam was already in bodyguard mode, scanning stalls, looking for anything unusual; new vendors, new products, unfamiliar faces, gaps a person could emerge from or be dragged into. He was doing his job. For the first time she understood more fully what that meant. He was *always* doing his job. He *would* always be doing it. Protection was ingrained in him. It was a reminder of all that *did* stand between them. He'd called it enemies and darkness.

May idly tested the apples in a bin. 'I'll take two pounds,' she told the apple seller, distractedly. Her gaze went to where Liam stood a few feet away, covertly conducting his surveillance without hovering; so tall, so bold with his blue eyes and that tiny scar high on his left cheek proclaiming him as a man of bold action as well as words. He'd opened himself up to her completely last night so she could decide. Could she live with the man he'd become and all that he might bring with him? Was he worth the danger?

How could she not want him? Every time she looked at him, her stomach did a queer twist, her skin tingled when he touched her, he could make her cry out with sensations only he could awake, but his attraction went deeper than the physical. He *knew* her. He knew her secrets, he knew her youth. He'd had experiences with her no one else ever would. When she was old and grey, he would know how she'd ridden neck-for-nothing across a sunlit meadow, how she'd lain in a field of wildflowers looking up at the sky on a summer day. He knew what made her mad, he knew how she thought, how she fought.

He knew her soul and all of its own flaws. He knew she wasn't perfect and he just might love her anyway. He'd not said the words, not since he'd come to Scotland, but he had loved her once and he said he didn't hate her. As for her, she greatly feared she loved him. Had never stopped loving him, although some days it had been harder to love him than others.

She loved Liam Casek. May dropped the apples. She watched them scatter on the ground, her mind numbed to anything but that one thought. She *loved* Liam and she was going to love him for the rest of her life whether she was with him or not. This feeling was going to be with her for ever. He was the other half of her soul.

Liam was beside her, kneeling down to pick up the spilled fruit. 'May, are you all right?' He piled the apples in her basket and moved her out of the way of other shoppers.

'I'm fine. I just realised…something.' She

didn't dare look at him. What if he saw? What if he knew? Would that solve all their problems or create more? Not yet. She couldn't tell him yet. She pulled herself together. 'I need to get some buttons—shall I meet you outside the inn in twenty minutes? I won't be long.' It was the best option for snatching some time alone. The notions shop was the shop Liam liked the least. Run by a fussy old widow, it was small and cramped with hardly any room for customers let alone tag-along escorts. She could use the time to compose herself.

Buttons took longer than she'd intended. Apparently, everyone needed buttons today and Widow Graham had talked to everyone *excessively* in turn. It was as though the woman knew May was in a hurry. Finally, her six buttons secure in the basket, May headed out on to the street. All of her attention was fixed on getting to the inn two streets down. If she let her attention wander, it might return to her earlier thoughts and that was not where she wanted them.

The streets were crowded. The fishing boats were in for a few days before setting back out and that made everything busier. She was jostled from all sides, not unusual on days like this. A rough hand pressed up against her back, another hand gripped the arm not holding the basket. At first, it registered only as the roughness of a busy crowd. When that grip persisted and she was shoved off balance towards a narrow alleyway, she got angry. When she found her back up against the rough-hewn brick of a wall, she gave that anger vent.

'Liam, I have had enough of this! You can't just go about hauling me off the street because I was a few minutes late and you absolutely have to stop pretending everyone you meet is trying to abduct me—' The last word died in her throat. This man wasn't Liam. Her gaze drifted over his shoulder to the right, where a hulk of a man stood, blocking the street from her gaze. He wasn't Liam either. The coldness of fearful realisation settled in her stomach. She didn't know these men, but she knew who had sent them.

The man pressing her to the wall gave a harsh laugh. 'Boss was right, Casek's with her. She must be the one, then.' He turned his attention to her, every gap-toothed, foul-breathed ounce of it, his eyes dark and beady. 'Seems no introductions are needed. We know who you are and since you're with Casek, you know who we are.' He leered. 'No one told us you were so pretty, though. I wouldn't want to have to hurt you. Burt, tell her what the plan is.'

The big one at the alley entrance swore. 'No names, Ivar.' He grunted. 'The plan is simple. You're coming with us for a little visit with the boss. All you need to bring are the ledger papers. We know you have them. Casek wouldn't be here otherwise.'

Not quite true, May thought, adrenaline fuelling her brain to high levels of activity. Liam was here to protect her because Roan wanted her for leverage against Preston. If she had the papers, all the more power to Roan, but Roan would want her regardless—something to trade for his own freedom and the return of the ledgers. If she couldn't protect herself from Roan, she could at least protect the papers Preston had risked his life for. 'I am Preston Worth's sister, but I don't know anything about papers or ledgers.' She put on her best perplexed, scared female look, buying time. These men didn't look terribly smart.

Surely Liam would be worried that she was late, surely his gaze would have been riveted on the button-shop door watching for her. Unless they'd already got to him? Was Liam lying hurt somewhere? Dead somewhere? She couldn't dwell on those thoughts, but neither, she realised, could she depend on Liam to charge in and save the day. What had he told her the day he'd swept her off the street? No one had seen it happen? Had he, too, not seen it?

'Best check, Ivar,' Burt suggested with a leer. 'She could be lying. If she's not, we'll go out to the cottage and we can all get better acquainted.' That leer left no mistake as to what the nature of the acquaintance would be. 'I don't think she likes you, Ivar. Maybe she'll change her mind when she sees the size of your—'

May brought her knee up. It was time to fight and her knee took Ivar hard in his supposedly large male parts. These bastards weren't getting close to her, to the cottage, to Bea or the baby. Ivar went down with a cry, but she had no time to get the pistol out of her pocket. Burt was on the move. She grabbed the apples from her basket and threw them rapid fire, anything to delay him, to keep him from getting close to her. Distance was her only advantage against a man who outweighed and outmuscled her, distance would give her time to get her pistol out.

She had the gun free of her pocket at last. She brought it up, bringing his advance to a halt. 'I *will* shoot.' Her hand closed around the trigger, her mind willing her body to stay calm long enough to get a shot off. Surely at this near distance she wouldn't miss. Surely she'd hit something, even though she was nervous.

'May!' A loud voice sounded from the open end of the alley, loud and deliberate, drawing Burt's attention for a split second, a second that cost Burt. A knife flew, it found purchase and Burt went down, less likely than moaning Ivar to get up any time soon. Liam sprinted past the two fallen forms to reach her. She was shaking by then, glad for the strength of his arms. 'May, give me the gun. Let me take it.' He closed a hand over hers and pried her fingers loose, his tone low. There was danger and calculation in his eyes even as he soothed her. She was glad to give up the weapon, glad to let him take charge for a moment, her mind suddenly numb. *Just do the next thing. Get out of the alley.*

Liam pushed her into the daylight of the street. 'Can you move quickly, May? They'll be down for a bit, but it won't buy us much time. When they're able, they'll drag themselves back to Roan.' His arm was about her waist, supporting her, urging her on as quickly as possible. 'We need to get home quickly. Can you ride?'

The ride restored her sanity. She didn't think about pulling a gun on Burt, didn't think about the horror of being at the mercy of those two, or how close the danger had come, or how ruthlessly, immediately, Liam had thrown that knife with unerring accuracy. That was all in the past now. She only thought about what happened next: get to the house, grab the ledger pages, get Bea and the baby to safety.

'How long do you think we have?' May asked as they pulled the horses to a stop in front of the cottage.

'Depends on how long they'll let themselves wallow in their misery before facing Roan's wrath. We might have an hour, but I want us out of here in twenty minutes, tops.' Liam called instructions over his shoulder, already striding towards the barn. 'It's all the time I'll need to tack both horses.'

Twenty minutes! Her mind was a whir. The letters, a change of clothes, any money she could find, Liam's things, some food. There was so much to do! 'Bea, we have to go!' she cried, racing through the house, trying to use her time without panicking. 'Grab Matty's things.' She tossed pieces of the story to Bea as she packed frantically. Roan was here, he'd tried for her in village, they would come here next.

In the yard, Liam held both horses impatiently, barking orders. 'Bea, can you ride long enough to get to the Maddox farm? You'll be safe there.' He stuffed a small leather bag into Bea's hand. 'Money to get you through.' Then he tossed her up on the horse and handed the baby to her. 'It's not far and this big guy is tired. You should be safe enough. Go.'

'You're sending her away?' May exclaimed as Bea moved the horse on to the road and headed to the Maddoxes, away from the village. There wouldn't be a chance of her meeting Roan's men going in that direction.

'Yes, we are running for our lives now, May.' Liam cupped his hands. 'Up you go, we have to hurry. If we miss the ferry, we'll have to take our chances on the road and I'd rather not.'

She wanted to argue, to protest, but how could she? There was no other answer and yet part of her heart was breaking as she glanced once more at the cottage. It wasn't even hers, it was rented from a Penrose relative of Bea's, but she knew instinctively she'd never be back. To stay was to die. Roan would be furious now. All the fears Liam had warned of had come to fruition. Roan was here and he was hunting *her*.

May closed her eyes for a moment, taking one last mental image of the cottage. So much was left behind, she hoped her freedom wasn't one of those things. But she couldn't stay, she could only go forward. With Liam. May grabbed for her courage as her horse sprang after Liam and the road.

Chapter Seventeen

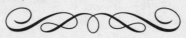

Cabot Roan bent and placed a hand on the bricks of the kitchen hearth. No heat, but definitely not cold. No heat from the coals either. The fire had been put out not long ago. He straightened, brushing his hands off against his trousers with a curse. Damn and double damn. May Worth had slipped through his fingers. If only Burt and Ivar had crawled back sooner, the snivelling cowards, never mind that Burt might very well still die from his wound. Casek was far better with knives than he was with swords.

He checked his watch. Half past four. It was nearly evening by winter hours. Dark was already settling. He and his men would have to start out regardless and they'd have to split up. He had no idea if Casek would take her by ferry, or if Casek would take the road. Roan weighed the benefits. The ferry was direct, but tricky. Casek would be reliant on the ferry's schedule and the tide. He might feel caged by those restraints, especially if he had to wait for the ferry to leave. While he waited, he and May would be trapped. They'd have to spend the night in the village unless they made the afternoon ferry. If they had, they were already on their way. If they hadn't, they'd have to wait somewhere. Casek wouldn't bring her back here.

'Do you know the ferry schedule?' Roan barked at his assistant. In his own mounting desperation, he'd driven his men hard, showing no quarter.

'It sails twice a day, boss. Once in the early morning and then once in the afternoon at two o'clock.'

Roan drummed his hand on the table. The ferry or the road? How good were the odds Casek *hadn't* made the ferry? He ran through the sequence of events in his head. He'd got the report from bleeding Burt and Ivar at three-thirty. They'd encountered May and Casek around one-thirty. There'd been the altercation, after which Casek and May had come back here to evacuate Mrs Fields, to pack and to get those damnable ledger pages, no doubt.

The horses were gone, proof indeed that they had come back and that they'd ridden to wherever they'd gone. If they had gone to the ferry, it meant a return to the village where someone would have seen them. There would be people who could confirm they'd got on the ferry. The ferry made them conspicuous even if it was faster. The road would make them more invisible.

Roan considered the other option: the road. The road would mean a longer trek. It would take two days to reach Edinburgh and Casek would have to be more cautious than the usual traveller. He might feel compelled to slow down and take less open roads. Roan gave a cold chuckle. Perhaps that's what Casek wanted him to think, that the road was the most logical choice. Perhaps Casek would risk the ferry after all. What a chess game this had become— thought and counter-thought. The game hadn't ended with his arrival here, as he thought it would. The game had just begun. Casek was proving to be a most worthy opponent.

Ferry or road, the next step was still the same. Roan strode through the house, his eyes taking sharp stock of everything left behind. It had all the signs of a Liam Casek getaway. Very little had been taken. Perhaps Mrs Fields harboured the belief she would come back and resume her life once the trouble had passed. She would be disappointed then. He hoped Mrs Fields had generous neighbours or relatives close to hand, because returning, even if she was an innocent bystander, was one thing he couldn't allow. If Casek and the chit were close, he wanted them to know he was coming. Stealth was effective, but even more effective was fear. In a panic, people were more inclined to make bad choices. Nothing like a little fire and smoke to induce that sense of heedless flight. He'd rather have Casek on the road where he could flush him out without too many witnesses.

'Men, take anything you find interesting. There's clothes for your girlfriends in the bedrooms, pots, pans. Help yourselves, but be quick. No more than ten minutes,' Roan called out, heading for the door. 'Then, fire the place.' He gestured to two men coming downstairs, arms already full of household items. 'Peters, Smythe, take two others and start on the Edinburgh road. If they're on it, they'll have to stop for the night soon. I'll take a group to the village and check the ferry.'

It seemed an exercise in futility to check on a ferry that had already sailed. But at least he'd

know. Even if he had to stay in the village tonight, he could cross over tomorrow morning
and still be in Edinburgh before Smythe and
Peters. It was the waiting he hated. He was
a man of action and it galled him that Casek
might be doing something while he was stuck
here, especially if that something was finding a way to send those ledger pages safely to
London.

'Are you sure they'll go to Edinburgh, boss?'
a man risked asking as his diminished group
turned their horses back towards the village.

'Very sure,' Roan snapped without offering
explanation. Casek's first job was to protect
May Worth, she was a prize with or without
the pages to leverage against her brother. She
alone would be leverage enough to drive Preston Worth to action. But if Casek was here,
Roan felt certain it was because the pages were
here, too. What better place to send them than
to Worth's sister who had disappeared from
the London map?

Ferry or road? The choice kept niggling at
him as they made the trip to the village. Were
there really only two choices? Sometimes it
was good to narrow down one's options to the
most plausible. It saved time and money. Other
times, it cost a man that same money and time.

Eliminating options could blind a man to other avenues. Was there a third way? Something he was overlooking? He wouldn't know until he started to eliminate the probable.

Damn! Liam swore in frustration, watching the ferry move out into the firth. In all probability, the chance of catching the ferry had been against him from the start, a game of minutes, and time hadn't been on his side. They'd missed the boat and now there wasn't another ferry until tomorrow morning. Beneath him, his horse sweated and huffed. He and May had raced the horses as fast as they dared to the dock only to come up short.

His mind was doing the racing now, going through the options: wait until the morning ferry, or take to the road and invest two days on the run hoping Roan and his men didn't catch them. He had his knives, his gun and May's gun. How long would they last against Roan's armed thugs? They'd take May alive, but he had no illusions how long he'd last. They'd kill him. Roan had been wanting to kill him for a while now, ever since he'd put the government on Roan's trail in Serbia. It had taken four years to build the case against Roan. Staying in the village was a death trap. He didn't think they could hide here until dawn. Even now, Roan could be on his way and they'd been seen. Discretion had not been part of their barrelling ride to the dock.

'Is there another boat?' he asked May, an idea coming to him as he scanned the busy wharf. Surely with all these boats there was one that would take them.

May's mare pranced nervously beside his stallion. 'There's only the ferry.'

'No, not a ferry, just any boat? A fishing boat?'

'The horses will never fit,' May protested.

'We leave them.' He didn't like the idea of leaving Charon and he knew May liked it even less. She'd been with her mare for twelve years. 'I'll get a boy to run a note to Beatrice. She can arrange to collect them later.' Horses would do them little good in Edinburgh anyway. Hadn't May said the fishermen were in port today, on a break between winter trips out to sea? The town had seemed busier than usual. 'That one.' Liam's eyes landed on a smaller vessel. He swung off his horse. 'I'll go talk to the captain.'

'Why that one? Why not something that looks a little *bigger*?' May dismounted and took the reins, holding both horses.

Liam flashed her a grin. 'Because that boat looks a little more desperate than the rest.'

It turned out he was right. For a little coin, the fisherman—captain was too exalted a title for the man who owned the boat—was happy to take them across. Liam couldn't be sure that coin would also buy a dose of discretion, but he was more concerned with speed at the moment. He wanted May out of the village and if he had to point a gun at the man the entire way across he would. It had been a damned bloody day already.

He found a boy and paid him to take the horses to the livery and to send word to Mrs Fields. He wanted to board and sail immediately. He was taking no chances of encountering Roan by going back into the village. Liam breathed a little easier once he had May on board and some distance between him and the shore.

He couldn't say the same for May. Her hands gripped the rail and her face was white. Not surprising considering the events of her day; she'd been attacked, evacuated from her home, and thrust towards a destination she had no desire to arrive at. She'd held up admirably all things considered. 'I don't like the captain.' She bit out the words.

'I'll shoot him if there's trouble.' But he'd spoken too callously. He'd not meant to. He'd meant to reassure her. One desperate sea captain was the least of his worries and easily handled.

'And the crew? Will you shoot them, too?' May kept her eyes fixed on the shrinking shore, but her thoughts were transparent. He'd tried to warn her last night, tried to explain what life was like with him, for him. Words could not adequately prepare one for the reality.

'I hope I won't need to.' He'd picked this boat because the crew was small and he felt he could take the other three men if he had to. He hoped for no trouble, but one never knew, desperation being what it was—a double-edged sword and a bitch to boot. If this fisherman had been desperate, had the man also sensed his client was desperate, too? Desperation had a way of seeking itself out. If there was going to be trouble, it would be midway between ports where he and May would be most vulnerable. If it was them or the crew, Liam knew unequivocally what his choice would be. But May needed a different sort of reassurance.

'I would never needlessly take a life, May. I never have. There's always been a reason,' Liam answered sombrely. 'My line of work might require the elimination of opponents, but it has never required me to demote the sanctity of life.' He reached for her hand. 'In fact, I think it may have enhanced my respect for it. I've seen first-hand how fragile life is, how it might be ended at any moment.'

'Like the man in the alley today?' May said with quiet steel, her words not quite a challenge. 'Will he die?'

'He might,' Liam answered honestly. The knife could have struck an artery and there was always the threat of inflammation and fever. 'What would you prefer I have done? Let him harm you? Harm me and leave you defenceless?' He squeezed her cold hand. 'Those men assaulted you and intended to do worse to you in the course of doing their job for Roan,' Liam answered matter of factly. 'If it's a choice between us or them, I'll choose us, May, every time.'

He'd been frantic when he'd realised she'd disappeared from the street. He'd been more frantic still when he'd caught sight of her in the alley, her pistol drawn, her hand trembling. Whether May realised it or not, she'd never have got an effective shot off. May should never *have* to fire a shot. Preston had put his sister in an untenable situation. Or perhaps *he* had. The thought that this was all his fault had lingered today. Perhaps he should have noticed the men sooner, should have gone looking for her sooner.

May gave him a considering look, understanding settling in her eyes. She finally saw what he'd endeavoured to tell her. Perhaps it was best she saw him for what he was, what he'd become: not quite a military man, but not quite a civilian either. The government had put him into a limbo of sorts, belonging to neither world. It was easy enough to do with men who were expendable, men with talents and a hunger to prove themselves who weren't scions of noble houses. She had no words for him, but she leaned against him and rested her head on his shoulder in a pondering gesture of acceptance.

The waves were rougher now as they approached the mid-portion of their journey. Liam brought out his pistol and made a show of reloading it. A visible weapon was a keen deterrent to anyone who hadn't yet decided to commit villainy.

May was watching him, thinking, searching for words to put to her thoughts. 'This is your world, isn't it? Weapons and mayhem, getaways and bad men.' She smiled ruefully. 'No wonder Preston loves it so much. His other life, being the grandson of an earl, is so boring. I'm not the only one wrapped in cotton wool, you know?'

Liam cocked an eyebrow, waiting for her to go on, one eye fixed on the man working ropes at the railing.

'Preston wanted to join the army when Napoleon was afoot. He was furious when his friend Jonathon went. Jonathon was a diplomatic aide, but Preston was still jealous. He and my father fought most ferociously for the first time ever. Did he tell you that?'

Liam nodded. 'Not in so many words, but it came up.' Preston had been supportively jealous about the chance to go to Serbia.

'He was thrilled to head up the commission in charge of the coast, but he always felt as though he was settling.'

'Catching the likes of Cabot Roan is not for men who "settle".' Liam rubbed at a smudge on the pistol barrel. He tossed a grin at the man at the rail and raised his pistol for a practice sighting.

'No, clearly, it's not.' May smiled wryly and laughed for the first time since breakfast. She hadn't much to laugh about. He'd upended her life today, taken her away from all the roots she'd just barely managed to put down.

'They didn't like you much in the village, anyway,' Liam tried to joke.

'No, they didn't. They liked Bea better,' May admitted with another laugh. 'I'm too brassy.'

'Is that why London didn't like you either?' he said more gently this time. May was beautiful to him, all the things a woman should be. It was a mystery to him why she hadn't been snatched up. Did he dare hope it was because she'd resisted? That she'd been waiting for him? Did he *want* that to be the reason? Was it fair to want that, knowing the limits of what he could offer her?

'Yes, most definitely. I made sure of that.' She smiled again, but this smile was brittle.

'You drove them away on purpose? Why?' He wasn't sure he wanted to hear it. Perhaps that had been his fault, too. Because of him, she'd been forced to push away eligible suitors: young handsome rich men, safe men. He'd taken her virginity and left her, thinking it would be for her own good, thinking it was what she wanted. If she was happy, he could live with that. But she hadn't been happy. She'd isolated herself, she'd retreated from the life she was supposed to have.

'Why not? There was no one who interested me and the surest way to avoid insipid men who wanted a doll on their arm and a dowry in the bank was to cut them down to size.'

He shouldn't laugh, but it was hard not to. He allowed himself a small chuckle—the image of May telling suitors exactly what she thought of them was too humorous to ignore. 'It's not funny, but it is,' he confessed. 'Surely one of them was worthy of you.'

'No.' May slid her glance his way. 'Not one of them. The problem was, none of them was you and you were long gone by spring.'

She'd missed him. After the anger had cleared, *she'd missed him.* Even five years later, hearing that did strange things to his stomach. 'I'm sorry you missed me.' He saw her shiver. 'You're freezing. Come here.' He pulled her to him and took her against his body, sharing his heat with her as darkness closed in. The lights of the port of Leith glittered in the distance. It appeared they'd arrive safely, after all, without needing to shoot anyone. Apparently the captain was only desperate, not malicious. Maybe May was his good-luck charm. He wasn't used to things going right.

Chapter Eighteen

When had things gone wrong? This was exactly where she *didn't* want to be. May stepped off the boat, with her head up, shoulders back, her body simultaneously alert and exhausted. The day had been beyond imagining. She felt Liam's hand at her back, strong and reassuring. She could feel the vigilance of his body, tense and alert beside her as he scanned the dark docks, ready to protect her from whatever local danger roamed the docks after daylight. His voice was at her ear. 'You're safe now, May.'

But she wasn't safe. What about the unseen? There were things here he couldn't protect her from, like the parents who waited at the town house. Here, she didn't know what came next. Did they hide out in Edinburgh trying to avoid her parents and Cabot Roan on their own? If Liam went to any British authorities for help with the latter, it would be impossible to avoid the former. If he didn't seek help, what chance did they stand against a man intent on harming them?

Harm might be too tame a word. Then it struck her—Roan wanted *her* alive. She was leverage. She needn't fear death at Roan's hand, not immediately any way. But Liam did. He was an obstacle between Roan and his goal. Perhaps even something more now that he might have killed one of Roan's men and there was a history between them. Roan would be out for Liam's blood.

Liam found them an inn a few streets off the docks, as quiet and respectable as they were going to find without entering Edinburgh's New Town tonight. He paid for a room and ordered dinner. May let him handle the arrangements. She had mental arrangements of her own to make. Of all the revelations that had been made recently, the last was the hardest to fathom: Liam could die in the act of protecting her. His life would not be spared. She'd had a few weeks to adjust to the idea that Roan would come after her. While it seemed surreal that he had actually done just that, it was more devastating to realise the danger Liam was in—danger she could do much to prevent. She could protect him with one simple choice. They had to go to her parents. Her father could protect them both.

Upstairs, the room was simple but clean. Liam busied himself laying a fire, unwilling to wait for a maid to come up and do it for him. 'Dinner will be up soon.' He paused from his work and looked about the room. 'I'm sorry, May. I know it's not what you're used to. But I think it's the best we can do tonight.'

The words made her mad. After all she'd been through today, the last weeks, the last months, accommodations were the least of her worries. 'I won't break, Liam. I wish you could see that about me. I may have been raised wrapped in cotton wool, but I don't need to be treated that way. I don't *want* to be treated that way.' She faced him, hands on hips. 'What do you think I'm used to anyway? Silk sheets and china plates? You saw the cottage. Beatrice and I lived quite simply.'

A knock at the door interrupted them, announcing the arrival of dinner. A maid and two boys hurried in with trays and laid the table. The smell of hot food nearly undid her. She was hungrier than she'd realised, more tired than she realised. Hot food sounded good, seemed so 'normal'. She was suddenly struck with a fierce wave of longing for her cottage kitchen with its hearth, for a simple night of eating stew and bread at the little table. She felt tears threaten and fought them back. It was silly to be sentimental over such a small thing when there was so much else to be thankful for. She and Beatrice were safe. The baby was safe. She and Liam had eluded Roan, they were alive and free.

Liam held out a chair for her by the fire. 'No one would blame you if you did break. Today would have broken a lot of people. As for silk sheets and china plates, I saw how the mighty family of Worth lived. Those things are your due, May. I would not have you be less than you are.' The old argument again, the old barriers again, subtly inserting themselves between them. Not in anger or hot words of accusation this time, but in caring and concern. That was something, wasn't it? They'd begun three weeks ago with wary scepticism of each other, blaming each other for the disaster five years ago, and now, they'd moved past the blame. But they were still left with the choices. Would she choose to give up a life of safety and luxury for a life of danger with Liam if he asked? After today, would he ever ask?

May met his gaze evenly. 'You are my due,

Liam.' She removed the cover on the tureen, breathing in the warm steam rising from the stew as she ladled it into bowls for them. It smelled like venison. Venison and heaven. 'I don't know how many ways I can show you that.' What would it take to prove to him that he was what mattered to her?

Liam took the bowl. 'Trust me with the truth, then, May. Why were you opposed to coming to Edinburgh?'

'Is there wine?' May glanced around the table.

'There's two.' Liam produced a bottle in each hand.

'Good. If I'm going to tell you the answer to that, I'm going to need wine and you are, too.' She waited until he'd poured glasses for each of them. She'd like to wait until they'd eaten, until they'd drank a few glasses and the wine had taken the edge off the day. Maybe it would take the edge off her decision, too. But Liam was looking at her intently, waiting.

'My parents are here,' she said simply. Maybe that's all she'd have to say. Maybe Liam would divine all those four words implied. His eyes merely narrowed, but she thought she saw his hand tighten around the stem of his wine glass. She was going to have to say more.

'The day you arrived and the letter from Preston came, there was another letter, too, from my parents. They "invited" me to Edinburgh to join them for Christmas,' May explained. 'I don't know why I didn't see it before. King George's visit to Edinburgh in August has made the city popular, has made *all* things Scottish popular.' Her own thoughts in August had been with Bea and wanting to keep her friend safe from scandal. She'd not been paying attention to current events or thinking about how they might affect her parents' decision in allowing her to come north. Her parents would want to follow the popular trend, too. Of course they were spending the festive season in Edinburgh, especially when it served two purposes.

'They're here?' Liam gulped a swallow of wine. She almost laughed at the sight. There was Liam, the fearless bodyguard who'd taken on two armed men in the alley for her, suddenly turned into Liam the would-be suitor, faced with the universal panic of suitors everywhere; meeting the parents, most specifically, meeting her father, a man who had shown himself once before to be quite fierce.

The moment of uncertainty passed. He was once again the bodyguard, all of his thoughts on her. 'We don't have to go to them. We can stay quietly in the city, somewhere.'

She didn't bother to test the logistics of such a possibility. There was no need to. Her mind was already made up. 'Yes, we do.' She reached across the small table and put a hand on his sleeve. She whispered her one hope, 'Preston may be here. We can turn the ledger pages over to him.' Once they reached the sanctuary of her father's home, the chase would be over.

'Roan will still want you as leverage,' Liam warned.

'Yes, but I think it will be much more difficult for him,' she said earnestly. Did he give no thought for his own life? Surely, he'd arrived at the same conclusions she had. May felt compelled to point out the other benefit. 'You will be safe, too.'

Liam's hand covered hers. 'What about you, May? Will you be safe?' He wasn't talking about Roan now. He was probing. She'd only told him half the reason she didn't want to be in the city. It wasn't merely the presence of her parents, although heaven knew they were a big enough threat to her continued independence.

May gave a throaty whisper, eyes engaging his. 'I've never been safe.' She didn't want to tell him about the suitor who was waiting. She'd convinced herself he was inconsequential. She was just going to drive him off like she had every other potential gentleman. She wanted distraction now, for both of them. No more questions. 'Did you say there was more wine?'

Liam reached for the second bottle, sensing the change in her mood. He held it up. 'You're quite the drinker, May. First the brandy, then the wine.'

She tossed him a coy smile and moved around the table, coming to kneel in front of him. 'Who said the wine was for drinking?' She ran a slow hand down the front of his trousers, moulding the fabric against the length of him.

Liam's eyes glinted. 'Whatever else would we do with it, vixen?'

May began working the flap of his breeches. 'I've always wondered if wine could be licked or lapped.' She ran her tongue across her lips, playing the flirt with a coy pout. 'It's too bad I don't have anything to try my hypothesis on. I need something to lick.' She felt him grow hard. She batted her eyelashes and was rewarded with a wicked grin. 'Perhaps you might oblige me?'

'I think I might have a sudden *need* to be licked.' Liam's tone had grown darkly seductive, reminding her she didn't play this game alone. The pleasure seeker and the pleasure giver were dependent upon one another. 'Maybe it's you who is obliging me?'

'Maybe it is,' May whispered, pressing his thighs apart and tugging his trousers down past his hips. 'You're so big and hard, definitely in need of licking.' She thumbed the swollen tip of him, liking how it caused a bead to form, liking how it made him grunt and shift.

'You'd make aspic hard, May.' Liam gave a rough growl.

'As long as I make *you* hard, the aspic can do what it likes.' She laughed, feathering his length with a teasing breath. 'The wine, please.'

She took the bottle and dribbled the wine along the length of him, eager to take him in her mouth before the drops could stain his trousers. 'Mmm…' She sighed, stroking her tongue languidly down the hard stalk of him, licking up the droplets, tasting the mingled flavour of salt and tannins. This was an intimate ambrosia indeed.

Liam groaned for her, his body sliding lower in the chair, his legs wide, his hands in her hair as he began to pant, the leash of his self-control beginning to slip as her mouth took him further from the shores of reason. He made a long, guttural sound, part-pleasure, part-disbelief, as if he was shocked to discover such pleasure existed. His body began to clench, she could feel it in the tensing power of his thighs, hear it in the raggedness of his breathing, in the cry of her name on his lips, a desperate sound as if he would be lost without her.

He was losing her. She was sacrificing herself for him. *You'll be safe, too.* He moved his hand idly through the tangle of her hair, her head resting on his thigh in the aftermath of their pleasure. His thoughts slowly assembled themselves. She'd poured herself into his pleasure as if there would never be another chance to do so. That worried him greatly. He understood it, of course. Her family was here. In general, their presence would curb her freedom. Their demand for her company would pull her away from the freedom of her cottage and her life on the firth. They would not allow her to go back to Beatrice. They'd want her to come home with them in January. May would see that alone as a very real threat to her. He suspected there was more to it than that, however. There was something more she wasn't telling him, something that had indeed convinced her tonight would be their last night.

The thought nearly broke him, his hand stilling in May's hair. He'd barely survived losing her the first time. They were just beginning to find their way back to one another, their way back towards hope and possibility where they might be able to consider again what they could be to each other. Tonight could not be the last. He would fight for her this time in ways he'd not been able to fight for her the last time. He'd fight the Cabot Roans of the world, he'd fight her father and he'd fight her if need be, starting right now. *If she wanted*. But that was a concern for another day.

Liam shifted, signalling he wanted to get up. He had plans for them that didn't involve a chair or hard decisions. May lifted her head and gave him room. He rose, drawing her to her feet. 'Come to bed. We're both wearing too many clothes entirely.'

The tenor of wicked play that had marked the early evening was gone. This was serious lovemaking. There would be no rush, no roughness, no foray into experimenting with the more decadent arts of intimacy. May stood before him, her gaze searching his face for direction. She sensed the change in mood, but was unsure how to proceed.

'Allow me,' he whispered, his hands at the laces of her gown. Allow him to undress her as a bridegroom undresses his wife on that first night, allow him to make love to her, allow him to be her champion, to fight for her, for them. 'I've never undressed you before, May.' In the loft, she'd been the one to undress him. He let his fingers drift over her bare shoulders. He pressed a kiss to the delicate bump of her collarbone as he slid the straps of her chemise down her arms, pushing the thin garment to the floor, aware that she trembled beneath his touch.

He was trembling, too. His usually steady hand shook just the slightest bit as he put a hand to her breast. To see her naked like this did something indescribable to him, something primal and fierce even as it reduced him to a man trembling with reverence, with a divine need to worship. Wordlessly, he took her hand, fingers interlacing, and led her to the bed. He would worship her here, would make the bed an altar to his devotion, his body an offering to her pleasure. He stirred, already recovered, already eager.

Liam rose over her, wanting to memorise the details of this precious moment: the glitter of her green eyes as she looked up at him, the feel of her arms about his neck, the scent of her skin all lavender and rosewater mingled with the lingering musk of him, the gentle invitation of her open thighs, inviting the supplicant into the goddess's inner sanctum.

He bent his mouth to hers, whispering his vow against her lips, as he took her with a kiss and a thrust. 'I will fight for you, May.' And this time, he would win. All that remained was for May to decide she would have him. With each thrust, he was determined that she would.

Chapter Nineteen

He wasn't going to let her go. The knowledge was both a buoy to her spirits and an albatross around her neck as they stood on the front steps of the Worths' rented town house. To have him with her gave her courage to enter this home where plans to see her married off awaited. Liam would be safe here and that made the thought bearable. After last night, though, it was harder than ever to contemplate a life without him. Even if she eluded her parents' intended suitor, Liam would be no more welcome in her family. He might even be blamed for her rejection of whatever suitor lurked at tonight's dinner table. Well, there was no other way around, only through. She wouldn't know how all of this ended if she didn't take the next step. May raised her hand to the brass knocker and let it fall, trying not to think too much about the man on the step below her and the last time he'd seen her father.

Liam was in bodyguard mode again this morning, perhaps in an attempt to present himself professionally to the parents who despised him, perhaps because it was such an intrinsic part of who he was. His back was to her and the door, all the better to keep his watchful eye on the street, his body tense with impatience, although she wondered if it was more than impatience that had Liam on edge. Cabot Roan aside, this couldn't be easy for him. No matter how old one got, no matter how much of the world one had seen, one probably never got over being nearly caught *in flagrante* by a lover's father.

A butler, a man who must have come with the house as May didn't know him, answered with a disapproving glance at her clothes. He clearly thought she belonged at the back entrance. May's chin went up, her tone frosty. 'Miss May Worth, to see her parents.'

It was rather amazing what one forgot in the span of four months and freedom. She'd thought she'd looked rather fine this morning in her warm wool riding habit. It had been serendipitous that she'd had to flee on market day when she'd already been dressed in a decent outfit for town. She'd done a good job of brushing out wrinkles and the travel wear the clothes had acquired yesterday, but now, seeing herself through the butler's eyes, she was forced to rethink that assessment. In his eyes, she'd look like a countrywoman, perhaps a shopkeeper's wife who could afford some small, occasional luxuries, but certainly not someone who could call at the front door of the mighty house of Worth unannounced. Even if the house was rented.

The door opened again, the butler's face neutrally blank as if he hadn't insulted her with his expression the first time. 'Right this way, Miss Worth.' He swept her in, saving his questioning stare for Liam, but decided against making a second mistake after taking in Liam's height and breadth up close.

The town house was spacious, no doubt the best money could rent, that much was obvious in the walk up the stairs to the drawing room. The drawing room itself was elegantly cavernous, done up in shades of peach and grey with hints of turquoise to lend a splash of colour, just exactly the sort of subtle decorating her mother approved of. The furnishings looked new, the wallpaper bright and fresh. Even in winter, there were bouquets of cut flowers in vases on tables throughout the room.

'Those flowers would feed a family in St Giles for two weeks,' Liam muttered crossly, his old habit coming out, probably on purpose, a sign of how much this solution galled him *and* how necessary he felt it was. Social consciousness, he called it.

The drawing-room door opened and her mother swanned in, arms outstretched, 'May! Oh, my darling girl, you're here at last.' She was impeccably dressed in forest-green silk trimmed in jet; at her throat were discreet jewels appropriate for receiving morning guests, her hair put up in a sophisticated twist. She looked ageless and elegant at a distance. It was only up close that one could see the tiny lines about her eyes.

'Mother, it's good to see you.' May searched her mother's face, looking for signs. Was Preston here? Was he well? Did they even know?

Her mother took her hands, just hands, never a hug. Women of her station were not given to hugs. 'We've been so worried about you. Your father wanted to go after you, but Preston insisted...'

'Is Preston here?' Liam turned from the window, his words excited and terse, drawing her mother's attention. The softness in her mother's face turned hard upon recognition. The past flamed into life.

'Preston is here.' She eyed Liam as if he were a repellent insect. 'He told us he'd sent you to May—that you might turn up.' The disdain was evident. How dare this boy from the streets deign to step foot inside such a fine home, let alone claim association with a daughter of its house.

May felt her temper rise. She disengaged her hands and moved towards Liam. 'He saved me yesterday, Mother. We are here only because of him. Roan's men came upon us in the village. Liam was able to get Beatrice and the baby to safety and us as well. He is deserving of our thanks at the very least.'

There were no thanks forthcoming, only redirection. Her mother was determined to ignore Liam. 'She's had the child, then? At least that's over with and we can get our lives back to normal.' She shook her head. 'It's such a distasteful business. I don't know what Edith Penrose was thinking not to keep a more watchful eye on her daughter and now they have a bastard in the family. Shall I call for tea?' She made a fluttering motion with her hand towards Liam. 'Cook will have something hot in the kitchen, if you need breakfast.'

Liam inclined his head, managing to look regal and feral as he stared down her mother.

'Breakfast will have to wait. We have business that must be discussed. Please, call for Preston and for your husband if he's available. We must decide what to do about Cabot Roan. Your daughter's safety depends on it, as does your son's.'

May wanted to applaud. When was the last time anyone had contradicted her mother? Had such an occasion ever even happened? May went to the bell pull and rang. The best way to make your wishes come true was to simply act as if they were already in motion. Her mother had taught her that. When a maid appeared, May gave the orders. 'Tea for five. Send for my brother and father at once. Tell them to join us here.' She shot her mother an imperious look. If Liam was willing to fight for them, then she needed to as well. She still hoped there might be a time when she didn't need to choose between Liam and her family, but until then she had to do her best to span both worlds.

Some of the iciness in the room dissipated with Preston's arrival. He saw Liam first. 'Case!' Liam went to him and Preston embraced him with a joyous laugh. Preston was a hugger, much to their mother's chagrin. 'Gently, now, old friend, I'm still tender.' Preston stepped back, hands on Liam's upper arms.

'You brought May and the pages through safe, I knew you would.' He turned towards her, slowly. Stiffly.

May was starting to notice how slowly Preston did everything. She followed Liam's lead and went to him, not wanting to wait for Preston to cross the room. Preston hugged her, too, wrapping her in his arms. He murmured his confession low for her alone. 'Forgive me, May? For getting into trouble and dragging you along with it? I had to protect you and I thought I might as well send the papers. Liam could only protect both if they were together. I hope I did right?' He was seeking absolution for more than causing her trouble, it was for sending Liam to her. She'd never been sure how much Preston had been told. Preston only knew they'd fallen into infatuation, that May had been furious when Liam had left, if not all the reasons why. Even so, he would have understood that seeing Liam again would raise a touchy subject.

'You did right, Preston. Liam has protected me with his life.'

Preston smiled then, tossing a warm glance at his friend. 'As I knew he would.'

'How are you? Liam told me you'd been stabbed.' She led Preston to the sofa covered in peach damask, careful to match her steps to his, noting how thin he felt through the barriers of his clothes. Now that the excitement and relief of seeing him had passed, she noticed the little things: the way his clothes hung slightly off on his body, the paleness of his face, the pronounced sharpness of his cheekbones. She slid a quiet glance at Liam. He noticed it, too. 'You're still recovering,' she said, as much as reassurance for herself as a prompt for Preston. She found herself reluctant to let go of her brother's hand.

'Yes, I am sure Liam told you we were set upon on the road. We were outnumbered, but we managed. Liam got me to a farmhouse and sewed me up.' Preston's eyes went to Liam. 'The family did their best for me. We were lucky in finding them.' There were secrets in that gaze and May was sure more would be said in private.

Her father entered the room, his sharp eyes immediately taking in the assembled group, a personal greeting for each of them in that hawkish gaze; a questioning glance to her mother, a soft look of sad joy upon seeing her and a look of pure dislike when it fell on Liam. Her father, with silver at his temples, reminded her of an alpha wolf defending his pack as he stalked towards them, ageing but powerful, still strong in his own right. She could feel Liam bristle in his chair across from her. Perhaps a battle of sorts was inevitable, but it would have to wait until the larger problem was resolved.

'Casek, I believe we owe you for our son's recovery.' It was as close to a thank you as her father was willing to go. May heard the subtle negotiation in the words as well. The family owed Liam for Preston's survival. In return, they would allow his presence in the house, tolerate his brief but temporary association with them. It was unlikely that tolerance would extend to him courting their daughter.

Her father sat, taking charge of the conversation and planning as the tea tray arrived. 'What news do we have?'

May let Liam recount their getaway yesterday, it was still too unbelievable for her to adequately put into detail beyond what she'd told her mother. 'We arrived late last night,' Liam concluded.

'And Roan?' her father asked, spearing Liam with a look that said he didn't appreciate the delay in coming to the house no matter how dark it was. 'When should we expect his arrival?'

'As soon as he realises we didn't take the road. He could be here as early as today.' Liam made his report with professionalism.

Her father nodded. 'The sooner the better. I want this over. We'll reel him in. We'll let it be known that May is here. That will push Roan to recklessness. He'll be doubly desperate at this point. I doubt we're the only ones looking for him. As much as I don't like the idea, May will be the bait and we'll be ready to pounce. We'll have him and his ledgers in London to stand trial in the New Year.'

Bait? May didn't like the sound of that at all. 'Exactly how am I supposed to be the bait? Can't you just hunt him down?'

'I'd rather not give him a reason to run. If he thinks he's being hunted, he might go to ground and give up on the ledgers. If he leaves the country, where would our justice be? It would be in France and that's no help to us. He'll keep selling arms, keeping financing war and he'll always be a threat to us,' her father explained. 'You will be our distraction. If he's focused on finding you, perhaps he'll be less focused on us finding him.' Her father's face was pensive. 'Don't think I like it for a moment, May. But don't worry. We just need you to be yourself. Go shopping, be visible.

Tease him with the invitation that you could perhaps be caught.'

'Wouldn't he suspect something? He knows that I know he's after me,' May argued. 'Why would I suddenly act unaware now?'

It was Liam who answered. 'Because now you think you're safe. We won't leave you unguarded—that would be too obvious to him. But we'll create moments of "unguarded opportunity", shall we say, when he could choose to act, and when he does, we'll be there. Waiting for him.

'*I'll* be there, May.' Liam's eyes on hers, dark and intense. She did not doubt him, but she didn't want him taking unnecessary risks.

'I know,' May said, not bothering to censor her comments for the sake of her parents. She had disavowed him once. She wouldn't do it again. 'That's what worries me.' She shifted her gaze to Preston and made her argument. 'Roan will kill him if he has the chance.'

Preston nodded, his expression sombre. 'Then we won't give him one. This won't be over until the ledgers are in London and Roan is apprehended. He can't be brought in for questioning until the Home Office has evidence to suggest there is a reason to suspect him.' Preston drew a deep breath. 'Which is why I will leave for London within the hour. The sooner the papers are gone on their way, the better.'

May threw a glance at Liam. She saw the dilemma in his eyes: go with Preston or stay with her. This was her chance to protect him, to get him away from Roan, despite his pledge to be beside her. 'Liam will go with you. You can't travel alone and you're still recovering.'

'No.' Preston's answer was swift. 'Liam needs to be here with you.'

'You need to be here,' her mother argued. 'You're still recovering. You can't be out on the road, with no one to watch your back.'

But Preston had an answer for that, too. 'Roan doesn't even know I'm in the city. If I leave before he arrives, he won't think to be looking for me on the road.' Preston rose. 'I'll pack. Father, call for the coach.' He shot a consoling glance at May. 'This could all be settled in ten days.' Four to London, two to see the right people, and four days back barring any catastrophes on the road. May counted them silently in her head. Her mother was right. Preston shouldn't be travelling.

Liam rose. 'Take May with you. Get her away from all of this. It's hardly fair she was embroiled in it to begin with.'

It was her father who answered with an impatient explanation. 'She's the lure to keep Roan in Edinburgh. If he can't find her in town, the first place Roan will look for her is on the road. The longer he's here searching, the safer Preston is and the more likely we can keep him from fleeing.' Her father raised a dark eyebrow. 'Perhaps, Casek, you should have taken him in Serbia when you had the chance and saved us all the bother.'

Liam's gaze narrowed, his words even. 'I had no orders to do that, sir. My orders were merely to observe.' May knew better than ever now what those words cost him.

'The rules have never stopped you before.' Her father's voice held a veiled challenge. They weren't talking about Serbia now. May moved to intervene.

'It's been a long morning after a very long day. I think I would like a chance to freshen up while Preston packs.'

Her mother took the cue, looping her arm through May's. 'I have your trunks from London and a few new dresses I had made for you. We have parties to attend, starting tonight with the Balforths' dinner...' May hardly heard her. She was too busy thinking about how she and Liam were going to survive the next ten days, a very relevant question considering the words floating out into the hallway, her father's voice carrying easily. She didn't envy Preston and Liam just now.

'What were the two of you thinking?' Albermarle Worth pushed a hand through his hair, a gesture he shared with his son. 'Forget that. I don't want to know because that presumes you were thinking at all, an assumption I don't think it is safe to make.' He let out an exasperated sigh. 'Good God, Preston, what possessed you to do such a thing?' Liam exchanged a look with Preston. Neither of them thought for a moment that Albermarle Worth was referring to Preston having sent May the papers. It was quite clear the 'unthinkable act' had been sending *him*. Preston's father was an intimidating man when he chose. He lived in a world of power and influence and knew how to wield both. He was choosing to do so now.

Once, Liam had allowed himself to be overwhelmed by the power of Albermarle Worth, but he was not that boy-man any longer. He was now a man who had seen the world—far more of it than its elegant drawing rooms—and he chose not to be intimidated. Liam met Albermarle Worth's gaze evenly, calmly. 'I am the best protection in the Kingdom, as my record proves time and again.' He dared Worth to argue with *that*. Worth knew as well as he did that Liam had yet to fail a mission. Everyone he'd ever been sent to protect had been protected. Everyone he'd been sent to kill had been killed.

It was not what Worth had wanted him to say. Worth had wanted him to argue that his feelings for May would ensure her protection. If Worth wanted to make this personal, he would have to take it there himself. Liam would not do it for him. Professionalism was the moral high ground here, a chance to show May's father that he had grown from being an angry youth into a man who'd made the most of his opportunities. To show him less would be to admit Liam had failed to rise above his birth.

Worth held his gaze for a span of long moments, a silent battle ensuing between them before Worth relented. Liam did not take that as a surrender, merely a tactical retreat. Worth was a lion, never more so when it came to his children. 'I assume your protective efforts will extend to the peremptory as well?' He raised a dark brow, slim and arching like May's when her temper was up. 'The best way to protect May is to flush out Roan before he has a chance at her. You need to find the bastard.' Then he added, 'Before anyone else does. Roan's enemies will simply kill him and that does us no good. We need Roan alive and able to stand trial.'

Liam nodded. His own thoughts had been running in that direction. Knowing that his enemies would be hunting him, too, Roan would be doubly hard to find. It was part of the man's success that he was able to make himself invisible, and fast. The man could slip a trap with the cunning of a fox. 'I'll comb every inch of the city.' And likely beyond. Unless Roan was more desperate and prone to more carelessness than his usual cautionary behaviour, Roan wasn't likely in Edinburgh proper. Illegal arms dealers didn't exactly hide in New Town and walk the high street at the crowded hours.

Worth turned his attention to his son, his hard gaze growing in some measure softer with fondness and concern. 'Are you certain you are strong enough to travel? Those pages need to be in London but not in lieu of your strength. I can take them.' The profound depths of Worth's devotion to his children was mirrored in those four words. He would take them, he would take Preston's place and all the risks that might be incumbent in doing so for the sake of his son's safety. In that honest moment, Liam thought he might forgive Worth anything. His heart ached at the idea of having such a father, such a family. It was no wonder May was reluctant to part with it and no wonder it held such sway in her decisions. He wished Preston would take the offer, but Preston was as stubborn as his father.

'No, sir. I will take the pages. This is my assignment and I will finish it.' Preston rose and shook his father's hand, very formally. For all the silent affection the Worths held for one another, they never touched. 'I will be back in ten days. We will all be together for Christmas and, with luck, this whole episode will be behind us.'

He turned to Liam and Liam refused to stand on the same ceremony as father and son. Liam embraced his friend. 'Godspeed, Preston. Be safe.'

'You, too. Take care of May for me. Don't let her do anything foolish.' Preston smiled. 'I expect you'll be here when I get back.' In other words, Liam wasn't supposed to let the family chase him off, or May for that matter.

'I can manage a few critical days.' Liam grinned and hoped he was right.

The next few days would be critical. Cabot Roan set up his headquarters at an inn in Leith.

He didn't dare go into Edinburgh on a more permanent basis. Headquarters was a relatively exaggerated term for the private parlour and the rooms he'd take upstairs, but this would be his hub, the place in which he assembled his orders and designed his actions, and from which he was forced to use others as his eyes and ears.

He was in a foul mood this afternoon. The morning ferry had been delayed and it was already one o'clock. He'd hoped to be in town much earlier. Despite the delay, his group was still the first to arrive. The other group, on the road, wouldn't arrive until tomorrow. The one bright spot was that his men did have confirmation the Worth chit and Casek had come this way. A quiet inn up a few streets reported a couple taking rooms late last night and leaving early this morning, although the couple did not say where they were going.

Roan tapped his finger on the rough table surface in thought. Not knowing where they were worried him. Had they gone on? Perhaps to London? Had they simply moved into Edinburgh once it was light? And why would they do that? Did Casek have help here? If so, he had to be doubly on guard. He didn't want the Edinburgh Watch on the lookout for him—another reason he didn't want to go into town unless he had to and another reason he wanted to stay close to the port. He felt better knowing the *Sweet Mary* was bobbing at anchor, waiting to spirit him away if need be. It felt like the whole world was after him at present.

He drew a breath, counselling himself to be patient. His men were out looking for signs of May Worth. He could do nothing until then. But when it was time to act, he would do so swiftly, dividing and conquering. Preston Worth was a devoted brother. Roan did not think he'd let his sister suffer over a few ledger pages. If he was still alive.

Chapter Twenty

Divide and conquer. Her parents' strategy was painfully obvious before the fish course was on the Balforth dinner table. May had not seen Liam since the awkward morning tea in the drawing room. Her mother had kept her busy going through gowns and trying on new ones. Preston had left and her father had disappeared into his study. Liam wasn't with the outriders and footmen her father had assigned to escort them across town to the party. When asked why in the carriage, her mother had merely cooed, 'He'd just have to eat downstairs with the servants. We couldn't possibly ask Lady Balforth to upset her table with an extra man.' Then her mother had taken her arm with a glance to her father and a conspiratorial smile. 'There's someone we want you to meet tonight. Alfred Dunbarton, Viscount Haverly's son, dashing young man. Not the heir, of course, but Haverly has him overseeing the family interests up here. They have an estate not far from town and he's expected to inherit something of his own from his mother's side, his maternal grandmother thinks highly of him and she's over eighty. Likely to die any day.'

It was shocking how her mother could sit there and tally up poor Alfred Dunbarton as if he was nothing more than the embodiment of a column of figures, then dismiss his grandmother. For that matter, how could her mother dismiss *her* as someone who would be impressed with only those qualities? 'I'm not marrying him,' May said firmly. She wondered what her mother would say if she pointed out the similarities between her and Liam. Her mother had found Liam's crass price assessment offensive in the extreme. But her own habit was not much different, only worse because it was done with people instead of objects.

Her mother laughed. 'Not tonight. You haven't even met.'

'Not *ever*,' May said staunchly. Her mother patted her hand and sighed.

'Just meet him, May, and please be polite. These are your father's friends.'

That was her mother's mantra the next night and the night after that. *These are your father's friends.* Translation: These are the sorts of men who are worthy of you. They had money and they had prestige. There was Phillip Lacey to meet, heir to a shipping industry and looking to marry up to the peerage in some way, and Robert Quinsey, royal barrister, also looking to marry up, and another round with Alfred Dunbarton hanging on her arm. They were decently attractive, well-mannered men raised in the best traditions of their stations. Not one of them could match Liam Casek.

May knew what her mother saw in them. Here were acceptable men who were willing to take a non-virginal bride to get what they wanted. Another girl would be desperately pleased with their attentions, thrilled to be mentioned in the society pages as the festive season's loveliest girl, but not this girl; the girl who'd seen her friend through a difficult pregnancy and delivered a baby, who had learned to cook and liked it, who walked to market and did her own shopping, who was just as comfortable in warm wool skirts and sturdy half-boots as she was in the rich brocades and winter velvets she wore to dinner. It didn't help that that girl had also lain beside Liam Casek, giving and receiving true passion. It was impossible to imagine exploring those passions with any of the gentlemen. There was a knock on her bedroom door and May tightened the sash on her dressing gown, preparing herself for battle. A glance at the little clock on her vanity told her who it was before the door opened.

Her mother glided in, ready for the evening in a deep burgundy velvet. She smiled, but May wasn't fooled. This was just the beginning. 'You're not dressed! Did your maid not come to help you?'

'I sent her away. I'm not going out tonight.' It was time to take a stand. She wasn't going out unless she got what she wanted.

Her mother gave her a patronising smile and started towards the wardrobe. 'You haven't worn the blue velvet yet and there's that gorgeous white ermine fur to go with it.' She laughed over her shoulder. 'Furs are the best thing about winter, don't you think?'

This was her mother's way. When met with opposition, Mrs Worth just ploughed right over it, ignoring its existence. May stood and repeated her argument. 'I am not going out tonight. I am not going to meet any more eligible men and, when this is over, I am going back to be with Beatrice.'

'I know the men are not heirs to titles,' her mother offered consolingly. 'But they are wealthy and well placed in their own right. I think you would agree it's the best we can hope for given your circumstances. Fortunately, you're still young, very pretty, very well connected and have a substantial dowry. Second sons are happy to forgive a youthful indiscretion in light of that.'

'Liam Casek was not a youthful indiscretion. I love him.' May's temper burned. Her mother had never spoken so bluntly about the loss of her virginity before. It was as offensive to May as her categorisation of the suitors. Was everything to be classified and bartered as goods? Liam was rubbing off on her.

'Do you love him still? Really? After all he's done to you? He left you and now he's back because your brother ordered it. It should be obvious to you that after five years, he had no intention of coming back for you at all. He only did it for your brother. If anything has occurred between you in these last weeks, it's only because you're convenient to him.' Her mother was positively vituperative. 'Good heavens, May. Didn't I raise you to be smarter than that?'

'You raised me to think for myself.'

'Well, that's obviously a highly overrated skill. Young ladies who think for themselves end up like Beatrice Penrose. Not even a second son will have her. She's ruined beyond repair.'

May saw with a flash of insight that this was about so much more than Liam. Certainly, he was a large part of it. Her mother was using this visit as a chance to put her beyond Liam's reach for good with a marriage that suited her family, but her mother was also using this as a chance to break off her friendship with Beatrice and to end her independent living. She sat down on the bed. Her fears were coming true. There would be no going back to the cottage.

She'd known this was what would happen. It had been the biggest reason she had decided to ignore the summons in the first place. If Roan hadn't flushed them out, she would still be there, baking in her warm kitchen, braving the cold weather for the laundry, rocking Baby Matthew by the fire, knowing Liam was just outside, chopping wood and watching the road.

Her mother picked up the dress again. 'What do you think will happen when this is over, May? When Roan is caught and the mission is complete. Do you think you will marry Casek? That we would allow such a thing? That the granddaughter of an Earl would marry an Irish street rat?'

'He's not from the streets any more,' May said quietly.

'He'll always be from the streets, May. Nothing can change that.'

May glared and reached for the dress. 'Invite him to dinner and I'll come. Let him speak for himself, let him prove he's risen above the streets.'

'The table is already set,' her mother protested. 'Guests will be arriving in an hour.'

May put down the dress, every inch as stubborn as her mother. 'It seems I've developed a headache.'

'Oh, very well. We'll invite him to dinner and perhaps then you'll see, when he's shoulder to shoulder with Alfred Dunbarton and Robert Quinsey, just how lacking he is.' She waved a hand at the well-appointed bedroom. 'This is your world, May, and he'll never fit into it.'

The dinner coat was never going to fit, not comfortably any way. Preston was narrower enough through the shoulders to make a difference, an uncomfortable difference. If he stood straight and didn't move too quickly, no one would notice. They'd chalk the tightness up to 'good' tailoring. Tight coats for gentlemen were all the rage this year. It was ridiculous, really. A man couldn't pull a gun from this jacket, or even hide one in it. If Roan came through the front door tonight, Liam would be at a disadvantage.

Fortunately, he and Preston were nearly the same height. Trousers weren't a problem, except for the fact that Preston was also slimmer through the hip. He turned in front of the long pier glass, trying to get a glimpse of his backside. The trousers felt tight. He hoped they weren't obscene. At least the long tail of the dinner jacket would hide his backside. As long as he didn't bend over or eat enough to pop a fragile button on the snug ice-blue paisley-silk waistcoat, he would manage. He wouldn't embarrass May and that was what he suspected was at stake tonight—the game within the game. She had arranged this for some reason.

Liam tugged at the waistcoat one last time, watching the buttons sparkle. Sweet heavens, were those diamonds? Probably. He couldn't imagine Lady Worth allowing a fake imitation. On the road with Preston, staying at inns, many of which were not high quality, and risking their necks to bring a smuggler in, one tended to forget the life Preston really led. It nearly boggled his mind to think what he could do with one diamond button. People from his part of the world would work their entire lives to afford one such button—yet another reminder of whose world he was in now.

As if he needed that reminder. The Worths did nothing by halves. The reminders were everywhere. Even the rented town house was the height of elegance and good taste, the servants as solicitous and careful as if they'd worked for the Worths their entire careers.

He'd been 'here' before; the summer at the lake when he and Preston had tried to pass him off as a gentleman's son from Oxford, and later his work when he'd returned from Serbia. It wasn't always dingy inns and dirty smugglers. Smuggling had its elite circles, too, and anyone who worked with Preston Worth at the Home Office often had to report to other lords at fine dinner tables or over brandies at London clubs. He could put on the clothes and say the words, he could pick up the right fork and sip the wine instead of swigging it down. But it wasn't him. Deep down, the 'clothes' were always too tight.

'Sir, it's time to go downstairs.' The polite valet who'd helped him dress stepped into the room, a stack of clean, pressed white shirts, all identical, draped across his arms. It still astonished him how many white shirts a gentleman thought he needed.

'Thank you.' Liam gave him a short nod, the type Preston had taught him to make in between teaching him to read and do basic mathematics.

Downstairs, the clock chimed seven as he stepped into the drawing room, the Worths already assembled to greet their guests. Lord and Lady Worth were arranged at the fireplace, a large white-marble piece streaked with grey veins to match the peach and grey décor. Lady Worth's burgundy velvet was a lush contrast to the subtle tones, but it was May who stole his breath.

She sat alone in the centre of the sofa, a queen on her throne, dressed in a stunning gown of royal blue that brought out the green of her eyes against the cream of her skin and turned her already dark hair darker. A delicate pearl pendant hung at her neck, daring a man to follow that innocent teardrop down a not-so-innocent pathway to the swell of her breasts. He was certain more than one man tonight would take that dare. This was her world. This was where she belonged. How could he ever think muted green and blue wools suited her when she positively sparkled here among the elegance of the room? How could he even think of competing with this? It was one more reminder of the gap between them, of how much a fantasy their days at the cottage had been.

'Liam, come sit with me. I haven't seen you for days,' she invited, lifting a hand that already held a glass of ratafia.

'Brandy, wine, ratafia. The list of your vices grow.' He whispered his censure, 'Careful, May.'

'I can hold my drink. You needn't worry,' May whispered back with a delightfully wicked smile. He felt himself stirring already. He shifted on the sofa. Between the ill-fitting trousers and May, it might be best if he spent the night standing.

'Are your trousers tight?' May enquired, her tone deceptively innocent.

'And likely to get tighter if you don't behave yourself.'

'Hmm. That's a tempting possibility.' May's eyes drifted indelicately downward. He wasn't going to make it to dinner at this rate before he'd have to excuse himself.

'Be careful, May. Your parents are watching us. I have no desire to be berated by your father as if I were an errant schoolboy. This is all your doing. Care to explain why I'm coming to dinner?'

'I told my mother I wouldn't come if you didn't.' Another time, he would have made a bawdy comment out of her remark, but the Worths' drawing room was hardly the place for crass entendre.

'I wanted to see you,' May confessed. 'What have you been doing? Whenever I ask about you I'm told that you are out.'

'I've been out looking for Cabot Roan. While he's hunting you, I'm hunting him. Cautiously, of course. We don't want him to run.'

'And if you find him? What then?'

'If it were up to me, I'd gut the bastard, May, for what he's done to you and Preston, what he's done to the country and who knows how many innocents. But that doesn't serve the government. I can follow him, I can warn the Watch and you of his next move. I can keep him from running and hope to bring him to justice.'

Something lit up in her eyes. 'It's day five. Preston is safely in London by now. You haven't found Roan, he hasn't found me. Perhaps Roan didn't follow us into the city after all.'

Liam gave her a polite smile. 'It's a nice fantasy, May, but he's here. I will find him. Sooner or later he has to come up for air and when he does, I'll hear about it. What about you? What have you been doing?' He hated talking to her as if she were a stranger with whom he could only make small talk. He wanted to drag her off to the nearest closet, the nearest wall, and take that dress off her, he wanted to pull down the carefully constructed art of her hair until it spilled around her like a dark curtain. She was his and he craved her. He missed her sharp tongue, the way she'd argue with him at the cottage. He missed the warm kitchen, the lavender-pressed sheets, the suspiciously nice mugs of hot drinks, the simple knowledge that she was near and in reach. They were living in the same house, but there might as well be a continent between them—a frigid one from the looks being cast in their direction by her mother.

'Dinners, parties.' May shrugged. 'Nothing exciting.' He didn't miss the shadow that crossed her face, or how her eyes drifted nervously to the door.

'Expecting anyone?' His own voice was a growl as his suspicions rose.

'Expecting too many someones.' She tossed a furtive glance her mother's direction. Her voice dropped. 'My mother has invited some gentlemen she believes might be of interest to me.'

'Are they?' He was not particularly keen on the answer to that question. Had these days reminded May of her 'real' life, the life she'd left behind when she'd gone to Scotland? 'Why am I here, May? To see all that you'd be giving up? To see how much better these men are than me?'

There was no chance to answer. The butler announced, 'Mr Robert Quinsey, Esquire.' Her mother moved from the fireplace, hands outstretched, a flick of her eyes commanding May to join her. May rose from the sofa and sailed away.

Dinner was uncomfortable for too many reasons to list. His clothes to start, May to finish, and in the middle of all that discomfort, he had to manage making conversation with two women who were most definitely more interested in the fit of his clothes than the fish. Halfway through the roasted beef, the woman on his right got her hand on his thigh, letting it drift high enough to test the 'tensile strength' of the trouser fabric at the seams. During the cheese course, the woman dropped her napkin and whispered as he bent to retrieve it, 'We've taken Number Five Princes Street for the season. My husband is gone on

Tuesdays.' He'd remember to avoid Princes Street on Tuesdays.

But he couldn't avoid the sight of May across from him, courted on one side by Quinsey, the royal barrister, and on the other side by Alfred Dunbarton, whose qualifications were dubious beyond what was apparently his wit. Liam didn't find him funny at all. It became very apparent what May had spent her days doing. Tonight wasn't the first night spent in matchmaking.

'What of yourself, Mr Casek?' Dunbarton enquired. 'What brings you to Edinburgh at this time of year?'

'I'm here on business for the Home Office,' Liam answered truthfully and then, to dissuade any further conversation, he added, 'I'm afraid I can't say anything more. Confidential.' He looked at Quinsey, deftly shifting the conversation away from himself. 'I'm sure you can understand that, as a barrister. You must have interesting cases.'

It was a fine conversational opening and one Quinsey took, but what those interesting cases were, Liam couldn't have recalled. May's foot had decided to crawl up his leg and stay there until the cheese was cleared away. Suffice it to say, brandy was far less interesting once the women left the room, but no less potent than the message the Worths wanted to send. He didn't fit in here.

If he and May were going to be together, it couldn't be in these circles. He'd never fit in. He could mingle on their periphery, join them on occasion, but he could not resign his life to this luxury and leisure. Was that May's message, too? Was that why she'd invited him? But, no, May wasn't that subtle. He had questions of her and questions of himself. After seeing this, how could he ask May to give it all up? Followed by the more important question: would she? He'd asked those questions before.

His body stirred as he remembered how she had answered that question in their dingy inn room a few nights ago and how she'd answered it in the cottage loft. Neither had been an answer in truth, but oh, how glorious her response.

How in the world was he going to get up from the table now? Which was followed by other questions throughout the night: how was he going to sit through cards and make nice with men who wanted to marry May? How was he going to refrain from hauling May out of the drawing room and having his wicked, lower-class way with her when she kept running a foot up his leg under the card table. She wasn't even his partner, but Dunbarton's, something he was sure her mother deliberately arranged to prove a point. And eventually, there was the question of sleep. How was he going to sleep when so much weighed on his mind? May, Cabot Roan, the future. He simply wasn't. His mind was simply going to run through the scenario one more time: what had changed and what hadn't since the first time he'd laid out his heart for May.

What *had* changed was what he could offer her. He was employable now on a scale that would keep May in comfort. They could afford a home—just one home. There'd be no estates in the country, but there could be a decent town home in London, or he could apply to be posted somewhere else in the great wide world of the British Empire: India, the Caribbean, Canada. There were choices if they didn't want to stay. Or couldn't. He could even be posted here in Scotland. Unless her father wanted to ruin that, too. One word from a powerful M.P. like Worth and his career could be adversely affected. But he rather thought Worth would leave it alone. His career had been one of his own making, with help from Preston, *not* from Worth, and Worth did respect a self-made man.

Would it be enough for May? Would she come to hate him if her father continued to take a hard line and banish her? The life they would create together could never rival the generations of wealth that formed the world of Worth. Would she look back one day and wish she'd chosen a man like Robert Quinsey? A man whose very presence didn't force her to choose between love and family. No matter how he asked the question, the answer was still the same. Yes. Yes and yes. And the conclusion was still the same, too: He had to give her up. It was the only thing and the right thing to do.

They were hard thoughts to fall asleep on. It was no surprise that the sleep that came was restless, filled with May's presence, so warm, so real it was hard to tell where the line between fantasy and reality existed.

Chapter Twenty-One

She had to claim him. Nothing else would be right until she did. May shut the bedroom door quietly behind her. If she and Liam were not allowed to be together in the day, she had no choice but to seek him out in the night. In the dark, she could just make out the bed and the tossing figure in it. Movement helped. It wasn't a nightmare that plagued him but it was disturbing, whatever it was.

She undid the sash of her robe, letting the silk drop from her body, letting the cold raise her flesh briefly before she slid beneath the covers. It was warm in the bed. It was always warm beside Liam. His body was a veritable furnace. She put her arms around him, pressing herself against his back, her voice quiet in his ear. 'Shhh… Be still. I'm here.' His restlessness seemed to subside and so did hers. She let the tension of the evening leave her. Nothing mattered but being with Liam. He was not the only one disturbed.

Dinner had left her angry *and* decisive. It was time to end this limbo and claim what she wanted, and that was Liam. She could only imagine dinner had left him feeling the same, not only because her parents' efforts to match her with someone else were so obvious, not only because those same efforts were designed to belittle Liam, but because she was regretting her evasive answer at the inn in Leith. She and Liam did not know explicitly where they stood with one another. Because of that, dinner tonight might have been a disaster. Had dinner created the impression that he should not be sure of her? She feared it had, when taken in conjunction with their past. Was he worried that once she'd seen all she was giving up, she would not choose him?

He should not doubt her, but if he did, she had to accept the blame for that. He'd asked for answers and she'd not given them. The circumstances might not be all that different than they were in the past, but she was. Wasn't that the motto of the Left Behind Girls Club? Nothing changed until you did.

May kissed the back of his shoulder. Loving him would cost her. Her parents had made that very clear tonight. She was prepared to pay the price and hope her parents would relent sometime in the future. It was a risk and she was willing to take it. It was a sign of how much she'd changed, how far she'd come in five years. She rather hoped it didn't come to that, that her family would accept her choice, that somehow she could bring the people she loved most in the world together.

May kissed him again, her hand moving down to cup him, enjoying how delightful it was that Liam slept in the nude no matter the season. He stirred in her hand. She stroked him, whispering wakeful love words in his ear.

'May?' He woke with a foggy start. She smiled against his shoulder in understanding. He thought he was dreaming, thought her hand on his rising member would disappear if he woke.

'You like to dream of me?' she whispered wickedly. 'Do I do this for you often in your sleep?'

'It's so nice.' His voice was drowsy, hoarse, barely coherent.

'Then wake up and enjoy it,' she encouraged. 'I'm real, Liam. I'm here in your bed right now and you're missing it.' She nipped at his ear, hard enough to prove it. He came awake with a start.

'Good heavens, May, what do you think you're doing?'

May laughed, low and throaty, as her hand closed over him. 'What do *you* think I'm doing?' Her body pressed against his.

His next words came slowly as he registered the fullness of her presence behind him. 'You're naked.'

'Yes. So are you.' They were going to be naked in more ways than one before this conversation was through. She was quiet for a moment, just holding him, just feeling him against her before she spoke. 'I came to tell you something.'

He took her hand off him and rolled over to face her. 'Are you measuring me against Quinsey and Dunbarton? Am I supposed to trot out my earthly value and make *those* kinds of arguments in my favour? Or have you already decided?' He sounded cynical.

She overlooked the snub. 'Don't, Liam.' She understood. He was hurting *and* doubting. Her fears had been justified, all the more reason she'd been right to come to him tonight. 'I came to reassure you that nothing has changed between us.' She drew a deep breath and whispered the words, 'I love you, only you.'

'You shouldn't, May. I can only cause you pain. You know that.' He drew back the covers, letting the cold air speak for itself. 'You should go before we're caught.'

May shivered. Something was wrong. This was not the response she'd anticipated. 'Liam, I just told you I love you and you're throwing me out of bed?' It was too fantastical to even be angry over. Yet. She was being careful not to get angry too fast. There was something else at play here.

May grabbed for the covers. 'I'm not going anywhere until you tell me what's going on. We are together, Liam. You and I. We decided as much at Leith.' That wonderful, glorious night in the inn when they'd set aside their worries and the danger.

'Reality, that's what's going on.' His tone softened. They moved away from the edge of a fight and that worried her even more. 'You love me now, May. I don't doubt that. But you won't love me, not if being with me forces you to leave all of this, your family, your wealth.'

'You were willing enough to ask me to part with it five years ago,' May argued, but her wits were slow, confused.

'I was young and selfish. I should not have asked, should not have put you in that position. I see that now and I will not put you in that position again.' He put a finger to her lips. 'Listen to me tonight, May. For once.' He paused, waiting for her consent. She nodded. 'May, if you leave all of this, you will come to resent me. I've thought about what I can offer you. It will never match this. There will always be the danger of association, always the stigma of living on the fringe of society if we stay, always the loneliness of being so far from your family if we were to leave. You can't win in loving me, May. You will look back and regret the choice.' Desperation edged his voice, a sure sign that he meant every word.

Something akin to nausea moved in her stomach. 'You're giving me up?' The words hurt to say. Her throat had gone dry. For the first time, she realised how close she was to losing him, how she'd never really let him go all those years apart. The lack of resolution brought about by the nature of their parting, a parting that was forced and coerced by her father, had kept alive some stubborn flame of hope. She'd not realised how stubborn until now.

'I am, May.' His words were even and slow.

'I won't pretend it's what I want or that it doesn't hurt. This isn't easy, I think you know that. If tonight showed me anything it was that, yes, you love me. Yes, I love you. But we can't make it right. That love will destroy us.' He got out of bed, beautiful and nude in the dark shadows. He came around to her and held out his hand. Dear God, he was going to walk her to the door. She was suddenly struck by a hundred thoughts at once. This might be the last time she saw him naked. Ever. He was dismissing her. The moment she stepped out the door, everything would change. Again. Then she wouldn't step out. She wouldn't go. She would use the old trick, the one that made things right between them if only for a short time.

May took his hand and tugged him to her, her body ready for him, but he resisted. 'No, May, not this time. I think we've proved sex can't solve our problems, only prolong them.' At the moment, she'd take prolonging.

His grip was tight on her hand. 'Come, May. Go back to your room.' He bent and with his free hand picked up her robe.

She snatched it, her anger starting to get the better of her. 'I hate it when you're rational.' But there was no anger in her words, only thick tears. Rational and right. How could she argue with him on those grounds? 'You're wrong, you know. I won't ever hate you. I will love you, always.'

'You might, May. You're stubborn enough to do it.' A wry smile cracked his lips. 'And I'll love you, we just can't do it together. You and I, it just doesn't work.' They were at the door now, and he opened it.

She tried one last time. 'There has to be another answer.'

Liam shook his head. 'There isn't. I will protect you until Roan is brought to justice and then I'll go. Goodbye, May.'

It was over for good now. He'd seen to it. All that remained was to catch Roan. Liam stamped his feet to keep warm. He blew in his hands to keep his fingers from getting stiff. His woollen gloves only covered part of his hands, his fingers exposed. All the better to handle a pistol or knife hilt if he needed to and in this part of town one never knew when one might need to.

He'd been standing outside in the shadows of this pub for over an hour, after following a lead and then eventually a man back to this destination. He had great hopes he'd found a connection to Cabot Roan. The sooner this was wrapped up, the sooner he could leave, the sooner he could put physical distance between him and May. His decision had been the right one, but that didn't mean it wasn't hard. Some relationships were just doomed. This was one of them. The inn door opened and Liam came alert. It was time to shove those thoughts aside and focus on the task at hand.

Two men exited dressed in greatcoats, mufflers pulled up over half their faces against the cold as they headed towards him. Liam turned towards the wall, pretending to take a piss. No one bothered a man doing his business.

'Roan's in a good mood today. About time,' one of them said. 'He's been a right bloody bastard these last weeks, no matter how much he's paying us. He broke old Joe's hand just yesterday for bad news,' he groused.

'I'll be glad when this business is over. The party can't come fast enough for me. We'll grab the girl and Roan can take it from there,' the other also groused. 'Scotland's bloody cold.'

Party? What party? Liam put himself back together, careful to make every move look casual. He sauntered away from the wall, searching his mind for any mention of an upcoming entertainment. But parties hadn't exactly been on his agenda the last time he and May had talked.

Under other circumstances, he would have gone straight to May. But under these circumstances, he thought detachment was best for him and for her. He needed complete objectivity to do his job and that was to keep May safe. He also needed the distance to ensure she didn't see how much it took to hold to his decision.

At the house, Liam went directly to Worth's study, ignoring the butler's request that he wait to be announced since Worth was busy at present. 'He's not too busy for this,' Liam said and kept walking, long purposeful strides that outpaced the aged butler. That was the problem with stately, older butlers. They just weren't very fast.

Liam pushed the study door open without preamble. 'I have news you need to hear.'

Worth's eyes flicked dismissively to the young man scribbling furiously on a tablet. 'You may go. We can finish later.'

Worth waited until they were alone. 'Well? You have news that is important enough to defy convention, apparently. What is it?' Worth did not ask him to sit. The slur was duly noted. Nor had Worth bothered to rise.

'I believe I have found Roan's headquarters. He's at an inn in Leith. What is more important is that he will make a try for May at a party, something soon. What is on your social calendar? Is there anything here? Perhaps something your wife is hosting?'

Worth looked at him with dawning realisation. 'The Christmas Masque. Tomorrow night. We're hosting it here.'

Liam began to pace. 'It would be ideal for Roan. This is an event she has to be at, unlike another event where she could cancel at the last minute if we suspected anything. A masque offers the perfect opportunity for unknown guests to slip in.' But not just any guest. He began to worry. 'I think Roan might try for her himself. He can't send street thugs. They'd stand out.' A man would have to know how to dance, how to comport himself at masque. The man would have to make himself agreeable to May, coax her out to the garden or some place where he could get her alone long enough to take her. Roan could be charming. Roan would like the dare. He'd appreciate the parallels of what he was attempting to do: stealing into Worth's own home the way Preston had stolen into his and taking something of great value.

'Still, I'll have my footmen vet the guests when they arrive,' Worth offered. 'I'll have guards posted at the garden gates. He can get in, but we won't let him get out.'

'Absolutely. We have to be sure of it,' Liam said sternly. When the man attempted to leave, he'd have May with him. This was the only part of the plan Liam was uncomfortable with. He didn't like the thought of May in any amount of danger. How far would Roan go?

'Even inside your home, your daughter could be at risk,' Liam began. Perhaps Worth simply didn't see it. 'Cornered, Roan will fight. He might not hesitate to harm her in exchange for his own freedom. The man is deadly with a knife.' He was, too, but he was held to government scruples—bring the man in alive. Roan had no such ethic.

'We'll have men everywhere.' Worth nodded his assurance.

'Very well. Do I have your permission to organise the men? A day is not much time.' He didn't like asking Worth for anything, but this was what detachment required of him, that he follow the rules. He had to treat May's father like he'd treat any other person he was assigned to work with, to protect.

'Yes. Report to me when everything is planned so that I am fully apprised of the arrangements.' Of course. Worth wouldn't tolerate not being in charge in some way.

Liam gave a short nod of his head. 'As you wish.'

He set to work immediately, immersing himself in what he did best: protecting others. There were perimeters to check, entrances and exits to calculate. How many ways were there into the house? What rooms would be open to guests tomorrow night? Had Lady Worth hired outside help for the evening? Who would be the strangers among them? If Roan didn't come himself, perhaps the kidnapper would be someone sent ostensibly from an agency to help with the service, someone to work in the kitchen, or someone to circulate with trays of drinks. That someone wouldn't need to pass themselves off as a gentleman. 'I want names and I want lists,' Liam barked the orders, 'and I want them now.'

Work was immersive. He could almost forget the quarrel with May, almost forget he was losing her for good. He managed to sleep a little, managed to eat a little, managed to keep going. It was nine days since Preston had left. If he could make it through the masque, this would all be over. Then it would be day ten and he could expect the arrival of some directive from London. Preston would be back or someone from Edinburgh could be in charge. He could be done.

The next afternoon, while florists and decorators ran through the house with vases of winter greens and roses, he laid out his plans to Worth, showing him maps marked with security. 'The footmen are ready, sir. Everyone knows to be on alert. Might I ask? How is your daughter faring?' He didn't dare use her name. Her father would find it too familiar and his heart would find it too hard to bear. Worth hesitated and Liam saw a shade of red so crimson it surpassed his hard-won detachment. 'You have not told her.' His voice was a deadly growl.

'If she worries, she might panic, might give away the game. It's best if she acts as natural as possible,' Worth answered. To argue would be to engage Worth's ire. He was a man who didn't like to be contradicted. Worse, if he argued, he might tip his hand and then be banned from taking any action. Worth didn't want May to know, that much was implied, but Liam had no trouble disobeying the implication. May needed to know.

He sought out May the first moment he could. She needed to know and that was not arguable in his opinion, although part of him acknowledged this might just be an excuse on his part to see her again. Alone.

He finally found her, lying down in her bedroom, a cool cloth over her eyes and blessedly alone. 'May,' he said softly, not wanting to startle her. 'It's me, don't panic.' His eyes ran over the room as he stepped into the dressing room, searching for signs of a maid.

May sat up, her face instantly angry. He shouldn't have expected anything else. Once she'd got over the shock, she would reach for her anger. 'What are you doing in here? Aren't you worried you might be compromised? You seemed very worried about that the last time we were together.' And her sarcasm, too. She looked—not herself. The usual signs of fiery life were not there despite her hot words. Without the cloth, he could see the purplish circles of sleeplessness beneath her eyes. Her face was pale.

'I don't want to talk about the other night.

We've both made our decisions, it seems,' May said stoically. It hurt him to see her like this. He wasn't giving her up because he wanted to, he was giving her up because he loved her, because he was not selfish enough to break her.

He shook his head. 'I'm not here to talk about that. May, listen. Roan is coming. He means to be at the party tonight. I believe he will be here in disguise as a guest with a mask. But he may send someone else. We are prepared on both accounts.'

May gave a slight nod. 'I suspected as much. There was more than Mother's usual activity today getting ready.'

'You needn't worry. We are prepared. He won't leave here with you. You have my word.'

She got off the bed and went to the window, drawing back the lace curtain. He tensed. 'I wish you wouldn't do that, May. Step away from the window. We don't need to give him any more help than he already has.' It was easier to scold her than it was to talk about the unspoken part of the plan, that she had to be compelling bait. It was harder still not to want to make amends, to take her in his arms and assure her that everything would be all right, not just tonight, but always, no matter what he'd said last night. They would find a way. But that would be a lie. There simply was no way.

'May—' he began, tempted to try. She cut him off with a sharp look and sharper words.

'You said you didn't come here to talk about *that*. So don't.' She nodded towards the wardrobe where a festive red-velvet dress with an enormous old-fashioned belled skirt hung, sumptuous and rich. A matching red mask, trimmed with brilliants, hung with it, a stunning ensemble. 'I am going as the spirit of Christmas.' She fluttered a hand. 'It's something esoteric my mother made up.'

'You'll be stunning.' He swallowed. She'd be more than that. She'd be ravishing. 'You'll be the most beautiful woman in the room.' She always was. 'Everyone will notice you.'

'That's the point, isn't it?' she said drily. 'We don't want Roan to have to guess too hard which one is me.'

'May, I won't let anything happen to you tonight. You will be safe.'

She looked down at her hands. 'Always the professional, aren't you, Liam? You and your damned objective, *rational* detachment.' She drew a breath and looked up. 'Well, it's good to know we have nothing to worry about between us. You know I'll do my job and I know you'll do yours.'

What had he expected? He stiffened his resolve. After tonight, he would find a way to move on. But until then, the evening was going to be hell.

Chapter Twenty-Two

The evening was a special hell, one full of juxtapositions and trepidation. Behind every elegantly adorned mask could be Roan. May saw the potential for danger everywhere, knowing full well every other guest at the party saw only the festivity of the occasion, the excitement of mystery—who was their partner now? Thank goodness, this torture would be over at midnight when the masks came off. If Roan was going to make a move, he had a small, specific window in which to do it.

Dear heavens, she'd finally caught Liam's paranoia; seeing peril in everything, in everyone, and she still had to find a way to be charming. Her current partner, a dullard of a dancer in a pine-green mask who'd stepped all over her feet, was asking if she'd like a cup of punch. 'Punch would be delightful. Perhaps I could find a place to sit?' To be alone for just a moment would be heaven. Surely, a few minutes in a crowded ballroom would be safe enough. She deserved a short reprieve. She'd danced all night, smiled all night and it was only ten o'clock. Had it really only been two hours? It seemed like days since Liam had come to her room and informed her Roan would be here. That was something else she had to pretend—that she didn't know. She was furious with her father for not wanting to tell her, but if she looked too stiff, too nervous, everyone would know she knew, even Roan. Roan would quietly drift away, unseen, if he thought she was aware of his intentions and all this would be for nought.

May scanned the room. Where was Liam at this moment? Was he masked and moving among the guests? Was he unobtrusively prowling the sidelines of the dance floor, scrutinising each man present? Maybe he was walking the outside perimeter in the cold, making sure everyone was in place if Roan made his move. No, not if. When. A little chill ran down her spine. She tamped down on the panic once more and tried to think about next steps. It was easier to think about the evening in a series of logical, unemotional events. Roan would grab her. Liam would grab Roan. It would be over before Roan even got her out of the house. She closed her hand over the rich full folds of her gown, feeling the weight of the little gun hidden in a secret pocket. Even if Roan managed to escape the house, she'd be prepared. That gave her assurance. *Unnecessary assurance.* How would Roan ever get her out of the house? She had bodyguards, her own gun, her own temerity and two hundred guests who would surely prohibit his leaving with a screaming, kicking banshee and she had Liam Casek with his perfect protection record. It seemed preposterous Roan would even try such an audacious trick tonight.

The dullard came back with punch. May thanked him and took a sip, smiling while he made small talk that matched his personality. She made the requisite answers: yes, she read Walter Scott—who didn't?—yes, she found the weather dreadfully cold; and, yes, she was looking forward to Christmas—how could she have answered otherwise without evoking even more conversation? No, she didn't find the room too hot. She was tempted to start giving him outrageous answers. She had just begun to contemplate telling him the room was indeed too hot and could he help her get out of this dress, when a footman approached with a small silver tray.

'A note for you, miss. From Mr Casek.' He bowed respectfully and May took the folded sheet. She flashed an apologetic smile at her partner for reading in front of him and opened the paper.

There's been a change of plans. Come to the rose sitting room so we can talk. Come quickly. Roan is on the move. L.

May rose. It wasn't hard to look flustered. 'I have to go. Something has come up that I must take care of immediately.' She walked as quickly as she could out of the ballroom without drawing undue attention. The further she got from the party noise, the faster she walked. The rose sitting room was at the back of the house. Of course Liam would want to meet there. No one would notice them, it wouldn't disrupt the party atmosphere, neither would anyone overhear them. There was no chance of tipping their hand to Roan or whomever he'd brought with him.

'Liam?' she whispered, stepping inside the room. She rubbed her arms, it was cold away from the heat of so many bodies. Only a few days ago, Liam would have wrapped her in his coat, in his arms. Never again would she feel the heat of his hard body. The room was dark, but she made out the form at the window, tall and broad. 'I got the message. What's happened? Where's Roan?'

The man turned, something silver glinting in his hand. 'He's right here. Allow me to introduce myself, Miss Worth. I'm Cabot Roan and you've led me a merry chase. But that's all over now.'

May stepped backwards towards the door, her hand searching behind her for the handle, her mind a kaleidoscope of thoughts, each one getting a mere fraction of her attention; this was Cabot Roan, this tall, commanding man whose face she couldn't see, but whose pistol she could. She understood the silver glint now—the barrel of a gun; Liam hadn't sent the note. She knew now how Roan planned to get her out of the house—she'd simply walk out unnoticed at gunpoint from a quiet, unpopulated portion of the house, the two hundred guests she'd counted on suddenly all for nought. This room exited out into the gardens—gardens that were dark and cold and unused tonight. There would be no kicking or screaming, or ploughing through a phalanx of guests. She'd made it too easy.

'I wouldn't try the door, Miss Worth.' He gestured with the pistol and forms materialised on the edges of the room. In the dark, she'd not seen them, so still were they. 'My men have been instructed not to let you leave the room without me.' She heard a match being struck. A lamp flared to life and Roan held it up, illuminating the room for her. 'As you can see, I have you surrounded. I prefer to keep this simple. You come with me, I send a ransom note to your family that suggests a trade—you in exchange for those ledger papers your brother has absconded with—and accounts will be settled.' He sounded almost bored, but his body was alert. She saw the tension in the lamplight.

'Do you do this often?' May met his eyes evenly. This was the man who'd attempted to kill her brother and Liam. He was dangerous indeed despite his superficial display of ennui. He did not take kidnapping casually. His eyes flicked past her shoulder towards the door. He was waiting for something, for someone.

'Often enough, Miss Worth. Occupational requirement in my line of business. Now, if you'll step towards me, we'll be going.'

'No.' Would Liam notice she was gone? Would someone have told him about the note? Was he, even now, darting through the house searching for her? He would be thorough, regardless of his feelings for her, his professional honour would demand it. She just had to give him enough time.

'No?' Roan's eyebrows went up. 'I'd heard you were something of a spitfire, Miss Worth. Unfortunately, that won't work here. If we can't do it the easy way, we'll do it the hard way.' He gave another imperious wave of his pistol. 'Gentlemen, if you please…'

Where the hell was May? Liam quartered the crowded ballroom, forcing himself to do it right, to slowly take in each group and search it carefully when what he really wanted to do was race his gaze over it. But that would risk unjustified panic, and in that panic he might sound the alarm and alert Roan when May had simply gone to the retiring room. How many times already had she thwarted his authority, refusing to stay where she was told? It had been her first line of resistance back in the village. Lord knew she'd been mad as hell when he'd left her this afternoon, not exactly the best of moods to cajole compliance out of her. The only time May was remotely compliant was in bed and, even then, she had her own ideas about how they should proceed. Not that they'd be proceeding in that direction any time soon, or ever again. Damn it! Where was she? How hard could it be to find a ravishing beauty in a gorgeous red dress, even with masks abounding?

There! He had her. She was by the window with a tall chap. He started towards her and then realised his mistake. Closer, the woman's hair wasn't nearly dark enough. The lights had played tricks on him. Liam retraced his steps, spotting one of Worth's footmen. 'Have you seen Miss Worth?' he asked calmly, casually.

'No, sir. She was dancing the last time I saw her.' All the footmen had been instructed to keep an eye on her.

'When was that?'

'Half an hour ago before I had to return to the kitchen.' The man nodded towards another footman circulating with a tray of cold drinks. 'Check with James, he came out with fresh drinks when I went in.'

James knew and the knowledge brought a tightening to Liam's gut. 'I delivered your note, sir. Didn't she show up?'

'I didn't send a note,' Liam growled. 'You didn't happen to read it, did you?' But it was a futile question. Worth would never hire servants who read his mail. He knew before a frightened James shook his head in shocked denial that the note had gone unread by everyone except May. Perhaps nosy servants weren't such a bad thing after all. 'Come with me.'

Liam was already moving, pushing his way through the crowd to the hallway. He looked up and down its length. To the right were the stairs and the front door. Masked guests milled about. There was always the option of hiding in plain sight among them, but the chances of getting May away quietly were slim. Liam turned left, running through the layout of the house in his head. He signalled for the footman behind him to check the rooms they passed for form's sake. He didn't think Roan would be in one of them. They were too close to the ball and they didn't have egress besides the hallway. Roan would want a room that opened out on to the grounds.

The rose sitting room at the end of the hall! Liam broke into a sprint. He hoped he wasn't too late, that Roan had not already lured May outside or forced her. If it were just him, he'd shoot first and ask questions later, but the Home Office needed Roan alive. If he shot, he had to shoot carefully. A dead Roan couldn't stand trial. A dead Roan didn't stop the arms cartel. Sometimes it was a damnable curse to have to put one's country first.

A crash like a vase shattering sounded. Good news and bad. May was still here. He wasn't too late. The bad news? She was in trouble and she'd chosen to fight a man who would show no mercy. Had he ever been this nervous facing down the enemy before? There was a scream and his heart was in his throat.

'Sir, you have to wait for help. You don't know how many men are in there,' the footman cautioned, pale and frightened.

'If I wait it will be too late.' He tried to calculate how many vases were in that room. May didn't have unlimited ammunition. When there was nothing left to throw, what would she do then? It didn't matter how many men were in that room. The woman he loved was in there. The thought of May struggling focused him. He gripped his pistol firmly. 'I don't have a choice.' More importantly, he didn't want a choice. He eyed the door. He had to assume it was locked. The next few seconds would be critical. He raised his foot and kicked as glass shattered on the other side.

It took his practised eye less than a second to take in the room. The ground was littered with glass from the broken window and porcelain shards. The man wrestling May bled from his forehead, one of her vases having found purchase as she struggled, pinned between him and a table. It was a fight she was losing. Liam fired without hesitation at her assailant, his body slumping off her. The bounder wouldn't be getting up any time soon, but there was another to take the man's place before May could flee to safety behind him. This man grabbed May and hauled her against him, a knife in one hand, her body a shield.

'Guns are only good for one shot, Casek. I thought you were smarter than that,' a voice drawled on his periphery as porcelain crunched beneath heavy boots. Roan. 'Or is it that you've simply not improved with swords since last we met?'

Liam turned, keeping his body between May's captor and Roan. 'Pistols are good for other things besides shooting,' he replied evenly. Clubbing men in the head, for instance, sometimes with deadly precision. Pistols were heavy. And Roan shouldn't underestimate the knife he hadn't drawn yet, wanting to keep an element of surprise. Knives were personal. He wouldn't hesitate to throw his if he could get off a good attempt without risking May. But that seemed impossible right now.

'They are. However, mine is still loaded.' Roan revealed his silver barrel. 'I don't have room in my carriage for you, Casek. Just the girl.' He raised dark eyebrows. 'Unless you have the ledger papers? Perhaps a deal could be arranged? No? It's too bad, but I didn't think Worth would have given them to you.' Roan's eyes glinted dangerously. 'Is Worth alive? I confess to a certain morbid curiosity there. And, quite obviously, you know we haven't found him or we wouldn't be here.' Roan gave a shrug.

Out of the corner of his eye, Liam saw the slightest of movements in May's skirts, her hand seeking something. He dared not concentrate on it too long or Roan would notice. He had to keep Roan focused on him and yet he wanted to warn May not to do anything ridiculous.

'Any last words?' Roan raised his long pistol with the ominous click of the hammer going back. Liam held steady, forcing his mind to ignore the fact that Roan's shot was meant for him. Perhaps his knife was meant for Roan regardless of what the government wanted. 'You've made my life a living hell these last months, Casek. Now, I shall send you there personally, and perhaps I'll make Miss Worth pay for that, too. Perhaps you can spend your last thoughts imagining what we might get up to in your absence.'

Liam weighed his odds. In a duel between a knife and a bullet, which would reach their target first? If he threw early, Roan would certainly fire in retaliation even if he was bluffing now. But if he threw late, he might never get the chance. Roan would not miss at this range.

'No!' May cried desperately from his left. 'I'll go with you, just leave him alone, leave him alive. Tie him up if you must. He can do nothing then.' She struggled against the man and his knife. Roan was amused, but too experienced to voluntarily divert his attention to her. Too bad for him. He missed May's subterfuge. Amid her other struggles, no one noticed her hand in her skirt until there was a muted pop and the man behind her went down clutching his thigh, moaning on the ground. It stunned him for a fraction of a second while his mind took in what happened. Good God, May had shot him! Through her skirts none the less. That fraction of time was enough to send the room into chaos.

Liam surveyed the room, counting: one man down, May behind him safe as long as he stood between her and Roan, two other men by the door. One of them rushed him, charging like a bull. Liam clubbed him around the head without hesitation. The other man behind him halted at the sight of his fallen comrade, the knife in his own hand temporarily forgotten in his shock. But Liam didn't stop. He threw aside his empty pistol and let adrenaline carry him, catching the man and slamming him up against a wall.

Liam grabbed for the man's wrist, banging it against the wall until the fingers released the knife, but the man eluded his first attack, slashing wildly, his blade finding purchase in Liam's shoulder, enough to hurt, enough to enrage before Liam captured his wrist. Liam brought his knee up into the man's groin and dropped him. Between the groin shot and being smashed up against a wall, the last man between him and Roan would be moving no time soon.

He had May behind him as he made a shield of his body. There was only Roan and him now. With luck, the footman would have gathered help. There would be reinforcements if he could hold Roan off *and* keep him here without killing him. But Roan was no fool. He wasn't going to stay. His eye was already on the garden door.

'I can't let you leave.' Liam's gaze flickered between the door and the gun runner. He was becoming far too conscious of the knife wound in his shoulder. Perhaps the man had got a better slash in than he'd thought. He was bleeding profusely, his shirt and jacket wet with it, and there was still Roan and his unfired pistol to contend with. Liam drew his knife at last.

Roan let out a harsh laugh. 'Always so noble, Casek. Country before self? That's going to cost you, I'm afraid.' He raised his pistol arm again, slowly, deliberately, to make clear his intention. He hesitated a moment too long.

The door flew open, Preston Worth, gaunt and travel worn, leading the charge with a wild yell worthy of the Highlands.

Roan fired.

Liam threw.

May screamed.

'No!' May pushed at him hard with all her weight, catching him off balance. He went down, May falling beside him as another shot rang out from an indeterminate spot behind him. Vaguely, Liam recognised assistance had come. Men poured into the room. His arm hurt, his shoulder blazed, black spots spun before his eyes. His right side was wet. He fought for consciousness, but he had a tenuous grip on it. He thought he saw Worth storming behind Preston, a flash of silver pistol in his hand. His mind pushed away his hurts and fastened on one thought: Protect May.

She lay just inches from him, still and unmoving. He dragged himself into position, levering his aching body over her, ready to keep her from being trampled. He fought his own pain, cradling her against him with one good arm, her body horrifyingly limp. 'May?' The activity around him blurred to the edges of his reality. May was all that mattered.

He swallowed, holding back nausea and his own unconsciousness. He couldn't let go now. Something was wrong with May. He saw the blood, a smear barely noticeable against the red of her dress. His blood. He must have got some on her. No. Her blood. *Her blood*. Clarity swamped him in a short, brilliant flash. Help had come too late.

He didn't care about Roan, about anything in that moment except May. He clutched May to him, determined to hold her here physically at the last in spite of his failure to hold on to her in all the ways that mattered when she'd come to him. What a fool he'd been to send her away two nights ago—had it only been forty-eight hours ago she'd been naked and warm in his bed? And he'd turned her away, told her their love was impossible. Now she was bleeding, perhaps mortally. He had to hold on for both of them. But whether he willed it or not, consciousness let go with a final thought: he'd never get to tell her he'd been wrong. She had been the one who was sure of him, of them. All along the doubter had been him. And now she would never know.

Chapter Twenty-Three

May would not die for him. Liam felt himself struggling towards consciousness. His body hurt. There was noise around him, men's voices. Someone was pulling at his arm. He wouldn't let go. They couldn't have May.

'Case, I've got you. You have to let them take her. She needs a surgeon, a good one.' It was Preston kneeling beside him. He could feel Preston's body next to his, Preston's voice at his ear, trying not to shake. 'Please, she needs help. You need help. You're both hurt, badly.' Preston kept talking, working his grip loose. 'We got Roan, Case. The Watch have him. Notice has been sent to London. Someone official will be here in a few days to transport him.' He was chattering away, getting an arm beneath him, helping him to rise. Someone else had May.

Liam knew a moment's panic. 'May! I have

to stay with her. Preston, please.' He grabbed for his friend with his good arm.

'People are taking care of her. We need to take care of you,' Preston argued firmly, dragging him to another room, the library from the looks of it. Worth was with them, following behind and shutting the door for privacy. 'Father, we need the brandy, quick.' Preston was already pulling off his own coat, then pulling at Liam's coat and shirt. In a pinch, an aristocrat's library converted neatly into an infirmary. Brandy was easily supplied from the sideboard and Preston's own shirt made a handy source of bandages. Liam mused they might be the most expensive bandages he'd ever have. He fought for consciousness again. The walk to the library had been taxing.

Preston had him propped up in a chair, his face level with Liam's as he knelt looking at the wound. 'Stay with me, Case. Talk to me, tell me everything that happened.'

'This is backwards,' Liam drawled. 'I'm supposed to be the one stitching you up.'

Preston gave him a wry smile. 'I figure I owe you one at least.' Worth passed the brandy. 'I think this is when you usually say, "this is going to hurt a bit".' He poured the alcohol on the knife slash and Liam grunted against the shock of pain. 'Lucky for you, I'm a dab hand at stitches and you don't need too many.' He nodded at Worth. 'Father, if you'd hold the light?'

'You'll do.' Preston stepped back when he finished tying the last of the bandage. 'The slash wasn't deep, thankfully. Give it a week.' Preston pushed a glass of brandy in his hand. 'Tell us everything.'

'What is there to tell, Preston?' Worth leaned a hip against the long reading table. 'Mr Casek nearly died tonight in service of his country, in protection of May.' Worth's green gaze settled on him. 'The three men in the room besides Roan didn't shoot each other, is my guess. You took them out?'

'May shot one of them.' The brandy went down warm. May would love it. In his current state, everything reminded him of May. He wanted to go to her. Liam tried to stand and nearly fell.

'What do you think you're doing?' Preston caught him by the elbow and steadied him.

'I need to see May. I need to know.' His words were starting to slur. Would she survive the wound?

Worth came to his other side. 'They've taken

her upstairs. Let's take him before he hurts himself trying to climb the stairs on his own. He's earned it.' If he wasn't so worried about May, he would have enjoyed the little victory with Worth.

Unfortunately, every worry he'd possessed was justified. The doctor had finished caring for her. A white bandage decorated her side, the beautiful crimson gown she'd worn had been cast aside on a chair, ruined. It had been sliced off her for expedience sake. But all the haste in the world didn't look like enough. May was pale and unmoving, the only colour was her dark hair fanned on the pillow. He and Preston were holding each other up now that their adrenaline was spent and they were faced with the danger May was in—a danger neither could protect her from.

May's father, who'd been unflappable, seemed to age as the doctor took him aside, murmuring news. Liam could guess what it was. She was in shock now, they would need to watch out for inflammation, there would be fever, it could claim her if they weren't careful and she'd lost a lot of blood. How many times had Liam delivered that same news?

Liam dragged himself to the bed, falling to his knees as his strength gave out. It would be days before May was out of danger and his strength was already failing. This was his nightmare come to life: that his strength would leave him when he needed it most, when *she* needed him most. He fumbled for her hand among the bedclothes.

She was in danger just when he'd thought she was safe. If she had stayed put, if she hadn't pushed him out of the way, she would be alive and well in her red dress. She should have let him do his job, should have let him take that bullet for her. But that wasn't quite right. The bullet was never meant for her. It was always meant for him. Surely she'd known that. What had she been thinking?

Liam would not die for her, for his perfect mission record. It was the only thought that mattered, the only thought that hovered on the edges of her consciousness. There were feelings, though. Hot, sharp feelings of pain. Breathing hurt. She didn't want to move. She was somewhere safe. But where was that? She didn't feel quite alive, but she wasn't dead. Dead didn't make any sense. Roan wouldn't shoot her, not fatally any way. He'd lose his leverage. He would shoot Liam. *That*, she could not allow.

There were more thoughts now, her consciousness able to grasp multiple details at once. She'd leapt for Liam, hoping to push him to the ground, hoping Roan would pull the shot. It had been too much to hope for. There'd been a pain in her side, she'd fallen and that had hurt, too. Falling among glass carried its own hazards. But the worst hazard had been the thought of Liam slaughtered before her eyes. Maybe she had done it to prove to him that she could, that she was brave enough, the same way she'd wanted to prove to him she could keep a house with her pressed sheets and lavender-scented pillowcases. It had been another way to argue. But maybe she had done it just because she loved him. She suspected the latter.

But what to do now? Liam had said their love was impossible. She did wonder if she could float here in this colourless world for ever. There was no reason to wake up if there was no Liam. The pain had become a little better. Perhaps in time it might go away altogether. It would certainly be easier than…than what? Waking up and finding Liam gone? *I'll protect you and then I'll leave.* Was it as simple as that? *Could* she wake up? Was this a dream? If so, she wasn't alone.

Someone was here, at least their voice was,

familiar and scolding as it called to her to open her eyes. Liam's voice, here in the darkness. He hadn't left. Yet. There was still time if only… His voice was loud now, exhorting her to wake, not to die. Was this some mystical limbo where she lingered, waiting to pass on? Not a dream like she'd thought? The last thought gave her a charge of fear. She didn't want to pass on. She needed to see Liam, needed to stop him from going. If he hadn't left already, maybe she could persuade him. He'd been hurt, she remembered that. Despite her efforts, he'd already been hurt before Roan had fired. She needed to know he was all right.

That was one decision made. She was going to find a way to wake up. Then, she was going to find a way to make Liam listen to her. Slow down, she cautioned. One step at a time. Just think about the next step. She had to find her eyelids. Had to force them to open even if it took days.

Ouch! The light was bright. She'd not planned on that. Her eyes shut, but not before someone had seen her.

'May? May? Are you awake?' The voice was rough and masculine, hoarse with hope and exhaustion and, oh, so very familiar. She tried again with the eyes, this time more slowly, wanting to savour the hope that existed between believing and seeing. In her mind, Liam was there, *had* been there all along. When she opened her eyes she would know for sure.

'Liam.' The one word was so very hard to say and she had a hundred other words that wanted to come out, but they stopped in her throat as she looked at him. He was all smiles, but she could see the worry behind those grins, in the circles beneath his eyes, the stubble of his beard at his jaw. She must have been hurt badly.

'May.' His voice was scratchy and a tear formed in his eye. A tear! 'I thought I'd lost you.' She felt the press of his hand on hers in the blankets.

She smiled softly. 'I'm right here.'

'Yes, you are. At last.' Then Liam Casek, the street rat who'd lived it all, seen it all before he was twelve, the man who'd fought in Serbia, who took on the work of the Crown deemed too perilous for others, who'd brought the notorious Cabot Roan to justice, who'd faced four deadly men in the rose sitting room just days ago, broke down entirely, tears streaming in his relief.

'You wanted to see me, sir?' Liam stepped into the town house library. Worth had summoned him after dinner, a celebratory supper even if the guest of honour, May, was absent, tucked in her bed upstairs. It had been an emotionally eventful day.

'Yes.' Worth waved to the empty chair across from him by the fire. 'Help yourself to a brandy.'

'No thank you, sir. I'm fine.' Liam took the chair and waited. He was ready for bad news. Whatever it was, he could bear it. May was safe and that was all that mattered. It was time to be moving on, after all. His job was done.

'May is going to pull through.' Worth smiled. 'Thanks to you.' Liam wanted to argue it was no thanks to him. She'd been reckless and he'd been unable to stop her, but he held his tongue.

'You kept her safe. Roan could have had her in the village if you hadn't been there. Who knows how that would have ended? I try not to speculate on it. It didn't come to pass. I wanted you to know how grateful May's mother and I are.' His brow furrowed. 'But I didn't call you here to congratulate you on a job well done. There is something more. My wife and I have not been fair to you over the years.' He held Liam's gaze and Liam returned it, seeing the man's sincerity.

'We underestimated your feelings for May

and hers for you. What happened in the sitting room showed us how committed you both are to each other. She was willing to die for you.'

Liam attempted to break in. 'Sir—'

Worth held up an authoritative hand. 'That's not all, Casek. You were willing to die for her. I saw the scene *before* she pushed you. When we charged through the door, I saw a man standing between my daughter and Roan's pistol. I saw three men dead or wounded on the floor. That was your doing. You faced incredible odds for her. You were willing to stand between her and Roan at the expense of your life.' Worth coughed to cover his emotion. 'A man like that is more than deserving of my daughter and my family. If you still intend to marry May, Lady Worth and I would welcome you.'

Liam was not often taken by surprise—except by the Worths, it seemed. May surprised him often. Preston certainly had on occasion and now Worth joined their ranks. He'd not been expecting this. For a moment he was speechless. Then he was elated. He wanted to caper around the room like an idiot. The repercussions of Worth's words rocketed through him; they wouldn't have to leave, May wouldn't have to choose. The next moment, reality had him in its clutches again. 'Sir, you do me a great honour with your blessing. But the events with Roan have shown me how my life puts May's in danger. My career has created enemies.'

Worth chuckled. 'Then you need a new career, Casek. I have some ideas about how you can continue to serve this country in a less dangerous capacity. As for your past, perhaps you should put that into perspective. Everyone is haunted by theirs to some degree. We all have enemies. I wouldn't underestimate May's ability to cope with that if I were you.'

Liam nodded. 'I will ask her when she's well.'

Chapter Twenty-Four

May came downstairs for the first time since the ball on Christmas Eve, dressed in a party gown, her hair up. It felt good to be out of her room. The house looked beautiful to her. Boughs of greenery decorated the staircase bannister, caught up at intervals with bows. Urns overflowing with winter flowers filled the niches and fireplace mantels throughout the house. 'I wanted the house to feel like our home,' her mother confessed in an uncharacteristically soft moment, helping her navigate the stairs.

May squeezed her mother's hand, feeling closer to her than she had in a long while. Together with Liam, her family had spent hours every day in her room as she recovered, reading books and playing cards with her. Perhaps, May thought, she wasn't the only one missing the traditions of a Worth family Christmas in London. But this Christmas would be special on its own. They were all together and lucky to be so. More than that, Liam was with them. Every day with him was a blessing. He'd not left. They'd not spoken of leaving, perhaps out of deference for her recovery, and she was willing to pretend it might never happen.

A fire roared in the drawing room, a yule log burning. The men were already assembled in their evening best although it would only be family tonight. This would be a quiet celebration. May's heart clenched a little at the sight of the three men she loved best gathered at the mantel, looking handsome and hale. Preston was filling out finally and Liam had taken off his sling. The men smiled at her and May sensed a current of anticipation. Something was up. Something good.

The family took their seats in the cluster of furniture gathered around the fire, the butler serving holiday champagne that sparkled in the flames. Her mother exchanged a smile and a knowing look with her father. May arranged her skirts on the sofa and Liam came to her, kneeling. She furrowed her brow. 'What is this?' She glanced at Preston, but he merely shrugged with a grin.

'I have to ask you something, May,' Liam began, his blue eyes serious. 'But first, I need your promise on something.' His hands covered hers where they lay in her lap.

'Of course.'

'I need you to promise that you will never take a bullet again for me.'

'I need you to promise that I won't need to. No more situations where that might be a necessity.' May was equally serious. She'd never been as frightened as she'd been that night in the sitting room, watching Roan aim that gun.

He gave her a boyish smile. 'Agreed. Now, for the bigger question.' He cleared his throat and May cocked her head. He was nervous. She'd never seen him nervous. He was always so self-possessed. 'I need to confess I was wrong a few weeks ago. Tonight I want to apologise for doubting you, for not trusting that your love was enough.'

'Oh.' She breathed softly. Her eyes began to mist, but what did it mean? Did she dare hope?

'May, I want to ask you tonight, on the holiest night of year, the night of all sacrificing love, if you will marry me, imperfect as I am.'

She made him wait, her eyes holding his with shimmering emerald drops as silence filled the room, her face filling with emotion. She glanced around at the shining faces of her family, knowing intuitively she had their blessing. 'May?' he prompted with a whisper when the silence outpaced his patience.

'Hush.' Her lips broke into a smile. 'I want to enjoy seeing you on your knees.'

'You could enjoy it a lot more often if you said yes,' Liam pressed.

Her smile widened and she raised her voice. 'Then, yes, most definitely. I will marry you.'

'When?' There was the pop of a champagne cork from Preston's direction, another bottle being opened.

'Tomorrow.' May laughed.

'Tomorrow's Christmas,' Liam reminded her.

'Then the day after,' May argued. 'We've wasted enough time already.'

Liam raised her to her feet and drew her to him, kissing her then in front of everyone. 'It hasn't been a waste if it's led to this. Merry Christmas, May.'

May beamed as her family rose, and hugged them each in turn. This was a night for miracles indeed. If Liam Casek could get the Worths to hug, who knew what other miracles might be in store.

Epilogue

The following May,
London

'For what purpose do you wish this knighthood? If it be for richness, for taking your ease, and to be held in honour without doing your honour, you are unworthy.' The old chivalric words rang through the receiving room, the chamber crowded and silent with the exception of the occasional rustle of clothing as Liam knelt before the King, making his ritual response.

'I desire to be a knight that I might serve my God, my King and my lady wife to the best of my abilities.'

Especially the last. His lady wife. Please, always let me serve May, he thought. In the solemnity of the moment and all it stood for,

Liam could overlook the blemishes of the event, that the old words were spoken by a fat monarch who by repute didn't have a chivalrous bone in his body, or that he himself was sweating profusely and uncomfortably, the combined results of nerves, a crowded presence chamber and being solemnly draped in a blue-velvet cloak lined in white ermine—the colour ceremoniously worn by those in the King's service—on a warm May day at the start of the Season. Those inconveniences didn't matter. Not right now. He only wanted to drink it all in as he'd been drinking in the joys of the last five months.

The moment he'd set foot inside the Worths' drawing room that snowy Christmas Eve, everything had changed. For the better and in ways he'd not thought possible, in ways he'd not even imagined he'd wanted. He had married May in January as soon as a London wedding could be arranged to her mother's satisfaction and theirs; a 'decent amount of haste' her mother had called it, which meant it had occurred with enough speed to appease him and May and with enough time to accord the occasion a sense of distinction.

No one could mutter behind their backs over the need for undue haste and an unseemly rush to the altar. There'd been imported white roses from a speciality greenhouse in the country—further proof that they could wait as long as they desired—and yards of satin ribbon festooning the elegant stretch of aisle at St Martin-in-the-Field off Charing Square. While the luxurious yards of satin had seemed a frivolous waste to Liam, the thoughtfulness of the locale was not lost on him as a sign of the Worths' acceptance of him—St Martin of Tours had been a champion of the homeless and downtrodden.

But if he and May had thought they could quietly retire to their newly purchased house north enough of Belgravia not to be middle class, but far enough south of the West End as not to be overly ostentatious, they were sadly mistaken. The house, the wedding location, all served a double purpose as did many things associated with the Worths. He would not change overnight, maybe not at all, and it would be wrong to think the Worths would either. All these things had been orchestrated first and foremost out of affection for May, acceptance of him and secondarily with an eye for the future.

If the wedding was proof of the former, today's ceremony at the King's drawing room was proof of the latter. This was his father-in-law's doing as much as the wedding had been May's mother's. The King raised the ceremonial sword and Liam bowed his head as the flat of the blade moved from shoulder to shoulder, bestowing on him the traditional colée, intoning the ancient, culminating words of the ceremony 'In the name of God, St Michael and St George, I create thee knight. Be thou valiant, fearless and loyal.'

Liam swallowed hard against the emotion welling. It wasn't so much the ceremony today in front of strangers crowded into the Chinese receiving room at Buckingham House that triggered the reaction, but the event that had led to it; how Albermarle Worth had gathered them all together in the drawing room of the Worth home upon his and May's return from a brief wedding trip and read the letter out loud. The letter had been his father-in-law's petition that he be recognised with a knighthood for his service to the country; for his role in bringing the notorious Cabot Roan to justice; for acting these last years on behalf of the empire wherever he was called; for his work in Serbia, and for his willingness to lay down his life for another without hesitation as witnessed in the events that transpired at the Christmas Masque in Scotland, all in the name of King and coun-

try. Albermarle Worth had set aside the letter, his hard green eyes unusually watery, and
recited the last of the petition from memory.
"'For these reasons and for my deepest convic-
tion that this man has more to give his country
in the years to come if given the opportunity to
serve, I hereby do affix my most solemn name
to this petition.'" It had not mattered to Liam if
the petition was accepted or not. It was enough
that his father-in-law had written it, had put his
name to those words.

The Worths had plans for him, not only because they wanted to make him into a person
worthy of social recognition for their daughter's sake but because they accepted him and
saw his potential. Liam would like to say it
didn't matter to him what the Worths thought
of where he lived or how he lived, but it did.
Mainly because it mattered to May, but it
would be dishonest to ignore the fact that it
mattered to him as well. He had a family now,
something he'd only ever imagined before.
He was rapidly learning what family meant.
Families meant compromise and sometimes
families meant difficult disagreements when
one stood up for what one believed in. But despite what families sometimes meant, he was
learning they *always* meant love, *always* had

one's back and *always* had one's best interests at heart. He had the acceptance that mattered to him. The ceremony today was just a formality, as were these final words.

'Sir Liam Casek, rise and be greeted as befits your station.' Liam stood and faced the crowd and the polite applause, his gaze going immediately to May, dressed in a spring blue trimmed in cool white lace, who stood in the front of the assembly, tears in her eyes. Custom or not, Liam went straight to her. Today was *because* of her, *for* her, as much as it was for him. No matter what else he and her family might disagree on in the future, and he could imagine there was potential for quite a lot, they would always agree on May. She was the thread that drew them together, held them together.

'Happy?' he whispered in her ear, taking her in his arms. Propriety could be damned. She had just enough time to breathe the words, 'so happy, so proud', before he kissed her. If every paper in London reported tomorrow that the newly knighted Sir Liam Casek's first act was to publicly kiss his wife, that was fine with him. He intended to do far more than kiss her as soon as he could manage it, which might not be as soon as he liked.

There would be the private reception at the

Worth home this afternoon, followed by the dinner for select guests and the charity ball tonight for poor relief. He was wasting no time in declaring his reform preferences. Albermarle and Preston were adamant he stand for Parliament at the next election in one of the family's pocket boroughs. He liked the idea, but not the method. He *would* stand for election, not in a pocket borough, but in his own district and on his own merits. He wanted to do this on his own, just as he'd wanted to purchase their house on his own. But he was not eager to think about politics just now. He only wanted to think about May. This kiss was in danger of getting out of hand.

May drew back, sensing they'd pushed propriety far enough, her face flushed. 'You're thinking about something,' she playfully accused, studying his face.

Liam grinned. 'I'm thinking about the carriage ride to your parents' home.'

May frowned, puzzled. 'What's so exciting about that?'

'It will be my next chance to ravish you,' Liam murmured.

'And the next chance after that?' May flirted.

'I was eyeing one of the alcoves in your mother's salon, perhaps your father's library—

the sofa looks like a prime goer.' Liam gave a throaty chuckle that drew a look of censure from a woman standing nearby.

May slipped a hand through his arm with a laugh. 'Then we'd best get on with it. Sounds like you have a busy night ahead.'

They teased one another until they were alone in the carriage. Liam took her hands, his expression solemn. 'Truly, May, do you mind all of this so very much? Everything is like a fairy tale on the surface: the wedding, the knighting, the parties—London can be intoxicating in its own way. But it's not what I thought we wanted.'

'What *we* wanted?' May gave a half-smile. 'I am still getting used to the novelty of there being a "we". The cottage in Scotland seems like a faraway memory, the fantasy of my greenhouse and selling vegetables in the village belongs to another time, another woman; in truth, Liam, that fantasy belonged to a rather bitter woman who had given up on the world, who was prepared only to see the world in two ways; her way and society's way.'

May sighed. 'Then, I only knew what *I* wanted. Even that was flawed, except wanting you, only I couldn't see my way to it, how to make it work with you without losing my family, because I saw the world as offering only two possibilities: my way and its way, two irreconcilable avenues.' She tilted her head and smiled. 'My friends and I have a motto: nothing changes until you do. For the longest time I thought that only applied to them. They needed to change. Claire needed to come out of her self-imposed shell and Evie needed to find her confidence. But I already had those things in abundance. I didn't need to change. I was wrong. I *did* need to change the way I looked at the world and the way I responded to it.' She paused and said in a whisper, 'It's amazing what can happen when you let love lead. That's made all the difference.'

Liam nodded. 'That makes two of us. You aren't the only one guilty on that account. So you're happy then? With how things turned out? With being a future politician's wife?' He drew her on to his lap, setting her astride. She grinned wickedly, her hips moving against him. He felt his body surge at the invitation.

'Most definitely. I am looking forward to hosting teas and discussing all sorts of reforms, even reform for women. The days of Bowdler and his ideas of expurgation have outlived their usefulness.' She kissed him softly, pulling on his lower lip with her teeth. 'A woman needs to take charge of her life in all ways and in all places.'

'Even in the bedroom?' Liam murmured suggestively.

'Mmm-hmm.' May slipped her hand between them, pressing it against his trousers. 'Especially in the bedroom. A woman should have access to birth control, to the choice of pregnancy.'

'I think I will look forward to Lady May Worth sexually educating the female portion of London.' Liam laughed. Life would be an adventure with her. There was no stopping May, no stopping them. May was right. It *was* amazing what love could accomplish. Love had taken a boy from the slums, an orphan with no family, no prospects, no hope and given him this beautiful spirited woman and a lifetime of possibilities to share with her, starting right now.

May flipped open the front of his trousers with a coy smile. 'I know something else you'll look forward to. A little knighting ceremony of our own.' She put her hand on him. 'I command thee to rise, Sir Liam Casek.'

* * * * *

If you enjoyed this story,
you won't want to miss the first two books
in Bronwyn Scott's
WALLFLOWERS TO WIVES *quartet*

UNBUTTONING THE INNOCENT MISS
AWAKENING THE SHY MISS

And watch for the fourth and final book,
coming soon!

MILLS & BOON®

&HISTORICAL

AWAKEN THE ROMANCE OF THE PAST

A sneak peek at next month's titles...

In stores from 1st June 2017:

- **The Debutante's Daring Proposal** – Annie Burrows
- **The Convenient Felstone Marriage** – Jenni Fletcher
- **An Unexpected Countess** – Laurie Benson
- **Claiming His Highland Bride** – Terri Brisbin
- **Marrying the Rebellious Miss** – Bronwyn Scott

Just can't wait?
Buy our books online before they hit the shops!
www.millsandboon.co.uk

Also available as eBooks.

MILLS & BOON®

EXCLUSIVE EXTRACT

Desperation forces Georgiana Wickford to
propose to her estranged childhood friend.
The Earl of Ashenden swore he'd never wed,
but the unconventional debutante soon tempts
him in ways he never expected!

Read on for a sneak preview of
THE DEBUTANTE'S DARING PROPOSAL

Georgiana couldn't really believe that his attitude could
still hurt so much. Not after all the times he'd pretended
he couldn't even see her, when she'd been standing
practically under his nose. She really ought to be immune
to his disdain by now.

'Did you have something in particular to ask me,'
Edmund asked in a bored tone, 'or should I take my
dog, and return to Fontenay Court?'

'You know very well I have something of great impor-
tance to ask you,' she retorted, finally reaching the end
of her tether as she straightened up, 'or I wouldn't have
sent you that note.'

'And are you going to tell me what it is anytime
soon?' He pulled his watch from his waistcoat pocket
and looked down at it. 'Only, I have a great many
pressing matters to attend to.'

She sucked in a deep breath. 'I do beg your pardon,
my lord,' she said, dipping into the best curtsey she

could manage with a dog squirming round her ankles and her riding habit still looped over one arm. 'Thank you so much for sparing me a few minutes of your valuable time,' she added, through gritted teeth.

'Not at all.' He made one of those graceful, languid gestures with his hand that indicated *noblesse oblige*. 'Though I should, of course, appreciate it if you would make it quick.'

Make it quick? Make it quick! Four days she'd been waiting for him to show up, four days he'd kept her in an agony of suspense, and now he was here, he was making it clear he wanted the meeting to be as brief as possible so he could get back to where he belonged. In his stuffy house, with his stuffy servants, and his stuffy lifestyle.

Just once, she'd like to shake him out of that horrid, contemptuous, self-satisfied attitude of his towards the rest of the world. And make him experience a genuine, human emotion. No matter what.

'Very well.' She'd say what she'd come to say, without preamble. Which would at least give her the pleasure of shocking him almost as much as if she really were to throw her boot at him.

'If you must know, I want you to marry me.'

MILLS & BOON®
are delighted to support
World Book Night

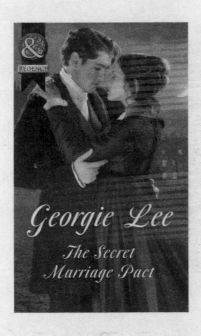

World Book Night is run by The Reading Agency and is a national celebration of reading and books which takes place on 23 April every year. To find out more visit worldbooknight.org.

THE READING AGENCY

www.millsandboon.co.uk